"News flash, Doc." Maggie's eyes danced. A thick resolve tinged her words. "The choice is mine to make. I decide who is best for me."

"So, tell me?" Grant matched her beat for beat. Challenge for challenge. How could he not? She was magnificent. And if he'd been in the mindset for falling for someone, he would've fallen even more for her now. "Tell me, Maggie. Who would you choose?"

Her gaze lowered to his mouth. A tremor worked over her bottom lip. And he knew. She felt it, too. Whatever it was between them. Grant lost his breath and forgot his words. *Walk away. Run.*

"Are you scared I'll pick you, Doc?" Her expression, intense and incredibly candid, kept him in place. The quiet frankness of her words speared right into his chest. A direct hit. But she wasn't through. "Or are you more terrified I won't?"

Dear Reader,

I recently heard a quote about how fate laughs when we make plans. I've said: I had the best plan, then life happened and changed everything. It's in those moments that I can hear fate chuckling if I listen close enough. I also know it's those moments when nothing is going as planned that I discover a strength I didn't know I had. Or I learn that laughter can get you through almost anything. Or I'm reminded how blessed I am to have my family and friends in my corner whenever I need them.

In *Falling for the Cowboy Doc*, Maggie Orr and Grant Sloan have each made big plans for their lives. However, when the spirited team roper comes boots to stethoscope with the reserved surgeon, more than career plans get uprooted. Now, if this dedicated cowgirl and serious-minded doctor can look beyond their differences, they might find the best plan is one they make together. It's summer in Three Springs, Texas, where the iced tea is served extra cold, the disagreements are good-natured, and there's always room at the dinner table. So, pull up a chair and make yourself at home.

I love to connect with readers. Check out my website to learn more about my upcoming books, sign up for email book announcements, or chat with me on Facebook (carilynnwebb) or Twitter (@carilynnwebb).

Happy reading!

Cari Lynn Webb

HEARTWARMING

*Falling for the
Cowboy Doc*

———

Cari Lynn Webb

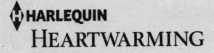

H HARLEQUIN
HEARTWARMING

HARLEQUIN®
HEARTWARMING™

ISBN-13: 978-1-335-58504-2

Recycling programs
for this product may
not exist in your area.

Falling for the Cowboy Doc

Harlequin Enterprises ULC
22 Adelaide St. West, 41st Floor
Toronto, Ontario M5H 4E3, Canada
www.Harlequin.com

Printed in U.S.A.

Cari Lynn Webb lives in South Carolina with her husband, daughters and assorted four-legged family members. She's been blessed to see the power of true love in her grandparents' seventy-year marriage and her parents' marriage of over fifty years. She knows love isn't always sweet and perfect—it can be challenging, complicated and risky. But she believes happily-ever-afters are worth fighting for. She loves to connect with readers.

Visit the Author Profile page at Harlequin.com for more titles.

To my daughters. Dream big. Make plans. And don't ever forget to enjoy the journey, especially those unexpected twists. They can turn out to be the best part.

Special thanks to my writing gang for responding to every text and email, especially the very late-night ones. To my friends: Diane S, Mike and Baker for answering my endless medical questions and texts. To my husband for his continued support and love. To my family for inspiring me every day.

CHAPTER ONE

"WE SHOULD LEAVE." Maggie Orr's sister sat cross-legged in the chair beside her. The toe of her teal cowboy boot flexed up and down. Up and down.

"We're already here." Maggie set her hand on Kelsey's fidgeting leg. Her sister stilled. Maggie added, "We might as well at least listen to what Dr. Toro has to say."

"But." Kelsey stretched every bit of her natural charm into the one word, then aimed her wide, round blue eyes at Maggie. "I'm fine. We don't really need to be here."

"Yes, I know." Maggie tried to ignore the disloyal doubt she was feeling. She really wanted to believe her sister. But ever since Tango had spooked and thrown Kelsey in a rodeo chute in New Mexico, her sister's shoulder had been far from right. Maggie reached for upbeat. "I suspect Dr. Toro will stroll in, give us a lively description of the best bulls bucking this weekend, and send us on our way."

At least that was what Maggie hoped would

happen. But what she really needed was Dr. To-ro's confirmation that Kelsey was in fact fine. Maggie's intuition was simply on the fritz.

"I'll wait another five minutes, then I'm out." Kelsey snapped open a lifestyle magazine and crinkled a page. "I don't know how many more times I need to tell you that I'm fine. That this appointment is unnecessary. We should be prac-ticing instead."

"There will be plenty of daylight left to prac-tice when we get out of here," Maggie assured her.

Kelsey's reply was a noncommittal hum. Only the flick of the magazine pages disrupted the still air between them.

Maggie hoped her suspicions about her sis-ter's shoulder were a by-product of her own guilt. After all, Maggie was keeping things from her sister too.

Not little things like: *Hey, Kels, I wore your favorite white lace blouse and spilled ketchup on it.*

Maggie shifted in her seat, snapped a hair tie off her wrist and tugged her tresses into a low ponytail. Unfortunately, her stress and panic weren't so easily contained.

Yeah, Maggie had secrets. And they were big, like: *Hey, Kels, our emergency fund is empty. We're barely getting by.*

They'd needed to use their savings for the string of bad luck they'd been having lately. Not in the arena, but out.

"I'm going to find Dr. Toro." Maggie jumped out of the chair, beelined for the exam room door and yanked it open. Only to run boots to stethoscope into a tall doctor built like a brick wall. "Sorry."

He smoothed a hand over his bold burgundy silk tie and kept her fixed in a stare that managed to unlock Maggie's yearslong determination to swear off men. "No problem. If you need the bathroom, it's down the hall on the right."

"I can wait." For bathrooms and romantic fantasies. Maggie retreated into the exam room, collapsed into the chair beside her sister and took a longer look at the polished doctor watching her. She'd never seen him before, and he was decades younger than Dr. Toro. "Are you Dr. Toro's intern?"

"I don't recall Dr. Toro having an intern with him when he was at the rodeo a few weeks ago," Kelsey mused, studying the handsome doctor as intently as Maggie was trying not to.

Dr. Handsome's clear-eyed stare widened slightly. "I haven't been an intern for over five years." He wore a crisp white dress shirt underneath his pristine white coat. His words, although polite, seemed dipped in starch too.

"Unfortunately, Dr. Toro had a family emergency. I'm Dr. Sloan and I'm handling Dr. Toro's patients until his return."

His summary of the situation was efficient, if not stiff. He was not an experienced rodeo circuit doctor like Dr. Toro. The older doctor resisted hardline diagnoses in favor of allowing his patients to tell him if they were still able to compete.

Dr. Sloan would give it to Kelsey straight.

Maggie slipped her hands underneath her legs and resisted the urge to fidget. Much as she wanted her sister to be healthy, they also had to compete to earn a bank account–saving endorsement. If only both could coexist.

"Wait. Sloan..." Kelsey tipped her head, and her smile stretched from cheek to cheek. "You're Ryan Sloan's little brother, aren't you? He and my sister Maggie are thick as thieves on the circuit." She smiled at Maggie. "That's a relief. For a minute there, I thought you had no clue about the rodeo." Kelsey elbowed Maggie with her good arm.

"Ryan is my brother." Dr. Sloan's half-smile barely dented his cheek, hinting that he kept his Sloan charisma, if he had any, in check and that he wasn't entirely pleased about the connection.

He was Ryan's brother. Ryan Sloan was one

of Maggie's best friends. Maggie wasn't sure she was happy about the connection either. Dr. Sloan was nothing like his no-holds-barred brother who Maggie's Gram would have described as the boot-wearing definition of devil-may-care. Ryan's brother was entirely too, well, doctorly.

Kelsey's grin stayed in place, perhaps she believed that Dr. Sloan was like Dr. Toro after all. Kelsey excelled at small talk. Always had. But then she'd always had an abundance of charm and cheer. "Ryan never told us you were working at this clinic."

"I'll only be in Three Springs temporarily," he said and turned his full attention to Kelsey's chart.

Maggie lowered her gaze to Dr. Sloan's sleek dress shoes and neatly pressed slacks and tried not to brush at the horsehair stuck on her jeans. And there it was. Evidence he was not her kind of doctor. After all, Maggie and her sister were more line-dried at the campground, and he was clearly dry clean only. Whatever he was about to say was most likely going to be expensive.

"Well." Dr. Sloan dropped onto a rolling stool, then regarded Maggie and her sister closely.

Maggie knew exactly what he saw. The Orr sisters had the same weary blue eyes and the same long hair with the same platinum blond color they'd been born with. Strong bone structure. Expressive features. All thanks to their mother. It was part of their marketing plan as team ropers and appealed to sponsors. What the Orr sisters didn't share was the same taste in spicy food or men. Apparently, Maggie was attracted to rigid doctors whose fancy shoes probably cost as much as gassing the truck for a month on the road.

"We're not twins. If that was what you were thinking." Kelsey chuckled and bumped lightly into Maggie's side. "Although we were both born in March, exactly one year apart. If you can believe that. And now, I suppose I'm the injured one, but it's fine. I'm fine."

The slight scratch of vulnerability in her sister's words tugged inside Maggie. She reached over and patted her sister's leg. "Kelsey might be older, but she's also prettier."

Dr. Sloan rolled his lips together as if he was working out the correct response, then he cleared his throat. "Perhaps we should discuss the results of your latest MRI, Kelsey."

Maggie held her breath. This was it. The moment Dr. Sloan confirmed Kelsey was fine. Or not... *Please don't be not.*

"I've reviewed the latest images and the rest of your file. Your rotator cuff is torn again."

Dr. Sloan focused on Maggie's sister. His voice strong. His words succinct. "You need surgery to repair the latest damage."

"But it was only a minor tear when I saw Dr. Toro two months ago. Dr. Toro called it small." Kelsey's words sounded earnest yet hopeful. "Dr. Toro approved conservative treatment and competition and this follow-up."

"Did he?" Dr. Sloan raised his eyebrows in doubt.

Suddenly Maggie was doubting Dr. Toro too. Or at least what his diagnosis had been.

Kelsey had met with Dr. Toro for a quick assessment two months ago while Maggie had gassed up the truck and checked on the horses. After her diagnosis, Kelsey had waved off Maggie's concern, climbed into the passenger seat and told Maggie to step on it. They had another competition to win.

Maggie hadn't pressed Kelsey too much. Certain Kelsey would've told her if her injury was serious. Or if her pain was unbearable. Certain also that she would've known. Would've sensed something. They weren't twins, but the sisters were connected. There had never been secrets between them. *Until now.* Maggie pressed back against the hard chair, but nothing dislodged the sudden pinch of unease.

"The tear in your shoulder is more than minor," Dr. Sloan countered. "And conservative treatment won't work in the long run."

Maggie glanced at her sister and wondered if the truth would finally come out, or if they'd continue pretending Kelsey was okay.

Kelsey cradled her injured arm in her hand as if she was guarding it from the good doctor and his ready scalpel.

The pinch inside Maggie strengthened.

"Dr. Sloan." Kelsey held onto her smile. Yet determination overrode any charm in her words. "Are you telling me that you don't recommend I ride in two weeks at qualifiers?"

"Your arm should be in a sling right now and the only role you ought to have in the rodeo is as a spectator in the stands." He folded his hands together on top of the closed file folder as if ending the discussion.

Silence crowded into the exam room. Maggie's heart pounded. The rest of her body went numb.

"I can't have surgery. I can't." Kelsey shook her head. "The recovery period will last the rest of this season and into next."

Maggie's heart pounded harder. She knew she should weigh in. A good sister would tell Kelsey to listen to her doctor. But the competitor in Maggie held her words in a tight rein.

"I can't tell you not to compete. But you need to understand that you're risking further injury to your shoulder if you do. Permanent injury." His gaze stayed on Maggie's sister, but nothing in his voice or posture softened. "Imagine not being able to lift your baby over your head because your rotator cuff doesn't rotate."

Maggie blanched. The sisters had promised to protect each other. Take care of each other. Now, her sister was injured, and Maggie had to either give her blessing for surgery or ask Kelsey to push through the pain. Risk even more. One more time. How could she do that to her sister? Yet given their precarious financial situation, how could she not?

Maggie and her sister were a top twenty nationally ranked roping team. Not to mention, one of the top five women's roping pairs competing on the rodeo circuit. Even more, they were set to secure their first major national sponsor. They needed to win in two weeks at the Stagecoach Pro Buckle Series and secure an automatic bid to the world championships in November. That fast-track opportunity to the world's largest stage would guarantee Denim Country, a national retail chain, saw them as an investment and not a risk.

There was no fallback plan. No retirement account.

Kelsey cleared her throat and stared hard at Maggie. "We are a team, and I must compete with my sister."

So, this was how this was going to play out. Maggie nodded, letting her sister know she understood and agreed, if reluctantly. They were risking it all.

Dr. Sloan crossed his arms over his chest, seemingly unconvinced and unwavering.

"The rodeo isn't a hobby, Dr. Sloan. Competing isn't a pastime," Maggie said. Without the rodeo and her sister, Maggie wouldn't know who she was. *Don't jump ahead, Mags*. She inhaled, seeking a little calmness to smooth her desperation. "The rodeo is what we do. All we've ever done. We've always done it together. We'll compete in two weeks." And deal with the fallout afterward.

The stubborn and too handsome for his own good doctor rubbed his chin, then braced his arms on his knees. He eyed Maggie in a way that felt less adversarial and more empathetic. "I don't suggest surgery on a whim, either. This is my specialty. My expertise. And just so we are clear, I'm one of the best there is in my field. You're welcome to ask Dr. Toro when he returns."

"We'll be sure to do that," Maggie assured him, wondering why she felt a bit breathless.

"I'll go to physical therapy twice a day if needed," Kelsey interjected. "I'll rest and ice my shoulder several times a day. That could work, right?"

Dr. Sloan held Maggie's gaze for another beat before looking at Kelsey. He held up two fingers. "You must wear a sling every single day for the next two weeks. That means no roping. No practicing. Stay out of the arena. And you can't miss one physical therapy appointment with the person I recommend."

Relief slipped through Maggie. Surely that would help alleviate her sister's pain.

"I can do all that." Kelsey's smile grew.

"This is not a guarantee," Dr. Sloan warned. "You need to understand surgery is most likely still in your future."

"But not right now." Kelsey stood and added, "We just need right now."

Yes, one more win. Then maybe Maggie and Kelsey could discuss their future. The one they'd only ever dared to whisper about on those special nights when they were still riding the high of a first-place jackpot.

Because in the light of day, the money went quick, covering expenses and horse care. And that dream future always seemed just a little bit more out of reach.

CHAPTER TWO

GRANT STEPPED INTO exam room four and for the second time that morning found himself completely blindsided.

Only this time it wasn't a wisp of a cowgirl with the prettiest, most expressive blue eyes he'd ever seen rendering him speechless. He'd gladly take a dozen more run-ins with his spirited cowgirl over this impending confrontation.

He regarded the older woman perched on the edge of the plastic patient chair. She was polished and perfectly poised from her dark hair that cut sharply across her cheek to her stiff, monotone power suit. A far cry from the soft woman he remembered from his childhood. But he knew her. Thanks to her contributions in the medical field, she was cited often in medical journals and featured in the media. There were few, especially in the medical realm, who didn't recognize the face of the renowned Dr. Lilian Sloan. Even her son, who hadn't seen her in person in well over two decades, recognized her.

Grant shoved his hands into the pockets of his dress pants and stepped straight into the heart of things. "Mother. What are you doing here?"

His words were blunt and brisk. Like the multiple stings of a wasp.

"Grant." Lilian Sloan uncrossed her legs and lifted her chin. "Your front desk is in a bit of disarray. I took myself to an exam room."

"The staff is filling in for the receptionist who up and quit over the weekend. We're waiting on a qualified replacement from the temp agency." Grant ground his teeth together. He owed Lilian Sloan no explanation. After all, his mother had never explained why she'd dumped Grant and his four brothers at their grandparents' house one summer when they were kids. Then never returned. But he refused to open that old wound. "I'm sure your medical clinic in New York City doesn't have such staffing problems."

Yes, the very woman without a heart had become one of the nation's leading heart surgeons. The irony was not lost on Grant.

Lilian tucked her perfectly straight hair behind her ear and studied him. "I can't believe how much you look like your father. I almost thought it was him when you came in."

Not going there either. Dear old dad hadn't

bothered to claim his sons either after the divorce. Grant didn't care. Old wounds and all—those scars had faded. The pain was forgotten. He repeated, "What are you doing here?"

"You haven't returned my phone calls." Her eyebrows creased together. Her voice remained neutral. "I left quite a few voicemails. I imagine cell phones now work in Three Springs."

His cell phone worked perfectly fine. Thank you very much. Grant had deleted her voicemails. Silence was supposed to send one heck of a message. Clearly his mother had missed that memo. Grant asked again, "Why are you here?"

"I couldn't very well walk into your brother's distillery, request a sample of his bourbon and offer him a surprise welcome home hug among all those customers of his." She chuckled. The sound was grainy and artificial. But the nervous flutter of her fingers reaching to tug on her pearl earring was not feigned.

Grant tucked his elbows against his sides. She could feel anything she wanted. Not his concern.

She continued, "I know your grandfather is at the Owl with Boone and that's also much too public. So, I came here instead."

To a cold and sterile exam room in a clinic that wasn't even Grant's. He could only hope his mother's return to Three Springs was as temporary as his time here. She had no place in their lives. Same as he had no place in his hometown anymore either. "I have patients with real injuries. Real pain. Patients who I need to care for."

Because Grant had gotten over the pain of his mom's abandonment years ago. And the only treatment he'd found that worked was *not* to go poking around into his past. Standing there within hugging distance of his mother for the first time in entirely too long was a jab too far.

"Have dinner with me." Her hasty offer tangled around her cultured tone.

You never came back for us. Not once. Grant leaned against the closed exam room door and muted that little hurt kid inside him. His voice hardened. "Why?"

"Can't a mom want to have a meal with her son?" She spun a plain gold band around her middle finger yet held his gaze.

"You haven't been a mother," he challenged. "Not ever."

She never flinched. Simply absorbed the insult like water on hot pavement. "I'm still your mom. You're still my son."

"Those are nothing more than labels," he said. "Doesn't mean we owe each other anything."

Ironic, she'd chosen his office. Grant was the least emotional of the Sloan brothers. The most clinical. If she'd wanted to reach Grant's soft side, she'd erred greatly. He didn't have one. That only served as a reminder of how little she knew of her own sons.

"Call it dinner between strangers then." She didn't plead. Her expression remained as contained as his. Her voice as impartial as his. She added, "Call it a chance to learn more about each other. To get to know each other better."

Grant stared at her. "Why would I want that?"

"Please, Grant. There are things that need to be said." She glanced around the small exam room as if sizing it up and still finding it lacking. "As much as we both live and thrive in our clinics, this isn't the appropriate place. I expect your nurse will be in any minute to take my vitals. Or a tech will arrive to take me to x-ray. I put carpal tunnel pain on my paperwork when I arrived, by the way."

Was there any place Grant wanted to hear what his mother had to say? Any place that would make him want to listen to her now? She was about two decades late. Still, Gran Claire had taught him good manners. Grandpa Sam had taught him family first. He'd do this for his brothers. Because he loved his brothers. Because his real family mattered.

"If I agree to dinner, then you'll leave here," he said. When she started to nod, Grant quickly added, "And you won't call my brothers either."

"They can come to dinner with us." Her smile was small, almost fragile.

Grant wasn't moved. He shook his head. This wasn't an invitation to open his brothers' old wounds too. Or to see them get hurt now. But it was the one thing Grant could do for his brothers before he left town permanently. "Evenings during a weeknight work best for me. But it has to be soon. I won't be in town much longer."

"Headed to the West Coast then." Her smile was one-sided, small but satisfied.

Grant worked to contain his surprise. Even though he shouldn't be. The medical community was vast, yet so very tightknit. Still, he asked, "How would you know about that?"

"Silverlining TeamMed is one of the premier sports medicine facilities in the nation." She eyed him. "They only take the best. Word is that you're one of the best. It's where I would've gone if I was you. You're making the right choice for your career."

He let that comment slide. Acknowledging her approval might encourage her. Every decision he made was for his career. He was only home short-term and intent on filling all his time with work. He had to stay sharp. Keep his edge. Aside from this one outing with his mother, he would allow nothing else to distract him. After all, his mother wasn't wrong. Everything he wanted was in California. "Text me a time and location for dinner."

She stood and brushed her palms over her pressed pants. "And you'll show up?"

"I'd give you my word, but we both know promises between us are pointless." *You promised to come back and never did.* Call that a lesson well learned. Grant retreated into the hallway and barely missed ramming right into his nurse, Aiden. Grant held up his hand, fingers spread wide. "I need five minutes. Just five minutes outside."

Grant headed out the side door into the back parking lot. He strode away from the building and dragged in a deep inhale of dust-tainted air. Seconds passed, and he lifted his gaze toward the cloud-filled sky.

He'd spent those first years at his grandparents' farm wishing on every star he could find in the sky. Every night he had wished. Over and over again. Always the same thing. For his mom to come back. He'd been relentless. Until he'd stopped caring about her. Then he'd stopped wishing for her return. As time went on, he'd prayed for her to stay away. To not come back and take him from his grandparents and the best home he'd ever known.

Now his mother was back.

As if she'd been invited. As if she was wanted.

Grant wanted her gone. Wanted even more to protect his family. He would go to dinner with Lilian Sloan. Tell her that there was nothing for her in Three Springs. Not anymore. If that truth hurt her, he couldn't be held responsible. Besides, it would be a fraction of the pain she'd caused her sons years ago.

He rubbed his ribs. His mind was set. She had to hear the truth. It was as simple as that. And he was the best one to deliver it. For the son was like the mother—unemotional and detached.

Besides, he had to get back to focusing on what he wanted. A position at the prestigious Silverlining TeamMed Sports Clinic in Los Angeles. Two more interviews—one that afternoon—and he would have the position secured and the future he always envisioned would begin. His mother's long overdue return wasn't going to interfere with his plans.

A horn blared somewhere on the other side of the parking lot.

Grant's gaze landed on the old, faded blue truck parked under a tree. Too many dents and scratches had tarnished any vintage appeal. A familiar blond cowgirl sat on the lowered tailgate. A cell phone was pressed to her ear and a notebook rested in her lap as if she always worked best outdoors. She looked comfortable, confident, and entirely too appealing.

Maggie tapped the brim of her cowboy hat up. Then lifted her hand in a sort of shy, tentative wave, aimed right at Grant.

There was nothing tentative about his fascination with that particular cowgirl. Grant turned toward the building and adjusted the knot on his tie.

Maggie Orr wasn't his patient. What she *was,* was more trouble than he wanted to handle.

Time to get back to his patients and his career. Because distractions like Maggie were hazardous to Grant's peace of mind. He was in the business of repairing bones and the body. Maggie, with her big expressive eyes, no doubt had an even bigger heart.

He'd seen her heart earlier in the exam room when her sister had chosen to compete instead of having surgery. Maggie had tucked her chin, chewed on her bottom lip. Her indecision had been clear. His cowgirl had been torn. The love and loyalty the sisters shared was admirable, even if Grant disagreed with their choice.

Usually, Grant bruised hearts like Maggie's more than he ever fixed them.

Besides, captivating cowgirls like her belonged with authentic cowboys like his brothers, not single-minded, headstrong doctors like him.

Still, Grant paused in the open doorway and glanced back at Maggie. One last time.

Because for the first time in decades, Grant wished he was someone else. Someone a cowgirl like her deserved.

CHAPTER THREE

"I'M GETTING SECOND OPINIONS." Kelsey lowered the volume on the truck radio. "I talked to Dr. Toro's nurse, Aiden, on my way out of the clinic. He told me he'd handle everything."

Maggie nodded and took the exit to Starfall Campground and their temporary home base on the outskirts of Three Springs. She'd thought her sister had gone to the bathroom before they'd left Dr. Toro's clinic in Belleridge thirty minutes ago.

"I want a rodeo doctor like Dr. Toro." Kelsey plucked at the bracelets on her arm. "Dr. Toro understands. He gets it."

Maggie wanted to believe Dr. Sloan didn't get it. Not at all. But she wasn't so sure. There'd been something in the way he'd watched her back in that exam room. As if...

Kelsey continued, "You don't need to come with me to the appointments."

That would free Maggie up to find a temp job at a local ranch or farm. Anything to press pause on the steady outflow of money. Whenever she brought up the financials, Kelsey always waved her off. *One more win, Mags, and it'll all wash out. You'll see.*

Maggie adjusted her sunglasses as if she just wasn't looking hard enough. "But I should be there with you, Kels."

"You need to practice, not hold my hand," Kelsey countered. "My medical issues have already taken up enough time."

A good sister would hold Kelsey's hand and be present for her. But Maggie was also her sister's teammate and business partner. As a teammate Maggie needed to practice if she wanted to compete at her best. And a good business partner would fix things without burdening her injured sister with more stress. Yeah, she had to handle the finances on her own and make it right for her sister. "We can decide when the appointments are confirmed if I go or not."

"You need to know my mind is set, Mags. No matter what the other doctors tell me." Kelsey brushed her blond hair behind her ear and tipped her chin at Maggie. "I will ride in two weeks. I won't let you down."

"You've never let me down, Kels," Maggie said.

Kelsey was Maggie's anchor. She had always been there for her. Always. But something felt different now. And that made Maggie worried. Worried that Kelsey's body was letting her down and there was nothing they'd be able to do to stop it. Maggie pulled into an open area in the mostly empty campground and released her tight grip on the steering wheel.

"The horses are going to be thrilled to get out." Kelsey opened her door and hopped down. "I know I need to move."

Maggie cut the engine and met her sister at the back of the trailer. "This isn't resting."

"I won't do anything that aggravates my shoulder," Kelsey promised and unlatched the portable corral panels secured to the outside of the trailer. "But the rest of me needs to move. You know it too."

Kelsey was only ever still if she was sleeping or adding rhinestones to something. Maggie's sister lived in constant motion. Her boots were rarely still, and her mind thrived when focusing on the big picture. She was always envisioning the next town. The next win. The next level.

And painting that picture for Maggie to believe in too. Kelsey had been doing it since their parents' divorce. Always giving Maggie something to look forward to. She'd needed that growing up. More than she could've known.

Lately though, Maggie found herself looking for a guarantee that it was all going to be worth it. That Kelsey's vision was going to be just as she described, if not better. *You need to have more faith, Mags. When have I ever led you astray?*

One of the camper tires looked low. Probably another leak. Yeah, a guarantee would be nice. Just this once. Maggie stomped on her disloyalty and got to work assembling the portable corrals.

Once their practice geldings were grazing in the first corral and Tango, Kelsey's sorrel American quarter horse, used in competition, was in the other corral, Maggie headed back inside the trailer. She worked her way to the last stall, smoothed her hands over her competition mare's sleek back and moved closer to the horse's head. That was when her heart sank.

Lady Dasher's right eye was completely swollen shut. Maggie shook her head. "No. No. Not today."

She tried to get a better look at her mare's eye. The usually easygoing mare was in no mood to cooperate. Whatever direction Maggie came from, the mare swung her head away. Finally, Maggie gave up and stroked the mare's neck. "You're right. It's time to call the doctor and get you help."

After a bit more coaxing than normal, Maggie guided her horse out of the trailer and walked her into the portable corral with Kelsey's gelding. "We need a veterinarian for Lady Dasher. It's her eye."

Kelsey dropped a brush into a bucket and hurried over to the mare. "That looks bad."

Her sister wasn't wrong. Maggie pulled her phone from her pocket and opened her text app. "Ryan will know who to call."

An hour later, Kelsey sat in a chair outside the corral. She sewed rhinestones and other bling onto an arm sling she'd found crammed in a cabinet inside their camper. Maggie clenched the top rail of the portable corral, her nerves stretched thin. She watched Dr. Paige Bishop, or Paige, as she'd told them to call her, examine Lady Dasher's eye. Three Springs's local veterinarian and all-around nice person kept up a running commentary for the horse full of praise and encouragement. Finally, Paige completed her exam then complimented the mare for her courage and patience.

"How bad is it?" Maggie asked and held her breath for the second time that day. The first had been with a different patient and a much different doctor.

"Corneal ulcer and infection." Paige offered one last long pat against the mare's neck. Then she stepped out from under the temporary tarp that they'd set-up over part of the corral to shield the mare from the sunlight. "The good news is that it will heal with proper care."

"And the bad news?" Maggie held onto the corral.

"There's a shortage of the medications we need. I'll put a call into Country Time Farm and Ranch Supply, but it's going to be a few days." Paige aimed her pencil eraser toward the sky. "The bright sunlight is going to cause her even more pain."

Maggie quickly calculated the time until the sun fully set. That would relieve her mare's discomfort temporarily. Only until the sun rose and another summer day descended over the barren, but affordable campsite. "I'm guessing you want her in something darker than our portable shelter."

"Yes, I do." Paige tapped her pencil against her clipboard and frowned. "Unfortunately, we don't have a stall open at the clinic. And my cousin's husband just took in four new rescues at the horse sanctuary he manages."

"I'm sure I can find someplace for her," Maggie said, not feeling confident of that at all.

"Not close and not any place I would approve." Paige braced her boot on the bottom rail of the corral and tapped her pencil against her clipboard.

Maggie chewed on her lip.

"Text Ryan again, Mags," Kelsey suggested. "He'll know someplace we can board her."

"Good idea, Kelsey. I'm sure the Sloans will have more than enough room in their private stables." Paige nodded and eyed Maggie when Maggie didn't immediately reach for her phone.

Then Paige continued, "The Sloan stables are the nicest in all the surrounding counties combined. Trust me. I know. I've been in more stalls than I can count around here. Lady Dasher won't find better accommodations."

Of course, the stables would be nice. The way Ryan had described his family's property, she'd expect nothing less. But it wasn't her horse stabling with the Sloans that concerned Maggie. It was her sister and Dr. Sloan possibly butting heads over her second opinions, as if she didn't trust his diagnosis or his recommendation. Maggie checked her phone. She had no signal. Was that good or bad?

"Even if they don't have room, Ryan will work it out." Kelsey sorted through her container of rhinestones. "Maggie can get Ryan to agree to anything. Any time."

Paige looked at Maggie, speculation lifted her eyebrows slightly.

"It's not like that." Maggie held up her hands and stepped back. "Ryan and I are just friends. Only friends. That's all."

They'd always been *just* friends. There'd never been that buzz of awareness with Ryan. The kind that could make Maggie reconsider her firm no-dating policy. The kind that she'd never experienced with Ryan. But Ryan's handsome little brother...

"Still, I'd like to see how you sway a Sloan, Maggie." Paige chuckled. "My sister is dating Ryan's oldest brother, Carter. And she tells me all the time she's never met a more stubborn bunch than Carter and his brothers."

"We met Dr. Sloan today." Kelsey frowned. "I'd have to agree with you, Paige. He was certainly stubborn and set in his ways."

Yet there'd been something nice, despite the formality, in the low timber of Dr. Sloan's voice. Something that hinted there might be more behind the designer suit label and fancy tie. Not that Maggie was interested in finding out what. It was just more of an observation about her best friend's little brother. Another phone check. Still no signal.

Paige tipped her chin toward the rhinestone-bedecked fabric on the folding table in front of Kelsey. Her voice was mild. "I take it from the arm sling that the appointment didn't go quite as you expected, Kelsey?"

"We're just used to Dr. Toro," Maggie said quickly, not wanting her sister to insult the Sloans and potentially offend Paige.

Maggie and Kelsey had been in more small towns than they could count. Yet one thing they could always rely on was that the communities were close-knit and looked after their own. Maggie and her sister weren't part of Three Springs' own. But they needed Paige's veterinarian care and the Sloan stables, it seemed.

"Dr. Toro is a cowboy's doctor," Kelsey added and smoothed her fingers over the rhinestones she'd sewn around the collar of her denim shirt last week. "Dr. Sloan looked like he should be hosting one of those medical talk shows on TV."

Dr. Dry Clean Only certainly had the look, presence, and confidence for his own TV talk show. But did that automatically disqualify him from treating her sister? Maggie wasn't as certain as Kelsey seemed to be.

Paige laughed. "Do not tell Ryan that or Grant will never hear the end of it."

Kelsey looked as if she was giving the idea too much consideration, then said, "It's hard to believe Dr. Sloan understands us."

But something in the depths of his very

clear, very alert hazel eyes suggested he got Maggie. Understood her. Maggie shook her head. *No*. Her sister was right. They were worlds apart.

"Talk show host looks aside, Grant is seriously one of the best doctors around." Paige spoke with assurance. "And believe it or not, there's more cowboy in Grant than in all of me."

Kelsey's eyebrows arched into her forehead.

"I'm serious." Paige ran a hand over her coveralls and held up two fingers. "I've only been here two years. Before that I was a city girl, born and raised."

Maggie took in the caring veterinarian. She wore a flannel shirt, mussed on one side, a pair of plain, broken-in work boots, jeans, of course, and held a cream-colored vet-kit as if it were an extension of her. More than that, Paige was at ease around Maggie's horse. So much so, Maggie would've assumed Paige had grown up around livestock her whole life. But her Dr. Dry Clean Only, well, he'd worn his suit as if it'd been custom tailored, according to his specifications, and looked as if he wouldn't come within a mile of any living animal.

"Well, I think Dr. Sloan turned his back on his inner cowboy," Kelsey said. "He's completely city now and for a cowgirl like me, farm-raised and rodeo-honed, it's hard to trust that."

Maggie wasn't sure what she trusted, other than Kelsey. She'd learned at a very young age that only her sister ever kept her promises to Maggie. But promises or not, Lady Dasher was a priority too. She'd just have to keep Dr. Sloan and her sister apart. One more phone check and she said, "I keep losing my signal out here."

"I've got it. I'll call the Sloans' farmhouse." Paige pulled out her cell phone, set it to her ear, and greeted the person on the other end of the line. She laughed then stepped to the side of the corral to continue her conversation. She turned to give Maggie an encouraging grin and a thumbs-up sign.

"Must be Ryan," Kelsey said. "She's laughing a lot. Can't be Dr. Sloan. He didn't look like he smiled much."

"It's all set. You can board your horses with the Sloans." Paige walked toward Maggie and held her phone out. "Grant wants to talk to you."

"Grant? You mean, Dr. Sloan?" Maggie took a step back. "I thought you called Ryan."

"I called the farmhouse, like I said I would." Paige shrugged and stretched her arm and her phone closer to Maggie. "Grant answered. Now he wants to speak to you."

This is for Lady Dasher. Maggie plucked

the phone from Paige's palm. The veterinarian walked over to Kelsey's crafting table and Maggie set the phone against her ear. Her voice was tentative. Cautious. "Hello."

"I need your phone number." The handsome, stiff, skilled doctor was straightforward and to the point.

"Excuse me?" Maggie stammered.

"Your sister's number was entered wrong in our system. Penny at Pearls and Presents in the great state of Oklahoma answered when I called it earlier." He paused and his deep sigh stretched over the phone line. "Let's just say that the temporary receptionist the agency sent over may have overexaggerated her skill set."

There was a quick pause. Then the sound of paper shuffling.

He continued, "It doesn't matter. I have the appointment information for those second opinions Kelsey requested."

Maggie winced. "Kelsey told me your nurse was taking care of that."

"He did. He told me about it." His voice was dry and flat. "I spoke to several of my peers to get Kelsey seen this week."

He personally got her sister in quickly? He didn't have to do that. It was kind and considerate. Now Maggie owed Dr. Dry Clean Only, who she could possibly like if he wasn't her sister's doctor. "Thank you."

"I don't like to see my patients wait for care, even if they don't want it from me," he said. "Give me your number and I'll text you the appointment information."

Maggie recited her phone number.

"Got it," he said. "And Maggie, I hope your sister finds the right doctor for her."

Now he sounded sincere too. *Don't make me like you.* She said, "I hope you're not offended."

"I wouldn't be a professional if I was," he replied. "But I stand behind my diagnosis and recommendations. I make my decisions based off the information and facts I am given. In this situation, it's clear cut."

And Maggie often made her decisions based on emotions. Talk about incompatible. "Do you ever change your mind?"

"No." There was a short pause, then he said, "Do you ever change your mind, Ms. Maggie Orr?"

The lightness in his tone added a warm layer to his deep voice. That she certainly didn't need to notice. Or like too. Maggie said, "I've been known to be indecisive occasionally."

Take right now. With you, for example. There were so many logical reasons not to find him the least bit interesting. And yet she did.

"That's good to know." The line went quiet, then he asked, "But I want to know, if I text you about something other than your sister's appointments, would you reply?"

"I guess that depends on what you put in your texts." Now her words sounded playful. Maggie pressed her lips together. This was surely a violation of her yearslong no-dating policy. She wasn't a rule breaker. Didn't intend to start now.

"Well, Maggie," he said. That lightness in his words curved over the speaker like a challenge. "It looks like I'll need to give you a reason to text me back."

Her chuckle was far from effortless. She blamed her sudden nerves. "Well, maybe I'll talk to you soon then."

"Good night, Maggie. We'll expect to see Lady Dasher soon." With that, he ended the call.

"Well, the Sloans have space." Maggie handed the cell phone back to Paige and tried hard to sound cheerful. "Looks like we have a temporary solution."

And what Maggie just had was a temporary glitch. But she was back to following her rules.

She was Team Kelsey.

And she would not fall for a handsome doctor who dressed better than a cover model and tempted her to polish her boots and peel back his layers.

No. She would not fall for Dr. Dry Clean Only.

After all, Maggie was just like her sister——farm-raised and rodeo-honed. And as such, she had more grit than that.

But just to be safe, she wouldn't reply to his texts either.

CHAPTER FOUR

THE NEXT MORNING, Grant set a medical journal on the kitchen table and stretched his arms over his head. It'd been one long restless night of tossing and turning. If he wasn't thinking about what ulterior motive his mother had for her return, then he was thinking about Maggie.

Just before dawn, he'd thrown back the covers, refused to check his phone for a text from Maggie and instead reached for an article on ligament reconstruction. The sun had risen, and he still hadn't checked his phone. Small success there.

Now he needed his usual large to-go cup of coffee and his truck keys. Surely, at the clinic, his work would divert his thoughts fully away from a certain cowgirl. A cowgirl he had no business thinking so much about. Clearly, his mind was too idle, as Gran Claire would've claimed. *If quick minds like yours are idle too long, they find trouble and it's not the good kind either.*

After that declaration, Gran Claire would always hand Grant a book and tell him to get to learning. *There's always more to learn, Grant, in books and in life*. The only thing Grant wanted to know—and had yet to learn—was what the good kind of trouble was. He'd never quite figured it out, even though he and his brothers had given it their best shot growing up.

Grant started the coffee maker and leaned against the counter.

Ryan walked quickly through the kitchen, yanking a t-shirt over his head at the same time. He tugged on his boots, opened the back door then called back to Grant. "Pour me a cup. Extra-large. Black."

"What's the rush?" Grant hollered.

"Mags is here." The door slammed shut on the rest of Ryan's reply.

"Maggie. Maggie Orr?" Grant rushed to the back door, wondering how his serial dating brother had become such good friends with Maggie. He watched a familiar vintage truck and camper horse trailer combo pull to a stop in the curve of their horseshoe-shaped driveway. An equally familiar blonde jumped out of the driver's seat. Grant was outside before he thought better of it.

Ryan jogged down the porch stairs. His voice rang clear and loud in the still cool morning air. "Mustang Mags, we had a deal."

Instantly, Grant found himself caught between wanting to cancel whatever deal his brother had with Maggie or wanting to walk back inside to get his coffee and mind his own business. He didn't move from his spot on the deck. Instead, he widened his stance and remained silent.

"You'll have to remind me about that particular deal, Ryan." Maggie rounded the hood of her battered truck. Her smile was as bright as it was refreshing.

Too bad it was aimed at his big brother. But Grant was used to being overlooked for Ryan.

Maggie added, "Because I don't recall ever making a deal with you."

"You wound me, Mustang Mags." Ryan slapped his hand over his heart then laughed. "But you're on my home turf now. And that means, I'm taking you out for a night on the town per our deal."

"I think you made that deal with Kelsey." Maggie tapped her cowboy hat higher on her head and headed straight for Grant's brother. "Because you know my nights end when yours get started."

"You just need a reason to stay up past nine," Ryan chided and spread his arms wide. "I've got a few for you."

Ryan picked Maggie up off her feet and held

her in a bear hug until she threw her head back and her hat toppled to the ground. Her laughter spilled toward the sky.

And her joy spilled through Grant like that first dive into the cold pond on a hot summer day. Bracing, breathtaking and energizing. He wanted to yell at his brother to knock it off and put his cowgirl down already. But really…when had any woman chosen Grant over Ryan? Accepting the inevitable, he slowly unfolded his arms and moved toward the pair.

The passenger door of the old truck swung open. Maggie's sister stepped out, wearing a sparkly arm sling and a frown. "Ryan and Mags, knock it off already. It's too early in the morning for you two." Kelsey's gaze skipped over to Grant. "Hey, Doc. Thanks for the referrals, but I want a rodeo doctor."

Maggie slapped at Ryan's hands then scrambled away from Grant's brother and over to her sister. She brushed the hair escaping from her ponytail and tucked it behind her ears. "Dr. Sloan."

"Maggie." He bent down, picked up Maggie's hat and handed it to her. Then he looked at her sister. "This is Texas, Kelsey. We're all rodeo certified around here."

"Well, no offense, Doc, but you sure don't dress like it." Kelsey propped her hand on her waist and shifted her weight in her boots. "Or act like it."

Maggie smashed her cowboy hat low on her head.

Ryan shook his head and moved to stand beside Grant.

"It's qualifications you should be concerned about, Kelsey." Grant folded his arms over his dress shirt and tie then tipped his chin at Maggie's headstrong sister. He was all for a strong mind, but not when it bordered on reckless. "Those jeans and boots you're wearing won't get you a clean catch on your steer's horns. But lifting your arm over your head and swinging your nylon head rope at the right time and angle will. That definitely gets you the win. Find the doctor who will give you that, Kelsey."

Kelsey narrowed her gaze on him.

He wasn't there to make friends. Even sugar-coating the truth wasn't always easy to swallow. So, he preferred to just stick to the truth. Grant's gaze shifted to Maggie.

Surprise flickered across Maggie's face.

Yeah, he knew a thing or two about team roping and the rodeo, and more than his surgical suite. But Grant wasn't there to prove himself to a pair of cowgirls either. He was qualified. More than. End of story. He kept his gaze fixed on Maggie. "Are you going to be here long? You're blocking my truck."

She opened and closed her mouth.

Ryan shoved Grant. "If you help and stop lecturing, we'll be done faster and will get out of your way, Dr. Sloan."

"It's only Lady Dasher who's staying here." Maggie motioned to the trailer then looked at Grant. "I can get her myself. No help required."

Translation: *you're off the hook, Doc. Now go away.*

Grant suddenly wanted to stand right in Maggie's way. Right in her space where she couldn't avoid him. Close enough where he could test the strength of that thread of attraction between them. He stayed where he was. After all, even good trouble was still trouble.

Besides, Maggie and Ryan were the logical choice for each other. They both shared a passion for the rodeo. Understood each other's drive. They were clearly friends. Grandpa Sam would call that a perfect pairing.

"Leave all four horses here," Ryan suggested. "We have pastures and stalls. And the horses are safer here than at the campground."

Maggie chewed on her bottom lip.

"Come on, Mags," Ryan urged. "You know I'm right."

Yeah, listen to my brother, Mags. Look at him,

not me. Because when Maggie looked at Grant, a mix of uncertainty and hesitation on her face, he wanted to get involved. Make things right. But Grant wasn't currently getting involved in much outside of his work and his career. Dinner with his mom was the only thing he planned to be involved in. And that was only to protect his brothers. They were building their own lives. Happy and successful ones. He didn't want his mom's unexpected return to interfere with all that. He didn't want her to hurt his brothers again.

Grant dropped his chin and headed toward the trailer. Time to move things along. He had his own day to get to. One that didn't include spending time with a pretty cowgirl who had the sweetest habit of biting her bottom lip. "If your horses have been traveling together for a while, they'll be more comfortable staying that way. It makes sense to leave them all with us."

Grant didn't have that problem. He'd been on his own for years now. Alone was his comfort zone.

"Doc is right," Kelsey said, although slightly less enthusiastic with her support. "Lady Dasher will be calmer with Tango in the stall next to her. Especially since we're waiting on her medicine."

"We've got an indoor arena, Mags," Ryan

offered, ever the gracious host. "We can get in practice. As much as you want."

Worked for Grant. He wouldn't be there.

"That's even better," Kelsey said then she eyed Grant. Her fingers drifted over her arm sling. "I'll be coaching Maggie from the sidelines, of course."

Grant nodded. Kelsey hadn't found a new doctor yet. And until she did, she remained his patient and under his care.

"You guys should just stay too," Ryan said. His voice decisive. "We've got plenty of room in the farmhouse."

No. Grant's eyebrows lowered. That definitely wouldn't work. Stables. Pastures. Arena. Fine. But inside the farmhouse. That was one line too many. Grant had no space in his life for a cowgirl like Maggie.

Apparently, she agreed too. Maggie held up her hand. "Stop, Ryan. Just the horses are staying. Kelsey and I are good in the camper."

"Right." Ryan grinned and tapped the rim of Maggie's cowboy hat. "I forgot how much you like to sleep under the stars."

Instantly, Grant wanted to know more. He reached for the latch on the trailer doors. As if suddenly ready to be helpful and accommodating.

Maggie moved to block him. "I got this. It's fine."

Grant eyed her.

Ryan elbowed his way between them and nudged Maggie toward the corner of the trailer. "We'll unload, Mags. Go with Kelsey to the side door and unload Tango and Lady Dasher. She needs you. Hurry up too. I'm starving. We need to go eat."

"You're always hungry, Ryan." Maggie chuckled.

"Keeping all this going takes lots of fuel, Mags." Ryan ran his hands over his chest and grinned. "I can't help it."

Grant rolled his eyes.

Maggie laughed.

And Grant discovered the appeal of being helpful. It wasn't long before the four horses were off-loaded and ready for their new quarters.

Ryan held the reins of a chestnut quarter horse and ran his hand over the gelding's muscular back. "Did I mention that Tess is cooking today? You guys picked the best day to come. Tess's food is amazing."

Maggie stood beside an impressive dun American quarter horse with a rich tan coat and deep black mane and tail. She glanced at Grant. "What is your day to cook?"

She sounded as if she wanted to avoid that day. Grant said, "I don't have one."

He couldn't be included in the cooking rotation when he wasn't going to be there long term. But he might make an exception if Maggie was his guest. If only for the chance to make her laugh again.

"Grant isn't into small talk or family bonding over leisurely meals." Ryan slapped him on the shoulder.

But Grant could be into a certain pretty cowgirl and learning more about her other than she preferred to sleep under the stars. If he was staying in town. However, he was chasing big goals in the city. And those city lights often blocked the stars. Just as he blocked his interest in Maggie now.

"Come on, Kelsey, we'll take this pair to the pasture. Grant is hardly dressed for the ranch today." Ryan bumped his elbow into Grant's side and chuckled. Then he took the reins of the two practice horses. "Grant, go with Maggie to the stables. Once we're done, we'll meet up with you guys at the house."

Kelsey handed over her horse's reins to Grant and considered him. "Maggie knows what to do for Tango."

Grant watched Maggie's sister chat easily and happily with Ryan as the pair walked off.

He shook his head. "Your sister doesn't like me much."

"She doesn't know you well enough yet to like you or trust you," Maggie said.

"That was straightforward." Talk about no sugar coating.

"You seem like someone who prefers that," she said and started walking toward the stables.

He caught her small grin before she turned her head to look around the property. She was starting to seem like someone he could prefer more and more. But he wasn't home to start anything. Home was only a layover until his real future began on the West Coast.

Inside the stables, he led her to the opposite end of the large, clean building and stopped at the last stall. "Paige told me you needed the darkest stall possible. This should work."

"It's perfect." Maggie guided Lady Dasher into the wide stall and checked the water bucket. Then her attention was on the mare's eye and ensuring the mare's comfort. And something in Maggie's expression said it was anything but perfect.

Grant led Tango into the stall beside Lady Dasher and removed the horse's halter. His brother would no doubt know how to make Maggie smile. Or laugh and forget her troubles. But Grant had never been like his brother. He gave the gelding a quick rubdown, checked both the water and hay buckets, then leaned on Lady Dasher's stall door. "We can contact my other brother, Josh. He's a horse trainer. He might have pain medicine on hand for Lady Dasher."

"Thanks, but I'll figure it out." Maggie ran her fingers through her mare's dark mane. "I'll take care of it."

"Do you always do that?" he asked.

Her hands stilled. "What?"

"Take care of everyone?" he asked. She'd jumped to her sister's side earlier before Kelsey had even said anything.

"I don't mind." She went back to concentrating on her horse.

There was a weariness in her words. Subtle, yet he'd caught it. But then noticing the details, even the most seemingly trivial, was part of his training. What made him good. But Maggie wasn't under his care. She wasn't his patient. She wasn't really even his friend either. And that meant he shouldn't care. "Well, I'll leave you to it."

He turned and made to leave.

"Dr. Sloan," she called out.

"Grant," he corrected.

She nodded then lifted her chin and eyed

him. "Cowboy doctor or not, any second opinion is going to be the same, isn't it? Kelsey needs surgery."

Grant rubbed his chin and watched her. "You look like you prefer to hear things straight too, Maggie."

"Most times," she admitted. "And now seems like one of those times."

"If a doctor is reviewing the same test results I did, and they will be because I sent each one Kelsey's complete file," he said, allowing only the smallest pause before he kept the straight talk going. "Then it's unlikely another doctor will recommend anything different."

Maggie's inhale was quick like the kind of breath a patient took before a shot in the arm.

Grant shoved his hands into the pockets of his dress pants. Not his patient to soothe. Not even his friend to hold.

"Thanks." Her eyebrows pulled together, yet her shoulders stiffened. "It's good to be prepared."

And now, so was he. He knew with certainty he wasn't the one who'd ever make Maggie smile. He headed for the stables' exit and walked to the farmhouse. He wanted his keys and his coffee and a quick escape.

What he got was his older brother's girlfriend, Tess Palmer, guarding the back door to the farmhouse. She pointed at him. "You're sitting down and having breakfast with your family this morning, Grant Alexander Sloan."

Grant folded his arms over his chest and arched an eyebrow at Tess. "Only my Gran Claire used my full name."

"She gave me permission," Tess countered.

"How do you know that?" he asked. "Gran Claire passed away years ago."

"I still talk to her," Tess announced. Her hand fluttered around in front of her. "Like this morning, I told her I was going to give you a piece of my mind. You know what happened?"

Grant rolled his lips together to keep his smile contained. He could see why Carter had fallen for the quirky but caring general store owner. She was really hard not to like.

"I'll tell you what happened," Tess continued. "My soufflé came out of the oven perfectly. Best one I've ever made. And it's still standing inside the kitchen now. That's your Gran Claire giving me her approval."

Grant motioned toward the door. "Can we do this later? I need to get to work."

"That's my point." Tess extended her arms over her head and up into the air, obviously exasperated. "You're never here. You're home, but not really. And there's an entire family inside that house who wants to spend time with you. Even if it's just for breakfast."

Yet, it wasn't *just* anything. Not with his family. And if he stayed for one meal, they'd expect him at the next. And then another. And then they might expect him to stay. To stay home for good. "Tess, I'm leaving soon. Everyone knows that."

"All the more reason you should be in there now," Tess argued. "With your family."

All the more reason he shouldn't be in there. He needed to be out west—it was at such a prestigious medical center where he'd refine his skills and build a résumé that would prove he was the top in his field. Then he'd finally be satisfied. Fulfilled even. Family breakfast, no matter how entertaining, added no real value to his work. And, therefore, his life. There would be other breakfasts.

Bonding with his family served absolutely no tangible purpose. Other than making the leaving all that much harder. Because he was going to leave. Besides, his family had been fine while he was away at med school. Thriving, really. They didn't need him intruding on all they'd built while he was gone. He was good, taking his meals when his schedule allowed, keeping his focus on work where it belonged.

Footsteps sounded on the deck behind him. Grant glanced over his shoulder, saw Maggie walking toward them and calculated whether or not he could slip past Tess. His keys were on the hook just inside the door. All he had to do was grab and go.

"This isn't over, Grant." Tess frowned at him then broke into a wide smile and greeted Maggie with a warm, welcoming hug. The clever shop owner never quite moved from her position in front of the door and said, "It's great to meet you, Maggie. Go on inside. Your sister is already at the table with the rest of the family."

Maggie looked from Tess to Grant. "Aren't you coming?"

Tess tapped her finger against her chin and narrowed her gaze on Grant. "We were just discussing that very thing."

"You're one of those people who juices, aren't you, Dr. Sloan?" Maggie said in an almost accusing tone and studied Grant.

It wasn't lost on him that she'd used his formal title. Guess that was appropriate for the not-quite-friends that they were.

Then Maggie added, "The skip the bacon, it's kale and chia seeds for me kind of doctor."

"Should you make those kinds of assumptions based on how a person looks? And just what do I look like, for that matter?" Grant set his hands on his hips, wondering what it would take for her to call him by his first name. As if he cared. As if he wanted her as a friend.

"You look like a host for a medical TV talk show." Maggie patted her stomach. "Juice for you because the camera adds ten pounds, or so I've heard."

Tess's eyes widened. Her shoulders shook. But her laughter remained silent.

Maggie arched a brow as if challenging him to prove her wrong.

She was proving how much he could like her. If he wanted to. If he was interested in connecting with more than his patients and his surgical team. "I like bacon. The crispier the better. My eggs fried and real butter on my biscuits." Grant walked to the back door, opened it, and motioned the pair inside. "Let's go have breakfast."

Tess cheered, albeit with only a wiggle of her eyebrows and a squeeze on Grant's shoulder. Then she hurried ahead.

Maggie followed.

When Maggie was beside Grant in the doorway, he leaned in and said, "And you, Maggie Orr, look like you could be trouble."

Unfortunately, even with all those books Gran Claire had given Grant, she'd never managed to curb his fascination with trouble.

"Now, that's something I haven't been called before." Maggie turned toward him.

Her gaze was shadowed by her cowboy hat. But her voice was pensive as if she just might be considering the merits of being dubbed *trouble*. And the trouble was that Grant didn't want to let her go just yet. He said, "You never responded to my text last night."

"I fell asleep," she said. No apology. No regret. "And I've been too busy this morning to reply."

In fairness, it hadn't been all that inspiring. Casual and brief. He supposed he hadn't passed her test. Grant rubbed his chin. "Guess I'll have to make the next one more interesting then."

Just like with his text, she didn't respond. Only spun on her bootheels and strode into the house. But Grant saw the hint of a blush on her cheeks.

And that was more than enough to make him want to stick around for seconds.

CHAPTER FIVE

MAGGIE WASN'T TROUBLE. But she may have caused some.

She should've gone right inside. Not stood on the porch and challenged Dr. Sloan.

Because she'd overheard his conversation with Tess.

Because she'd seen the distress on the woman's face from clear across the wide patio.

Or because she thought she'd seen a vulnerability in Dr. Sloan too. In the way he held himself, so still and contained. As if he wanted to be detached but wasn't and feared the smallest movement would give him away.

Worse, she'd given herself an even bigger dose of trouble. He was supposed to be starched, Dr. Dry Clean Only in her eyes, anyway. Not Grant, a man and beloved brother. With layers and hidden depth.

Nothing good could come from knowing that. Maggie cleaned her boots on the mat in the mudroom, then washed her hands in the laundry room sink. The sudsy water circled the drain along with her thoughts of Grant.

He could only ever be her Dr. Sloan. No more. No less.

After all, Maggie had made her choice years ago. She'd chosen her sister and she always would. She'd placed a Do Not Disturb sign on her heart, set love in the spectator section, and put all her attention on her team roping career.

Besides, falling for someone like Grant would come with a steep price. Love always did. And it was an amount Maggie wasn't willing pay.

The laughter and the lively conversation circled Maggie as soon as she walked into the farmhouse kitchen. She barely glimpsed the modern appliances and family room beyond when an older cowboy, with a pure white beard, approached, lifted his sand-colored cowboy hat to reveal his equally white hair, and offered her a hearty welcome.

"You must be Maggie." Sam Sloan's smile was kind, his gaze clever and the deep lines around his eyes wise. "We've been talking about you with your sister."

Maggie opened her mouth.

"It's nothing to worry about, Mags," Kelsey interrupted and waved from her seat at the end of a very large, solid oak table.

A full plate of food sat in front of Maggie's sister, and her arm sling sparkled. Kelsey looked happy and seemed entirely at home with the rest of the Sloan family, which included identical twins, Josh and Caleb.

Sam introduced Maggie to Josh, a talented horse trainer. Josh added that he was exactly eleven minutes older than Caleb and obviously better looking.

Caleb, the youngest and the tallest of the brothers, gleefully claimed his brothers were simply practice runs until he came along, and his parents found themselves with perfection inside and out. That earned an eye roll from Josh, followed by a light punch on Caleb's shoulder.

"That's enough about us." Caleb grinned at Maggie and tapped the empty chair next to him. "Come on over, Mags, and take a seat. Ryan has filled us in. Your sister too. Now we want to hear from you."

Maggie's gaze skipped around the table. She was uncertain about what the conversation had been like but was already feeling herself drawn to the good-natured family. Maybe breakfast wouldn't be any trouble after all. "Is there something I should know?"

"Nothing to worry about, Maggie. We've been having a bit of a debate with your sister."

The other older cowboy, seated beside Kelsey, waved his fork and waggled his salt-and-pepper eyebrows at Maggie. Then he introduced himself as Roy Sloan and said, "Now that you're here, Maggie, you can settle things for us once and for all."

Maggie glanced at her sister. Kelsey speared a piece of melon on her fork and gave nothing away. Until Kelsey's attention lifted over Maggie's shoulder and her sister's eyes narrowed ever so slightly.

Dr. Sloan appeared on Maggie's left. He wore dress pants, a sharp silk tie, and had the same bold presence as when she'd met him in his office yesterday. But his designer clothes didn't boost his confidence. He just was. He should've come off as brash. Arrogant. Yet he wasn't.

She wanted that to be a flaw. Another reason to keep her interest in the good doctor in check.

Sam's eyebrows lifted at his grandson. The thinnest thread of hope wove through his words. "Grant, you joining us today then?"

Maggie watched the self-assured doctor hesitate. He touched the watch on his wrist as if preparing to blame the time and his tight schedule for his soon-to-be absence. For skipping out on his family again.

Then his hazel-eyed gaze collided with Maggie's and held. There was nothing uncertain in his candid stare or his words. "Yeah. I heard Tess's egg soufflé is not to be missed. And you know I'm never one to pass up homemade biscuits and bacon."

Maggie looked away first. Cutting the connection. After all, she'd gotten Dr. Sloan to the breakfast table. Now she was out. It was up to his family to do the rest.

Sam glanced from his grandson to Maggie. Speculation flared across his face, then it was gone. Replaced by a smile that lifted into his white beard. "Well, let's get to eating. Can't ever have enough bacon. I always consider it the perfect start to a day."

Sam guided Maggie to the table and pulled out the empty chair beside Caleb. That left one more chair vacant next to Maggie.

But Dr. Sloan never sat down. Instead, he grabbed the coffee pot, refilled his grandfather's and uncle's cups, and then scanned the rest of the table as if food service had been part of his former work experience and returned to take up a spot at the island.

"Thank you, Mr. Sloan." Maggie smiled at the older cowboy.

"I answer to Grandpa or Sam. Only my Claire called me Mr. Sloan when I stepped out of line."

Sam's chuckle was wistful. His gaze filled with pride. He tipped his chin toward the other end of the table where Tess held hands with a dark-haired man whose reserve matched Dr. Sloan's.

Sam added, "Now *Mr. Sloan* is better suited for my grandson Carter, when he's handling his important distillery business and needs a little clout."

"I go by Carter, Maggie. Both here and at work." The distillery owner lifted his coffee cup in greeting to Maggie, never released his hold on Tess's hand and grinned. "Grandpa himself taught me the power is in how you treat people, not in a title."

A plate full of food was set on the placemat in front of Maggie, along with a cup of coffee. Her doctor was back in the kitchen before she could thank him.

"What about me?" Ryan asked. He sat across the table from Maggie. Amusement circled through his words. "I could answer to Mr. Sloan too."

"You answer to bucking broncs." Sam returned to his seat on the other side of Kelsey. "They don't care what your title is. Or your name. And they only respect you if you stay on for eight seconds and not a second less."

"True." Ryan shook his head. "And Mr.

Sloan makes me sound outdated. Carter can have it. He's getting up there in years anyway."

A biscuit sailed across the table from Carter's end. Ryan snatched it midair and offered his thanks.

"Can we not do this today? Please," Tess pleaded.

Dr. Sloan dropped into the chair beside Maggie. She should've felt crowded between the two Sloan men. Instead, she wanted to scoot closer to one and lean in. Maggie pressed her bootheels into the floor and locked herself in her chair. There was no leaning in allowed, especially not with her doctor.

Josh was reaching across the table before Dr. Sloan's plate settled on the placemat. The twin snatched two pieces of bacon from the doctor's plate.

Dr. Sloan's shoulder bumped against Maggie's, but the lighthearted warning in his words was all Grant. "The only rule here is eat fast. Otherwise, your plate will be empty, and you won't have taken a bite."

Maggie had a new rule too. Appreciate the sweet scent of vanilla and warm maple syrup covering her waffles, not the rich scent of Dr. Sloan's cologne.

"He's not wrong, Mags." Ryan swiped the last

of Dr. Sloan's bacon from his plate and laughed as he took a large, satisfied bite.

"This is what I'm talking about," Tess said. "We have guests today. Can we make it look like we're not a bunch of kindergarten kids for once? Please."

"Gran Claire taught us to share." Caleb plucked a blueberry from Maggie's plate. "That's all this is."

Tess frowned and pointed her fork at each of the brothers. "I know she taught you all how to dance, so she surely taught you manners too."

Grant left again and returned with the plate of bacon, setting it in the middle of the table. The bowl of blueberries he handed to Caleb.

As for Maggie, he left her with another brush of his arm against hers. Another inhale of his cologne. But starched, right-minded doctors shouldn't smell good and remind her of summer nights after a rainstorm washed the countryside clean. Maggie was sinking into that trouble again.

Josh leaned back in his chair, motioned to his twin, and considered Tess. "What do you want us to do?"

Tess intercepted another biscuit and frowned at Caleb. "There's nothing wrong with sitting down, eating from your own plate and talking."

"Okay, everyone. Tess wants us to talk."

Caleb cradled the blueberry bowl. "Let's get back to talking about Maggie and her pick."

Everyone around the table nodded, even her sister, as if Maggie had been in on the earlier conversation. But she'd been outside, with her doctor. Not at the table where she clearly should've been.

"We've been talking it over with your sister." Sam cut in before Maggie could decide if she was picking someone to help her clean stalls or to date.

"Ryan is the most logical choice," Kelsey offered, her voice clear-cut.

"But we're all qualified to help Maggie." Caleb tossed blueberries into his mouth, one after another in quick succession. "You don't have to pick Ryan because he's, you know, Ryan."

No, Maggie didn't know. Her bite of waffle got stuck in her suddenly dry throat. She reached for her coffee and took a long sip. That dust-coated sensation remained. "I'm not sure I'm following."

Beside her, Grant had gone decidedly still.

She sensed more trouble might be coming after all. Maggie reached for her coffee cup, trying to look unaffected and uncommitted. "What exactly am I choosing?"

"One of my grandsons." Sam toasted her with

his coffee mug. "You can't very well go it alone, my dear."

That sounded decidedly like choosing a date. Ryan had been lamenting for a while now that his grandfather's latest hobby was matchmaking. Maggie cradled her coffee cup in her hands and searched the hot liquid for a way out of the conversation. At the very least, a conversational detour. She considered grabbing a biscuit and throwing it at Ryan to continue the food fight.

"Gotta have a partner," Roy said from his seat beside Kelsey.

Maggie's knee bumped against Grant's under the table. Had he widened his stance? Better to shove a chair back for a hasty retreat away from this family's matchmaking maneuverings.

Roy continued, "After all, it's called team roping for a reason."

Maggie choked on her sip of coffee and glanced around the table. Finally, her gaze landed on Sam. "You want me to choose a roping partner?"

"Of course, we do." Sam straightened and studied her.

Roy reached over and patted Kelsey's good arm. "What with your sister and her bad shoulder and all. She can't practice with you. It's obvious."

Now Maggie knew where Ryan and Caleb got the mischievous glints in their gazes from.

Sam's gaze fairly sparkled from the far end of the dining table when he asked, "What'd you think you were picking?"

Her sister's shoulder shook, and Kelsey hid her chuckle behind her coffee mug as if enjoying her own private little joke. Maggie dipped her head and vowed sisterly payback. Then she shifted away from Grant.

Because beneath the minor misunderstanding was a not-so-minor realization. Maggie's first thought had been a date. Not roping. Not winning. Not her career. Where it should have been. Where it always had been.

Maybe Dr. Sloan had the right idea. And the next time she was invited to a Sloan family meal she should decline. Otherwise, she just might find more trouble than she wanted.

Sam waved at Tess. "Didn't Tess fill you in when she came to get you earlier?"

"No. Sorry." Tess laughed. Her eyes danced too. "We got to talking about TV shows outside just now and I completely forgot to tell Maggie that you all decided she needed a practice partner."

"Before you make your choice, Maggie, you should see my grandsons in action," Sam suggested and added several spoonfuls of sugar to his coffee.

"That's a fair point." Ryan rubbed his chin and nodded.

"Josh has built a first-class training center right here." Pride and affection infused Sam's weathered face and words. "We can take Maggie out there and you all can show off your skills. Then she can make her choice."

"We can get livestock to practice with from Evan Bishop." Carter pushed his empty plate away and looked at Maggie. "Evan owns a cattle ranch in town. He'll have steer we can use."

"Well, that's settled. Now we just need the when." Sam took a bite of his eggs, swallowed, then shook his piece of toast at Maggie. "What do you say, Maggie? When do you want to make your partner pick?"

"Give me back ten years and Maggie would've picked me." Roy brushed crumbs off his plaid shirt, then patted his curls into place. He waggled his eyebrows at Maggie. "I guarantee it."

Maggie wanted to pick the older cowboy now. But choosing one of the brothers? No. Kelsey was right. The logical choice was Ryan. Maggie's knee bumped against Dr. Sloan's. Maggie said, "I can manage on my own. With my roping practice." And her personal life.

"But we want to help." Sam's smile was encouraging. "Ryan says you're practically family."

Dr. Sloan leaned into her and whispered, "Welcome to the family. Bit of advice. Just go with it 'cause there's no stopping them now."

Just as there was no stopping the splash of warmth that curved through her at her doctor's words. *Welcome to the family.*

Roy rubbed his hands together. "How about this weekend for the partner tryout, Maggie?"

"Then Grant can join in." Carter drummed his fingers on the table and watched Grant. The challenge hung in the silence.

"Don't say you have to work either." Caleb frowned at Grant. "It's the weekend. The clinic is closed."

Grant opened his mouth.

Maggie sensed his refusal coming. She poked him in the leg to get him to cooperate and whispered, "Just go with it."

He poked her back and closed his mouth.

"Of course, you could merely watch, Grant." Caleb reached behind Maggie and shoved at Grant's shoulder playfully. "You have been spending more time in operating rooms than saddles these days."

Josh tapped his chin and considered Grant.

"We understand if you're afraid of a little competition now that you're a fancy doctor."

Maggie poked Grant's leg again. Couldn't he see all the hopeful looks aimed his way? His family wanted him there. Tess hadn't been wrong. And Maggie hadn't been wrong to push him earlier. Just as she was going to poke him until he yielded now.

But he was ready for her. She'd barely reached toward him, and he captured her hand in his and held their joined hands against his leg. His words were mild. "I'm not afraid, little brother. I can handle myself in and out of the arena. You aren't worried, are you?"

"Not even a little bit." Caleb chuckled and focused on polishing off his second helping of egg casserole.

Grant squeezed Maggie's hand and said, "Then I'll be there."

At the other end of the table, Kelsey pursed her lips. Her gaze once again narrowed on Dr. Sloan. Clearly, Kelsey liked the whole of the Sloan family, except one.

Maggie liked one of the Sloan family a bit too much. And the feel of his hand in hers, well, that was something she could get used to.

Now that left Maggie with a choice. Like always.

Maggie tugged her hand free. Cutting their connection.

After all, she had to keep chasing down steers and jackpots and sponsors. All the things that would make her and her sister a success. And connections like the one with her doctor, well, those were all too often broken anyway.

Kelsey picked up her cell phone, offered a quick apology to the table, and stood up. With her phone pressed to her ear, Kelsey's gaze showed alarm.

Maggie instantly worried.

"Now?" Kelsey spun around and rushed toward the mudroom. "That shouldn't be a problem."

But from the sudden static in Kelsey's words, there was a problem. And it was bigger than the handholding under the table kind. Maggie pushed her chair back and stood. "Sorry. I need to check on my sister."

CHAPTER SIX

NOT EVEN FIVE minutes had passed from Maggie leaving the kitchen table to reaching the camper and her sister. Five minutes. One phone call. And her sister was in complete disarray.

Kelsey's arm sling was up around her neck. The strap and her ponytail were twisted together. And still Kelsey kept yanking.

Maggie rushed forward. "Kels, what are you doing?"

"Help me." Her sister tugged on her ponytail and only tangled herself more. Her words were urgent and tense. "This has to come off now."

"It's supposed to be on." Maggie batted her sister's hand away and worked to untwist her hair from the strap.

"It can't be on, Mags." Kelsey's words became more strained. "Lewis Trumbly from Denim Country is coming to the interview this morning. The interview with *Lasso Your Lifestyle* magazine that you promised to reschedule."

Maggie winced. She'd forgotten. There'd been

new truck tires to find. Practice. Farrier appointments. More practice. Feed store runs. The list went on. Maggie had been doing her best to make sure her sister was doing the least. She hadn't wanted to cause Kelsey's shoulder any unnecessary pain. Maggie thought she had it all handled. She cleared her throat. "That's today?"

"Yes, and they're coming now." Kelsey's words snapped out like pebbles pinging against a windshield. She continued, "I told them we were stabling the horses here. They want pictures of us. Riding and roping. Doing our thing, as he put it on the phone."

"It was supposed to be a simple interview over lunch." Maggie freed her sister's hair and handed Kelsey her arm sling. "She called it a casual chat. A 'get to know the Orr sisters' sort of article."

"Not anymore." Kelsey tugged her hair tie out and shook the long strands around her shoulders. Then she gave Maggie a slow once over from her head to her boots. "We need horses saddled. And you definitely need to change."

Maggie glanced down at her plain, pale-pink tank top and favorite pair of work jeans. Her attire wasn't the so-called elephant in the pasture. "You can't ride, Kels."

"This isn't riding *riding* and anyway..." Kelsey brushed her hair over her shoulder as if she wanted to brush away Maggie's words. "I have to."

"But…" Maggie started then looked at Dr. Sloan, crossing the porch and heading straight toward them.

"What's going on?" he asked.

"We've got some rodeo business to take care of." Kelsey braced her hand under her right elbow as if filling in for her missing sling. If she was in pain, she gave no hint of it. "We have to saddle the horses. Prepare for a photoshoot and an interview. They should be by soon."

Maggie rubbed the back of her neck. The sun was already heating up. But not as much as the standoff between her sister and Dr. Sloan. Choices. It always came down to choices for Maggie. And it seemed she was always picking a side.

Dr. Sloan braced his hands on his hips and said, "You can't ride, Kelsey."

Her sister tipped her chin up. Her voice as firm as the doctor's. "It's not up for discussion, Doc."

Grant looked at Maggie and arched an eyebrow.

Time to pick that side. Maggie turned her sister toward the camper door and gave her a none-too-gentle nudge. "Kelsey, go. Go put on makeup or whatever you need to do to get ready for pictures." Then she swung back to face Dr. Sloan.

"Doctors fire patients." His gaze tracked her sister until Kelsey disappeared inside the camper. Then he looked at Maggie. "It happens all the time."

"But you won't." Maggie searched his gaze.

She'd watched him at breakfast. For a man who hadn't wanted to be there, he'd catered to everyone before they even knew they needed something. Refilling coffee cups. The biscuit basket. The fruit bowl. And he'd never looked put out that his food was getting cold. Right now, however, he looked more than a little exasperated.

Maggie kept her voice soft. "You won't fire Kelsey because you take care of people too, even the difficult ones."

His chin lowered as if she'd called out his weakness. He said, "Everybody has their limit."

"No one knows the severity of her injury," Maggie said. "Not our agent. Not our sponsors and most especially not the sponsor who's about to arrive with the interviewer for *Lasso Your Lifestyle* magazine."

Surprise widened his eyes. "You haven't told anyone?"

"I know. I shouldn't be lying." There were

those secrets again. Maggie threw her hands in the air as if that would free her of the guilt. But they were so close to turning that corner. To reaching their goals. To getting everything Kelsey had dreamed about. After all the hard times, it wasn't too much to ask, was it? She added, "I get it, but now isn't the time for a lecture. I need to saddle horses and get myself ready."

Ryan jogged over to them. "What's going on, Mags?"

"I forgot to reschedule an interview with *Lasso Your Lifestyle*." Maggie rubbed her forehead. "They're coming here now. Sorry to impose."

"It's not a problem. Use the arena. The light is good in there," Ryan said. "I've got to get to the sanctuary. There's a problem with the pregnant mare they took in. Caleb and Carter are heading to the distillery. Josh has a client."

"I'll stick around here." Dr. Sloan looked at Maggie. "You know. In case you or your sister need anything."

"Grant will take care of you guys." Ryan squeezed his brother's shoulder then grinned at Maggie. "Smile, Mags. Try to look like you're having fun and enjoying yourself. No pressure. It's just an interview and photo session with a national magazine. No big deal."

"Go. Go now." Maggie pointed over Ryan's shoulder. "Because you're not helping. At all."

Ryan walked backward and tipped his cowboy hat up on his forehead. "Mags gets really nervous in front of a camera, Grant. It's the strangest thing. Her smile gets all...and her face pinches up. Her eyes close."

"Still not helping," Maggie warned her friend.

"Make her laugh, Grant," Ryan called out. "Then her blue eyes get bigger. That's good for the camera."

Maggie slapped her hands over her face.

Ryan's laughter swirled around her.

"He wasn't teasing you, was he?" Dr. Sloan's low timbre spoken aloud settled inside Maggie.

She spread her fingers, peeked at her doctor, who unfortunately hadn't budged, then she lowered her arms. "Don't you have patients to see this morning?"

It was all he could do earlier to get out of breakfast with Tess. Now with Maggie, he looked as if lingering was his new favorite pastime. She never should've interfered. Poked him. Or held his hand. *Trouble, Mags. Nothing but trouble.* Everyone always made out trouble to sound like so much fun. Maggie wasn't having fun.

"My first patient isn't until ten thirty." He

glanced at his watch. "The temp at the front desk changed the appointment program to East Coast time. Everyone's appointments got moved back an hour. Don't ask." He paused before hooking his thumb over his shoulder. "Which horse do you want from the pasture? I'm assuming Lady Dasher will sit this one out."

Lucky mare that she was. Maggie had agreed to do the interview only when she'd been assured it was just a conversation. No photoshoot. "I'll saddle King. He's the chestnut with the full blaze. But I can get him. He can be temperamental, especially when he's happy out in the pasture doing his thing."

"I know the feeling." Dr. Sloan smiled at her. "We'll get along fine."

And Maggie would get along not knowing what a smiling Dr. Sloan looked like. She started to argue.

But the camper door swung open, and Kelsey hollered, "Get a move on, Mags. I need Tango's saddle. And you really need to change. I should have something with more color in my closet for you to wear."

Dr. Sloan's gaze tracked over Maggie's face as if he was searching for something. Finally, he lifted his gaze back to hers. "Better go and take care of your sister."

Pick your side, Mags. She said, "Well, it was my fault."

"Mistakes happen."

"Not on my watch." Maggie turned and headed for the camper.

She wouldn't make the mistake of falling for her doctor.

It always circled back to what mattered the most. One more ride. One more win. For her sister. For their team.

Because hearts were never on the line. And love had never been the goal.

CHAPTER SEVEN

GRANT WAITED OUTSIDE Maggie's camper and stroked his hand down King's neck. The gelding had been friendly and almost eager for the saddle as if he anticipated getting in some roping time. Or maybe that was Grant anticipating seeing Maggie on her horse. In her element.

The camper door opened. Maggie stepped out. And Grant stared.

Rude. Sure. But it was all he could do. She'd changed into a deep blue tank top. The vibrant color only enhanced her already striking blue eyes. A single row of rhinestones curved along the neckline of her tank top, adding just a hint of shimmer. Her blonde hair swept past her shoulders. And just like that his cowgirl swept his breath away.

"The makeup is too much, isn't it?" Maggie touched her face, then rubbed at her eyelids. "I knew it was too much."

"Maggie." Grant took her hand and tugged it away from her face. He waited until she focused on him, then said, "You were pretty before and you're pretty now."

She tugged her hand from his. "You can't say that."

"Why not?" He let his gaze trail over her face, slowly. Taking his time. As if she was the only detail he wanted to know. "I'm simply stating a fact."

A door slammed somewhere behind him.

Maggie blinked and retreated without moving. The softness in her gaze shuttered.

Instantly, Grant knew he was back to Dr. Sloan in her mind. That was probably for the best. He was really only there to watch out for her sister anyway. He could certainly do that and keep his thoughts about Maggie to himself.

Maggie's gaze focused on something behind him. Her mouth twitched. One side lifted.

Grant watched Maggie while he listened to the commotion. The tromp-thud-tromp of boots on wood. The impatient but secretly pleased commentary. Grant said, "Let me guess. Uncle Roy and Grandpa Sam are scrambling across the porch like there's a fire."

Maggie pressed her fingers over her mouth and caught her laugh. She nodded.

His grandpa hollered to hurry it along, you

two. Grant continued, "And Carter and Tess are saying goodbye."

Maggie's gaze skipped back to his. "They don't look to be in any rush. Or the least bit concerned."

Grant turned toward the farmhouse.

Uncle Roy scurried by them and touched his hat. "No time to chat. We're late."

"We gotta get to the Silver Penny and claim the book nook before the garden club. It's the historical committee's turn to use it for our meeting today. Not that the garden club follows the rules." Grandpa Sam was hot on Uncle Roy's bootheels. "See you two at dinner."

The cowboy duo was inside a deep blue truck before Grant could give his customary working late excuse.

Tess reached the gravel driveway and smiled at them. "If you have time, Maggie, come see me at the general store. I have new chocolate samples and I need taste testers."

That was all Tess got out before Carter swept her off her feet and spun her around for another kiss.

The truck horn blared, disrupting the couple's moment. Grandpa Sam stuck his head out the window and tapped his watch. "Carter, if we don't get the book nook for our meeting today, I'm nominating you to chair the historical committee for the next two terms. And you'll win too. I'll make sure of it."

Carter took his time releasing Tess then he faced the truck. "Grandpa, I'm only following your instructions. You told me *kiss her good morning. Kiss her good night. And whatever you do, never forget that one rule.*"

Grandpa Sam rolled up the window and trapped his reply inside the truck cab.

Carter settled his hat on his head and started whistling. Then he turned and nodded to Maggie. A grin worked across his face. "Best part of my day is that woman."

With that declaration, Grant's big brother continued walking and whistling as if he hadn't a care in the world. As if he didn't have wheat fields to harvest. A distillery to run. And any number of other business decisions that required his full attention.

Grant scratched his cheek and stared at his brother's back.

"You okay, Dr. Sloan?" Maggie asked. "You look like you don't recognize your own brother. It's the whistling, isn't it? Did you think he was going to be off-key too?"

Grant took in Maggie's quiet grin and shook his head. "Believe it or not, Carter used to be more serious than me."

"I can't imagine anyone being more serious

than you." Maggie reached for King's reins. "You sort of take it to new levels."

"That doesn't sound like a compliment." Grant walked beside her toward the stables. "I prefer dedicated and focused over serious anyway."

"Are you saying your brother isn't dedicated or focused?' Maggie asked.

"Not at all." Carter hadn't lost either his dedication or his focus. The distillery was performing even better than Carter projected. The wheat crop yield would be high. Still, Grant's big brother was different now. "Carter is in love."

"You don't have to sound so grim about it." Maggie chuckled. "You're supposed to be happy for happily in love couples."

Grant was happy for his big brother. Love suited Carter well and Grant was more than content to let his brother have it. All of it. Grant trusted those facts he found in his medical books. He relied on logic and good common sense. In his experience, love was unpredictable and flawed and nothing he ever wanted to trust in again.

Maggie bumped her elbow into his side, drawing his attention to her. Her words were playful. "Worried you might catch the love bug too, Dr. Sloan?"

"Not in the least." He grinned at her. "Love and I have an understanding. We've agreed. We don't want to be involved with each other."

Maggie laughed. "I like that."

Not as much as he liked the sound of her easy laughter. He asked, "What about you? Are you and love on good terms?"

"There are no terms between me and love. Love hasn't proven to me that it's worth my attention or my energy." Maggie brushed her hands together as if preparing to yell: *no deal*. "I still have too much to prove in the arena anyway. And that requires all I have to give."

Grant understood that too well. He had his own career to give his full attention to. His own future to build. That started with his patients in California. Not a cowgirl he met while passing through his hometown.

Kelsey walked out of the stables, her boots moving at a fast clip. "The magazine folks have just turned onto the Sloans' private drive. I'll meet them. Tango is ready and just needs his saddle."

"I'll do that," Maggie said. "Then I'll take the horses to the arena."

Kelsey nodded and ran her hand over her hair. "I guess we might see you later, Doc. We'll be back to look in on Lady Dasher."

"I'm not leaving." Grant smiled at Kelsey, not

sure if it was his grin or his words that ruffled Maggie's big sister more.

A shadow crossed over Kelsey's face. "I'm getting on my horse, Doc."

"I'm not here to stop you," he said simply.

"Why are you here then?" Kelsey countered.

"One. This is my family's home." Grant crossed his arms over his chest. "Two. I'll be here in case anything happens."

"Fine." Kelsey sighed.

Kelsey yielded quicker than he'd expected. Grant masked his surprise and studied Maggie's sister. Her jaw tensed as if she had clenched her teeth. Then she released the muscles and her features smoothed. That was her only tell that she was in pain. What Grant didn't know was how much pain she was in. And just how much she was hiding from Maggie. The sisters' dynamic and Maggie weren't his concern. He was only there now to look after his patient.

At least that's what he tried telling himself thirty minutes later in the arena. When something happened and it wasn't with Kelsey, his patient. And Grant found himself getting involved, despite telling himself not to.

Kelsey was off Tango and seated on a metal bench. She was having an animated conversation with Tasha Logan, the journalist from *Lasso Your Lifestyle* magazine and Lewis

Trumbly, the bald-headed, jovial representative from Denim Country.

Grant left Kelsey to her interview and walked toward the far end of the arena, where Maggie was seated on King. Her back ramrod straight. Her face frozen somewhere between a grimace and an awkward grin. The photographer, Betsy Jarvis, moved around Maggie and the horse, offering advice and encouragement.

The closer Grant got, the more he decided Maggie looked almost ill. Ryan hadn't been exaggerating earlier. Maggie had a surprising case of camera fright.

Grant stopped within Maggie's line of sight and rested his arms on the top railing of the fence that circled the arena. "Hey, Maggie. Let's have a story swap."

Maggie's eyebrows pulled together. Her hands tightened on King's reins. "Now?"

Grant lifted one shoulder and glanced at the photographer. "Do you mind?"

"I'm going to change my lens." Betsy sounded relieved and appreciative of the assist. "You two chat away. Pretend I'm not even here."

"Here's how it works, Maggie," Grant said. "I'll tell you a story. Then you tell me one. Got it?"

Maggie nodded then tilted her head at him.

Suspicion wound around her words. "What's the catch?"

Grant chuckled. "It has to be a true story and it has to be about you."

"You first." The color was slowly coming back into her cheeks, but she was still too stiff. Too tense.

"True story." Grant waggled his eyebrows at her. "When I was five years old, my brothers told me we were having an egg hunt in the morning. I wanted to win so I got up early and collected all the eggs from the chicken coop." Grant paused. He had her full attention now. He continued, "But it was Easter morning, and I had the wrong eggs."

Maggie's smile broke free like that first peek of the sun behind a cloud. "What happened?"

"Gran Claire crowned me the top egg collector in the house." She'd even made Grant an actual crown. Grant chuckled. "It became my job until I left for college. Your turn."

"True story. I was five too." Maggie's grip loosened on the reins as she leaned into her childhood memories. "I wanted to be royal. So, I only ate foods fit for a formal tea party. All my sandwiches had to be cut in triangles and my desserts had to be mini. I only wore princess dresses. And I made my family refer to me as her royal highness for an entire year."

Maggie lifted her hand. "I even perfected the wave of a princess."

"That's impressive." Grant grinned. Even more impressive was the photographer snapping pictures without Maggie seeming to notice. He kept her distracted and tried to keep his fascination with his cowgirl to a minor speedbump level. Nothing he couldn't manage.

"Okay. True story." He touched the faint scar on his forehead. "When I was in college, I told everyone I had to get seven stitches in my forehead because I fell off a bull while I was home for the weekend."

One corner of Maggie's mouth kicked into her cheek and her eyebrows lifted. "Let me guess. You tripped on the stairs."

"No. Not even close." He shook his head and worked to keep his expression impartial. His words uninteresting. "I slammed face first into a door, trying to outrun a bee."

"A bee." Maggie's eyes popped wide open. Grant nodded.

Maggie's laughter, bright and unrestrained, burst free and filled the arena. And Grant. All he wanted to do was capture the moment. Steal the snapshot of Maggie. Like that. Head thrown back. Joy infused. That speedbump got a little taller.

"Seriously," she said and sobered. "A little bee."

"I don't like them. Never have. It's the buzzing, but they're somehow soft too." Not as soft as the tender look in her striking blue eyes. Grant waved his hand. "Don't get me started. Your turn."

Maggie adjusted in the saddle and tapped her chin. "True story. When I was seven, I went outside to play behind my dad's woodpile. Where he told us not to play, by the way. But I was convinced fairies lived back there."

"Did you find any fairies?" Now, he grinned.

"No." Maggie rested her hands on the saddle horn and shifted forward. Her words enthusiastic. "But I did find a mama skunk and her four adorable kits. She wasn't happy when I reached in to pet one of her babies. Sprayed me something good."

Grant's shoulders shook. "Did you stay away from the woodpile after that?"

"No way. Even though my sister told me fairies don't exist, and to stop wasting my time on the impossible." Maggie's expression was wistful. Her words confident. "I still look for those fairies when I go home, even now."

His tough-minded cowgirl had a whimsical side. And she charmed him even more.

The photographer knelt and continued collecting images of Maggie from every angle.

Maggie arched an eyebrow at Grant. "Your turn."

"True story. Back in high school, I brought Jessica Bolton a big bouquet of flowers on our first date. She was the first girl I'd ever had the nerve to ask out." Took him more than a month to even find the right words. Funny how the words somehow came easy with Maggie. But this wasn't a date. Or the start of anything. Grant continued, "Turned out Jessica was highly allergic to daisies. She sneezed and coughed through the entire drive-in movie. And I ruined my chances for a first kiss."

Maggie pressed her hand over her chest. Her expression was full of sympathy. "Poor thing."

Grant had no time to ask who Maggie felt more sorry for: him or his date.

"That's a wrap." Betsy announced. The photographer let her camera hang from the strap around her neck, dipped her chin in gratitude to Grant and then grinned at Maggie. "Well, Maggie, you were terrific. These shots are going to be great. I'll check in with Lewis and Tasha. We'll meet you out front."

Maggie dismounted, thanked the photographer, and walked over to Grant. Relief washed over her face. "Thanks for that."

"Any time." That was out before he could tap the brakes and keep his thoughts to himself. *Any time* implied a next time.

"So." Maggie gazed at him. Curiosity slowed her words. "Did you ever get that first kiss from Jessica Bolton?"

"No." He opened the gate for her to walk King through. "Jessica decided she liked Ryan more."

"She told you that?" Maggie sounded irritated.

"She didn't have to." Grant walked beside her and stopped outside the arena to look at her. He hadn't been wrong earlier. Maggie was pretty. Inside the arena and now with the sun highlighting her hair. He continued, "I caught Jessica trying to steal her first kiss from Ryan behind the gym a week later."

Maggie frowned. "What happened?"

"Ryan refused. He told her that we weren't cowboy hats she could try on until she found the right fit." Grant ran a hand through his hair. "Then Ryan promised me I'd have more fun being single with him and my brothers anyway."

"Did you?" She watched him. "Have more fun?"

"More than I should have." He grinned. "Never gave Jessica another thought after that day." But he wasn't sure he was going to be able to say the same about Maggie when he left.

She waggled her eyebrows. "Well, you have to tell me now."

"Tell you what?" He took her in. Her smile. Her shining gaze.

"About your first kiss," she said. "Tell me it made up for Jessica Bolton's disrespect. That it was perfect."

If I asked to kiss you, would you agree? How could I make it perfect for you? Grant glanced at his watch and cleared his throat. "That's a story for another time. I need to change quickly, get to the clinic and my patients."

After all, his work was done here. He'd looked after Kelsey, even helped his patient's sister get over her anxiety. Job well done. And nothing about looking after a patient included kissing said patient's sister. Nothing.

Besides, kissing Maggie would move them from not-quite friends to something entirely different. And Grant was leaving soon for the West Coast. After that, their paths would have no reason to cross. City highways and country roads were worlds apart. Maggie and Grant were worlds apart.

That was reason enough to keep his distance.

"Well, Dr. Sloan, I guess I'll see you around," Maggie said.

Grant should've left it at that. Should've nodded and wished Maggie a good day. The same as he did with his patients and their family members at the end of every appointment. Simple and succinct.

Instead, he turned around, walked backward, and said, "Maggie, don't forget to check your phone tonight before you fall asleep."

"Why would I do that?" Her smile was quick and small. A flash.

He lifted one shoulder. "Might be a text there that catches your attention."

"True story," she said. "I'm looking forward to that text, Dr. Sloan."

Grant spun back around. And had the absurd urge to start whistling. He shut that down. Too bad his ear-to-ear grin wasn't as easy to quit.

CHAPTER EIGHT

KELSEY ORR WAS having a bad day. And she'd run out of things to bling, and that was putting her in a bad mood. She dropped into a stool at the Feisty Owl Bar and Grille, smiled at the busy bartender, then set her crafting bag on the well-worn, yet polished bar top.

Whenever Kelsey needed a mood booster, she reached for her rhinestone collection and opened her closet. Didn't matter what the apparel or accessory was, Kelsey could enhance it. The precision work calmed her mind. The finished products lifted her spirits.

Clearly, she'd been lifting her spirits a lot recently. There wasn't anything left in her entire wardrobe that didn't already have rhinestones or beads on it, including her pajamas. She pulled out a denim tank she'd shoved into her crafting bag that morning. Before the first of her doctor's appointments and the start of her bad day. But she wasn't interested in rehashing her disappointing afternoon.

She'd been a late talker as a child. Her dad

liked to say it was because Kelsey had waited until she was good and ready to let the words out. Nothing wrong with that, Dad always told her. Well, she wasn't good now. Nor was she ready to discuss anything. Not with anyone, even her closest ally—her sister.

And that, she supposed, was the reason she was hiding out in the Feisty Owl rather than returning to the campsite and Maggie. Kelsey ran her fingers over the beading she'd sewn along the cotton straps of the denim tank top and considered a new design.

"Evening, Kelsey." A deep, familiar voice came from behind her.

Kelsey twisted on the stool and took in the man she wanted to blame for all her recent bad days. Unfair, yes. It still didn't stop her from feeling it, all the same. "Dr. Sloan. You here checking up on me? I got my sling on and there's not a horse in sight."

"Just came by for dinner." He pointed to the sign hanging over the end of the bar. "To go."

Funny. The doctor looked like he could use a mood booster too. But Kelsey wasn't sharing her rhinestones or her sister. "It appears I owe you several thank-yous, Dr. Sloan."

His eyebrows raised slightly at that.

"I want to thank you for not revealing my injury yesterday morning with the sponsor and magazine people," Kelsey said, pleased she sounded sincere.

"It's not my truth to tell." He picked up a menu from the pile on the bar. "And there's a patient confidentiality thing we doctors tend to take quite seriously."

"You might not believe this, but I have really good reasons for why I'm doing this." None of which she needed to explain to him. She owed Dr. Sloan nothing. But Maggie, well, she owed her sister everything.

"I'm sure you do." He scanned the menu.

Kelsey frowned at him. Logically, she realized that Dr. Sloan was simply the person who'd told her the absolute last thing she'd wanted to hear. No one wanted to be told they needed surgery. No one wanted to face the end of their career before they were ready. And Kelsey knew that was the part Dr. Sloan hadn't said. Not yet, anyway. The whole situation made her surly. And Dr. Sloan, so calm and composed in his scrubs, made her even more prickly. Definitely not her best look. "Maggie told me the photographer wouldn't have gotten one decent picture yesterday without your help. Thanks for that too."

"Ryan told me to make Maggie laugh." Dr. Sloan set the menu on the bar top. "So, I did."

Except Kelsey sensed there was more to it.

Especially since Maggie had been equally as vague. Her sister's smile too secretive whenever Dr. Sloan's name came up. That only made Kelsey more touchy. And even more protective. "You should know that the rodeo is my sister's life."

"Yes." Dr. Sloan leaned his elbow against the bar and faced Kelsey. "I'm aware of that."

"But do you understand?" Kelsey asked. Dr. Sloan reminded Kelsey of the man who'd broken her sister's heart all those years ago. A man who could give Maggie the world, but only on his terms. Maggie deserved more. Kelsey had promised her sister more, and she fully intended to keep her word. "Do you really understand what that means?"

Dr. Sloan considered her. His face impassive. "I'm not sure why it matters."

Because someone had to look out for Maggie's heart. Kelsey lifted her chin. "I just think you should know. The rodeo is not a job. It's a part of who Maggie is."

"It's also a part of who you are." He watched her. His gaze steady and compassionate. "A big part."

Right. But Kelsey didn't want to talk about what she might be losing. Not with him. She said, "Well, like I said, I appreciate you looking out for Maggie yesterday."

"But…"

"But my sister and I have taken care of each other since we were kids." Kelsey stuffed the tank top back inside her bag. "When we leave here in two weeks, it'll be just us again. Like always."

"As I said earlier, I'm just here for dinner." Dr. Sloan tapped his finger on the menu, then said, "I'm not trying to interfere with your team, Kelsey."

But he already had. He already was. It was more than his medical diagnosis and treatment plan. And Kelsey wasn't sure how to stop it. "Then it looks like we do understand each other, Dr. Sloan."

The door from the kitchen swung wide, interrupting Dr. Sloan's reply. A man wearing a chef's coat that rivaled Dr. Sloan's in the crispy white division stepped through. His hair was a chestnut color with curls that looked like they hadn't been finger combed since that morning. But it was his smile—big, broad, and unapologetic—that made Kelsey do a double take.

His was the kind of smile that made Kelsey want to smile in return for no good reason. If she was being honest, she hadn't felt like smiling for a while now.

"Dr. Sloan is in my house. What an honor." Nolan, or rather Chef Davis, according to the embroidered name on his white jacket, reached over the bar to fist bump Dr. Sloan. Then rubbed his palms together. "Tell me you've got something fun planned, Grant. Because I want in."

If Chef Davis was going to be there, Kelsey wanted in as well. For the fun, she corrected. Not for the chef.

"Nolan, you're always where we are anyway," Dr. Sloan replied. "Your last name should be Sloan."

"I can't help it if I'm the life of every one of your family gatherings." Chef Davis laughed and shifted his amber gaze to Kelsey. His smile looked as if he'd locked it in place. "Going to introduce me to your date, Grant?"

"Dr. Sloan is my doctor." Kelsey touched her sling, extended her good arm over the bar to take Chef Davis's hand, and introduced herself.

"So, Grant is not your date?" The chef's smile widened further into his cheeks. He held onto Kelsey's hand and captured her full attention.

"Not. My. Date." Kelsey's words sounded flirty. She never flirted. Dating and a life on the road never mixed well. So, she'd concentrated on roping. Only now, she couldn't seem to not concentrate on Chef Davis.

"Well, look at that. My day just got that much

brighter and so much better." A half-grin played around Chef Davis's mouth.

"Can I get some food?" Dr. Sloan drummed his fingers on the bar top. "You are still the head chef around here, right, Nolan?"

Chef Davis held up his hand, quieting Grant. He never looked away from Kelsey. As if he was having the same concentration troubles as she was. Interesting.

"So, Kelsey Orr, are you waiting on a date to arrive?" Chef Davis asked. "Or your boyfriend perhaps?"

Kelsey shook her head. Chef Davis's thumb smoothed across her palm. And her stomach fluttered. But fun and flirting wasn't on her agenda. She had life-changing career decisions to make. Her sister's future to secure. Kelsey couldn't get distracted. Not now. Yet, she didn't pull her hand away.

"Let me move this along." Dr. Sloan leaned against the bar and waved between the pair. He gave a quick rundown of Kelsey's relationship status and her roping team ranking. Then he motioned toward Nolan. "Chef Davis is unattached. We've been friends since elementary school. Nolan is one of the most honest and dependable people I know. He also cooks some of the best food I've ever tasted."

"Some of the best?" Chef Davis lifted his eyebrows. "Why not the best, period?"

"Can I just get some food, please?" Dr. Sloan rubbed his forehead. "The service here is incredibly slow. I'll be sure to put that in my online review."

Chef Davis only laughed and ignored his friend. "Have you ordered, Kelsey?"

"Not yet." Kelsey finally pulled her hand free. Time to get back on task. Fun and flirting weren't part of her immediate future. For the first time in a long while, she felt a genuine twinge of regret. "But I need a to-go order for me and my sister. We're staying out at Starfall Campgrounds."

"Let me cook you dinner instead, Kelsey Orr," Chef Davis offered.

Yes. If you promise to keep smiling and give me a moment to forget. The strap of her arm sling rubbed the back of her neck. But there was no forgetting, not even for a minute. Kelsey said, "I don't date."

"It's not a date. It's dinner." Amusement coated the speculation on Chef Davis's face. "In the big commercial kitchen back there."

"Why?" she asked.

"Because it would be fun." Chef Davis braced his hands on the bar top and considered her.

"You don't date, but you still have fun, don't you?"

"I would have more fun if you took my order, Nolan," Dr. Sloan interrupted. "You know, because you're the chef. And cook the food."

Kelsey eyed Chef Davis. She wanted fun. But she had to be responsible. Like always. She'd been the one Maggie depended on since their mom had walked out and took all the fun with her. That was Kelsey's job, and she took it seriously. But Chef Davis tempted her now.

"Hey, Grant." Hope worked across her chef's face, lifting his eyebrows high. "Dinner is on me for a big favor."

Dr. Sloan narrowed his gaze on his longtime friend. "What kind of big favor?"

"You deliver dinner to Kelsey's sister so I can cook for Kelsey here," Chef Davis suggested. Then he glanced at Kelsey as if he knew her inner struggle and wasn't one to give up easily.

She admired his skill at removing obstacles. Still, she had to set boundaries. "I'll have dinner with you, Chef, if you let me add sparkle to your chef's jacket."

Chef Davis ran his hands over his pristine white jacket but didn't appear all that concerned. "You want to bedazzle this?"

"Yes." Boundaries were good. She shrugged

her healthy shoulder. "Then I'm working while I eat."

Chef Davis smiled and considered her. "Then it's not a dinner date."

Oh, he understood her. That could be a bad thing. But not if Kelsey didn't let her time with Chef Davis go beyond one meal. She had to eat, after all. Might as well enjoy herself while she did.

"I've got another jacket in the back." Chef Davis tipped his head toward the swinging door. "As well as a chef's hat. And aprons. Enough to keep you busy through dessert."

Kelsey worked to keep her smile contained and turned toward Dr. Sloan. "Do you mind taking Maggie her dinner? I don't have to stay…" In fact, she should just leave. Find herself a drive-thru and head back to her sister. Leave the fun for someone else.

Dr. Sloan scratched his cheek. "What is Maggie going to say about this? You just met Nolan."

Kelsey pulled back. Dr. Sloan sounded eerily like he was looking out for her. Like a big brother would. She wanted to continue being mad at him. Not start to like him. Kelsey frowned. "You vouched for Chef Davis yourself. You can't take that back now. Besides, it's only dinner."

Dr. Sloan's expression remained neutral.

"Fine. Here's the deal. Maggie and I had a long day. You can ask her about it. I don't want to rehash it," Kelsey confessed. "I'm here because I need space to think."

Dr. Sloan tipped his head toward the busy kitchen. "You plan to do that in there."

It would be better than being with Maggie and seeing all the ways she was letting her little sister down. She wasn't giving up. Never that. She just needed a night off. It wasn't too much to ask, was it? She wanted that time to be spent with Chef Davis. Silly, sure, but there it was. "Please, Dr. Sloan."

Finally, he nodded and sighed. "What does Maggie like?"

"I'll text Maggie and fill her in." Kelsey hopped off the stool, grabbed her bag and headed around the end of the bar. "As for what she likes, let me look at the menu."

"I'll take care of your order, Grant. Leave everything to me." Chef Davis held open the swinging door and waited for Kelsey to step through. Then he grinned at Dr. Sloan. "I'll be out in a flash with your food."

Chef Davis escorted Kelsey to a table in the corner. It was out of the staff's way but offered an unobstructed view of the commercial kitchen. It was spotless. Impressive. And Chef Davis reigned over it all.

Kelsey sat in the chair he pulled out for her, and she said, "Just so we're clear. This is not a date."

"Definitely not." Chef Davis dropped a fabric napkin on her lap and lit the candle in the center of the table. "Because if it was a date, this is the last place I'd be taking you."

"Where would we be going?" *If this was a date.* She wouldn't say the rest out loud. Wouldn't tempt fate like that.

He lifted one shoulder and grinned at her. "You'll have to agree to a date if you want to find out."

Curious. He made her very curious. And he knew it too.

What her chef didn't know was this was one night only. No second dinner. No encore. No impromptu invitation for a follow-up meal.

Tomorrow, Kelsey went back to being the hero Maggie had called her in an interview years and years ago.

Tomorrow, Kelsey got back to the business of not failing the only person who had always believed in her.

Tomorrow, Kelsey got back to making sure the dreams she had promised Maggie came true.

Kelsey's gaze landed on her chef. But not tonight.

CHAPTER NINE

MAGGIE WANTED COOPERATION. From someone. From something. It didn't matter. As long as she got what she wanted. What she wanted was an air conditioner that blew cold air, not hot. Or a freezer that wasn't a block of ice. Or a sister that would talk to her. Really open up about what she was thinking. What she was feeling.

Maggie cradled her tool bag under her arm and climbed the ladder onto the camper rooftop.

Problem was if Kelsey opened up, then Maggie would have to do the same. And Maggie's thoughts and feelings were not on the same page as her sister's. What was right for the team collided with what was right for Kels.

Surgery would fix Kelsey's shoulder but break their team. Bust their dreams.

Yet, asking Kelsey to continue to push her body past its limits felt all wrong. Selfish and wrong.

But if Kelsey wanted to compete... If Kelsey *chose* to compete, Maggie should support that decision as a good teammate. As a sister, Maggie was raised to put family first. Always. But what was best for her sister?

The stakes, well, those had never been higher. This was about reaching their goals. And finally being able to find a real home for the sisters to build something on. Not a crowded camper with too many miles in the rearview and not enough future in the dim headlights.

But they needed money to fund their dreams. That meant riding, roping, and winning. Again and again. Because it wasn't only about getting to the top. It was about staying on top. Maggie wasn't certain how many more rides Kelsey's body could handle.

But that was for Kelsey to decide. And for Maggie to support.

That was why when Kelsey had pretended to be asleep during the drive back from the doctor's appointments that afternoon, Maggie had been more than content to go along with the ruse. And leave it all unsaid and undecided.

Maggie picked up a wrench from her tool bag and crouched in front of the air conditioning unit. "That leaves you. I need cold air now. So you need to start working." Then at least Maggie would know she did something right.

Minutes later, the only thing clear was Maggie's lack of mechanical skill. She sat back and wiped her forehead. Her stomach growled. Her phone rang.

Maggie pressed the answer button on her earpiece without pulling her phone from her pocket to check the caller ID, and said, "I'm starving, Kels. You better be here soon."

"Last I checked, the camper had a proper kitchen." Her dad's voice rumbled over the speaker. "Sure sounds like you've got a problem you can solve for yourself."

"Dad." Maggie dropped her wrench and scrambled to yank her phone from her pocket as if she didn't know her father's voice.

"Of course, it's me. We talk every week." Her dad's voice always sounded gravelly as if the dirt from years of bull riding and ranching was stuck permanently in his throat.

When she'd been little, she used to climb on her dad's lap and press her palm against his neck while he talked. He'd ask her if she could feel the sandpaper he'd swallowed. Maggie would giggle until her tummy hurt. That had been before her parents' divorce. Before her father had lost his laughter completely. Maggie swiped at the sweat running down the back of her neck.

"You've been gone too long," her dad continued. "If you've forgotten all that I taught you."

Not likely. Howard Orr had the unique talent for turning everything into a life lesson. But at the core of every lesson was the same message: *always count on yourself first, second and last. Then and only then will you be happy.*

One thing she could count on was her dad's routine. It never changed. "Shouldn't you be at the livestock auction right now, Dad?"

"I'm still here. I got a preview of a heifer pair, Maggie." Excitement drove his words into a quick clip. "These two are real beauties. Special too. One of 'em is going to give me that champion. I can feel it."

Her father's passion project was breeding the next champion rodeo bull.

"With the right bull and the right heifer, it's a win-win." More of that excitement pushed across the speaker. Her dad added, "Proper breeding and patience. I told you we just needed to wait for the moment. It's all about finding the right match."

It was all about the bull leaving the chute and bucking like mad at the top rodeos. That was the only way a bucking bull earned a reputation and got paid. And that would take her dad's passion from a hobby to a sustainable business. But first, her dad needed to get his bulls to the chute to compete and stop breeding more. She tried to sound positive. "That's great, Dad."

"It will be great if I can get this pair tomorrow when the bidding is live." There was a small scratch over the phone line, then her dad said, "But I'm going to need a little help on this one, honey."

And there it was. The problem with her father's passion project. It hadn't paid out yet. Until it did, he kept coming to Maggie to keep the dream bankrolled. Maggie felt her patience running thin.

"Think of it as an investment, Maggie. In the bulls and in me." The slow cadence of his words made them all the more persuasive. "I know I can count on you, Maggie."

Can't let down your family, Maggie. Like your mom did to us. In this house, we're family first. Maggie dropped her head against her raised knees.

Her dad added, "We'll all be celebrating when one of these heifers births a real champion. I can promise you that."

The last dozen or so heifers were supposed to have bred champions. True buckers no cowboy could ride. At least that had been his promise when he'd asked for money back then too. So far, her father's bulls had bucked in his practice arena only. Nowhere else. Maggie wanted her father to succeed. She wanted him to be happy too. But their own finances were far from flush. Exhaustion pressed against her shoulders. "Now isn't really a good time, Dad."

"Still daylight, isn't it? You're practicing, aren't you?" His approval washed over his tone. "Gotta be at the top of your game, honey. Don't want to go and get distracted now. You owe it to your sister not to let her down either."

Next to his bulls, her father's other favorite topic was Kelsey. And when her dad got to discussing family bonds and obligations, the conversation became one-way. Her participation optional and certainly not required. Maggie kept silent.

"Kelsey saw what you two could be all those years ago," her dad rolled on. "Look where your sister has gotten you. Now even with her shoulder, she's still pushing. For you. For your team. Her family. What you have with her is special, Maggie. You have to treasure it. Honor it. You won't find that with anyone else. That I can assure you."

You were blessed with your mom's beauty, Maggie. Doesn't mean you have to act like her too. She had more quit than grit. But that's not you, Maggie. Don't ever let it be you. And if Maggie wanted to prove her love for her sister and her dad, she didn't quit on them or their dreams. Maggie touched her throat and kept to the usual, expected script. "I'll get you that money, Dad."

"Knew I could count on my daughter." He pressed more emphasis into *my daughter*, as was his way. "Tonight is soon enough to send the money, Maggie. You go and finish your practice now. I'll be sure to send you a picture of our new heifers."

With that, her dad ended the call.

Maggie flopped back on the trailer roof and stared at the twilight sky.

Howard Orr was a former jackpot-winning bull rider and as old school as they came. He claimed real cowboys rubbed dirt on their injuries, always got back in their saddles and never accepted defeat. Because real cowboys knew full well that love and respect was always earned, both in the ring and out of it. When it came to her father, Maggie wasn't worried about earning his love. But she was worried about keeping it.

Frustration crowded in. Fear too. She stomped her feet on the trailer roof. Tapped her fists too. She was allowed to give in. It would pass. She just needed...

"Maggie. You okay up there?" an all-too-familiar voice called out.

Rolling onto her stomach, Maggie scooted to

the edge of the roof and peered over. Dr. Sloan waited below. Still in his scrubs, he looked confident. Steady. So sure of his place. Right now. In the world.

Maggie felt like she'd been in one endless competition to earn her place. Always searching for her place to stand. But that would change when the sisters earned their sponsor. Bought their own ranch. Then Maggie would have a place. And finally be truly happy. Because surely at the end of their winning streak, when they'd reached their goals, that was where the true joy waited, right?

"Maggie." The soft rumble of Dr. Sloan's voice wrapped around her. "I can see you."

CHAPTER TEN

CLEARLY, MAGGIE WAS not going to catch a break. *Some people sit around and wait on luck, Maggie. We aren't some people.* Maggie pushed herself up, set her hands on her hips and took back control. "Are you here to gloat, Dr. Sloan?"

"I have dinner. Your sister sent me, and she texted you." He lifted a paper shopping bag and arched an eyebrow at her. "Check your phone."

Maggie opened the text app on her phone. Change of plans, sis. Just go with it. Have fun. I plan to. Her sister ended her text with dozens of heart and smiley face emojis.

"I'm not above gloating. Ask my brothers." He tipped his head and studied her. "What should I be gloating about now?"

Maggie refused to smile. "All your peers agree with you. You really are a leading authority in your field."

He ran his fingers over the back of his neck and shifted his weight. His expression turned neutral. "Kelsey's appointments were today."

Maggie watched him. Where was his *I warned you in the stable? You should've listened to me. I told you exactly what would happen*. She'd heard him when he'd told her the other doctors would most likely agree with his recommendation for surgery. But still, she'd held out hope for a different outcome. "There's more. Every doctor agreed with you, and then they all referred us back to you."

"I'm sorry." His words were genuine. As gentle as the cooing of an owl in the night.

No, *I told you so*. No pride. He looked as displeased as Maggie and completely stole her bluster. How completely unfair was that? Maggie crossed her arms over her chest. "My dad says you should never apologize for being the best."

"Why is that?" he asked.

Maggie lifted one shoulder. "Someone else's bruised ego can't be your concern or your responsibility."

"Fair enough." He locked his gaze on her. "What if I told you that I'm concerned about you?"

He did it again. Tipped her off-balance. Same as his text had tipped her off-balance last night. Yet, she hadn't continued their text conversation. Getting to know Grant Sloan the man would only make her like him more. Liking him more would be a temptation her heart might not be able to ignore.

Maggie knew the danger of opening her heart. Only to find out her kind of love wasn't enough. That was in the past. Now love belonged on the sidelines, along with her interest in Grant Sloan.

"The only thing wrong is a broken AC." As for her heart, she wouldn't allow that to be broken ever again. She lifted her chin. "So, you don't need to be concerned about me, Dr. Sloan. I'm fine. Good, even."

"Well, you can come down or I'll go up there," he said and motioned from the roof to the ground beside him. "Either way works, but I'd like to see for myself."

"See what exactly?" she asked.

"That you're fine," he said. "Or was it good?"

"I am hungry." Maggie admitted and patted her stomach. "I'll come to you." But only for dinner. Nothing more.

Maggie stepped off the last rung of the ladder and found her doctor waiting within catching distance. Close enough that he'd hear her secrets if she revealed them. *Would you hold me and tell me I'm enough as I am?* Maggie pressed her lips together.

He reached out and tucked her hair behind

her ear. His fingers trailed over her cheek. His touch there and gone.

A warmth curled through Maggie, whisper-soft and not entirely unwelcome. Nothing to do but ignore it. Surely her attraction would fade. And her interest too, if she didn't encourage it. She brushed her palms on her jeans, keeping her movements and words easygoing. "See. I'm fine."

"Then we should eat." He held up the to-go bag. "And you can tell me the story you owe me."

Maggie knew instantly which story he wanted. Last night, he'd texted her about his first kiss. Answering her question about whether it'd been perfect. Now he wanted to know about her first kiss. Then Maggie might want to know more about him too. Like his first car. Did he prefer highways or old country roads? Or his first night in college. What had he missed the most about his home?

Setting aside her curiosity, Maggie walked around the side of the trailer toward the portable outdoor sitting area. "How about you tell me what really happened? Why is it that you're here and not my sister?"

"Nolan Davis is head chef at the Feisty Owl. I introduced him to Kelsey." He set the food bags on the folding table. "Nolan wanted to cook Kelsey dinner, so here I am."

Maggie gaped at him. "You set my sister up on a date."

"She didn't seem to mind." He took out the food containers and checked the writing on the lids. "Doesn't your sister date?"

"No." Maggie dropped into the chair across from him. "Neither of us date." A warning for him. A reminder for her.

"Do you and your sister have a no-dating policy?" He handed her a napkin.

"We have goals. We need to be focused, and relationships disrupt that." *You start concentrating on too many things, Maggie, then you'll only ever be mediocre at everything.* Average had never been their goal. Not to mention Maggie had given up on love and preferred it that way. She clarified, "We have career goals."

"I get that." He sat in the other available chair and handed her a container of loaded chicken nachos. "Dating is a distraction."

"Exactly." Maggie should be thrilled. She and her doctor shared the same belief about dating. She flicked jalapenos onto the container lid and tried to skim over her quick jolt of disappointment at his conclusion. "Why are you here, Dr. Sloan?"

He lifted half of a grilled cheese sandwich

from another container. Avocado and tomatoes were stacked between the cheese and toasted bread. But his attention was on her. "I thought we just went over this."

"No. I mean here." She swirled her fork over the nachos. "Why are you here in Three Springs?"

"This is where I'm from." He shrugged and took a bite of his sandwich. "And my family is here."

"But it's not where you're staying. Living, I mean." That was a hunch. One she hoped was correct. Because a temporary Dr. Sloan meant there was a deadline on whatever this was between them. And that meant there was an expiration date on her interest too. When he left, her interest would end. In the meantime, she just needed to keep a tight rein on her curiosity about her doctor.

He took another bite of his sandwich, then said, "What makes you think I'm not staying or living here?"

Maggie dipped a chip in the guacamole. "You don't act like a person happy to be home."

"How am I supposed to act?" he asked.

"It's just Ryan always talks about dinners at the farmhouse. It's the one meal everyone shows up for." There was more too, according to Ryan. Movie marathons. Poker games. Pool tournaments. Ryan always filled her in on who won and who lost. And Maggie always thought it sounded like the family fun she'd craved as a child. She added, "Yet you're here with me, not your family."

"As a favor to your sister," he said.

"Who you ran into at the Owl," she countered. "You're still in your scrubs, so you most likely haven't been home yet."

"California." He polished off half his sandwich and wiped his hands on a napkin. "That's where I'm headed. To a prominent sports medicine clinic in Los Angeles."

That fit. She pictured him in his sleek suit. All that polish and refinement belonged in a big city. "When?"

"End of the month." He pulled a cup of sweet potato fries from the bag. "Maybe sooner. I have my last interview tomorrow."

That mirrored the same timetable as Maggie and her sister's. She had her expiration date. Two weeks. No more. She snatched a fry from his cup. "Is your family okay with you living so far away?"

"I haven't asked." He polished off more sweet potato fries, seeming almost indifferent. "It's not their decision to make."

"Don't you want their support?" Big decisions Maggie made with her sister. When they'd been living at home, those decisions had involved their dad as well.

"My family's support is nice to have." He considered the fry cup, then looked at Maggie. "But ultimately it won't change what's the right decision for me and my career."

"I envy you, Dr. Sloan." Her words slipped out before Maggie could block them with a nacho chip.

True to form, he didn't let her statement go by. Instead, he leaned his elbows on the table and watched her as if getting to know her was his only priority. His gaze, steady and thoughtful, held hers.

And Maggie felt like he saw her. Just her. There was power in that. Freedom too.

His voice was low, yet gentle. "Why would you envy me?"

"You're willing to leave your family and see where you'll be without them. I don't have that kind of courage." Maggie closed the lid on her nachos and her truths. This wasn't a tell-all. Confessions like that belonged between good friends. Between partners, really. Not here. With Dr. Sloan, who was…she wasn't sure what he was to her. Knew only that he couldn't become anything more. "Sorry. I'm not sure where that came from. The AC broke last night, and I didn't sleep well."

He reached across the table and set his hand on her wrist. "You can talk to me."

"No. No, I can't." *I barely know you. I can't trust you.* Trust took time to build. Time to earn. Maggie moved her arm and found her hand in his. And it felt right. But how could that be? Her words sounded weak. "We aren't even friends."

"You know my brother." He shifted, linked their fingers together. "You're his friend."

"That's different." Ryan didn't know her secrets. Ryan knew Maggie the competitor, and that's the person Ryan liked. And she'd never wanted to hold Ryan's hand. Maggie stared at their joined hands. Not like she wanted to hold onto Grant's hand now. She had to let go.

"Maggie." He tightened his grip as if he had no intention of letting her go.

"I can't." *I can't let my guard down. I could fall for someone like you, who belonged in a different world than the one she'd chosen.* That was exactly how to get her heart broken. She cleared her throat. "I have to take another look at the air conditioning."

"About that. I texted my brother for help when you were coming off the roof." Grant tipped his head toward the parking lot. The rumble of a truck filled the evening air. "That's probably him now."

The headlights of an approaching truck flashed across the table, highlighting their joined hands. Maggie tugged her hand free and shielded her eyes. The engine cut off. The headlights dimmed. Then Ryan hopped out from the driver's side and called out a gleeful greeting. "Sorry to interrupt your date."

Date. As if. Kelsey was on a date, not Maggie. "It's not…we're not…" Maggie waved her hands over the table. "This isn't…"

Grant opened a container of pretzel bites and watched her. Unconcerned by her stammering. And seemingly unwilling to correct his brother.

Ryan dipped a pretzel bite in the cheese dip. Amusement drifted across his face.

Maggie gave up and asked, "Ryan. Why are you here?"

"I'm here to fix your air conditioning, of course." Ryan toasted her with his pretzel bite, then popped it in his mouth.

"Where's Josh?" Grant frowned at his brother. "I texted him about Maggie's AC."

"Josh sent me and his toolbox." Ryan swallowed and grinned at Maggie. "Josh is at the distillery with Carter. They're welding something and he can't break away, so I'm here in his place."

"Ryan, when was the last time you fixed

something like an air conditioner?" Grant's words were more bland than curious, as if he already knew the answer.

"Never. I call Josh like we all do when things break." Ryan laughed and squeezed Grant's shoulder. "That's why we're going to call Josh when we get up there. He's supposed to walk us through the repair."

"We can't all go up there," Maggie warned. "There's a weight limit."

"I'll go. You guys can finish your dinner." Ryan turned toward the truck and started to whistle. "Just need my tools."

Maggie touched her forehead and watched Ryan stroll to the passenger side of the truck. "He doesn't know what he's doing, does he?"

"Not a clue," Grant admitted and wiped his hands on a napkin. "But he's good at following directions. And Josh is good at giving instructions."

Ryan kept on whistling as he made his way toward the back of the trailer and the ladder.

"We can't let him go alone." Maggie stood.

Grant sighed, pushed out of his chair, and walked over to Maggie. "This conversation isn't over."

It was very much over. Maggie never responded to prove her point and instead headed to the back of the trailer.

"You go ahead." Grant motioned toward the ladder. "You know more about your AC than any of us."

Maggie climbed the ladder, leaned her arms on the roof and called out, "Ryan, let me know how I can help."

Ryan slid his cell phone toward Maggie. "Hold my phone so I can work with both hands and tell me what Josh says to do."

Maggie pressed the call button and waited for Josh to answer. Within minutes, she was issuing instructions and watching Ryan sort through the tool bag, pulling out a meter and other implements. It wasn't thirty minutes later that the tools were packed up, and she and Ryan were headed down the ladder.

"What's the prognosis?" Grant asked.

"Josh says I need a professional AC technician." Maggie frowned. Worse, Josh hadn't sounded too convinced that the unit could be fixed this time after she'd filled him in on the previous repairs. "Josh has a friend in the service business, but he can't look at it until next Monday at the earliest. Welcome to summer and the busiest season for broken air conditioners."

Grant ran his hand over his mouth.

Ryan adjusted his grip on the tool bag and

started around the camper. "Nothing to do now but stay at our place, Mags."

Maggie searched for an argument. An out. And tried not to look at Grant. Certainly, that wasn't the solution he'd choose either. Maggie shook her head and followed Ryan. "No, we couldn't impose."

"You're not imposing. We have the extra rooms and working air conditioning." Ryan dropped the tool kit on the ground and faced her. "Besides, you moved your horses into our stables. Lady Dasher needs more time out of the sun to recover. Shouldn't Kelsey get the same consideration?"

Always. Her sister was always Maggie's priority. "I'll send Kelsey over to the farmhouse."

Grant frowned at her. "What about you?"

"I'll get some fans and stay here." Maggie tightened her ponytail and her determination. "It'll be fine."

Grant's eyes narrowed as if he was starting to dislike the word *fine.*

"I don't think that's a good idea, Mags." Ryan rubbed his chin, then looked at his brother. "Tell her, Grant. Tell her it's a bad idea."

Grant's gaze lifted briefly up toward the sky, then returned to hers as if he'd found a solution among the stars. "Maggie, you can come stay at the farmhouse or I'll stay here with you."

Maggie gaped at him. "You can't be serious."

Grant crossed his arms over his scrubs and looked about as unbending as a cinder block.

Ryan held up his hands, then hitched his thumb over his shoulder. "I'm going to put Josh's tools in the truck and let you two hash this one out."

Maggie glared at Ryan for leaving her alone with her exasperating doctor. Grant wasn't staying with her. No way. Not happening. Maggie stiffened her spine and the insistence in her words. "Grant, you're being unreasonable."

He arched an eyebrow as if surprised at her use of his first name. Then he countered, "Maggie, you're being stubborn."

Yes. Yes, she was. She wasn't giving in first. She stepped closer to him, intent on changing his mind. "We have air mattresses in the camper and no air conditioning. You can't sleep here."

"If it's good enough for you, then why not me?" He leaned toward her slightly. "Trust me, some of the places I slept during my residency weren't as comfortable as an air mattress."

"Why are you doing this?" she asked.

"Doing what?" he challenged. "Wanting you to be safe? Not wanting you to be alone out here?"

Caring about me. You aren't supposed to care. Not like this. It was supposed to be casual. If he cared about her, she might start to care about him too. She might forget all the reasons she'd put that Do Not Disturb sign on her heart.

"I know you've got this." He took her hand in his. Curved his fingers around hers. "I know you can handle yourself, Maggie. That you've been fine on your own with your sister. But this one time, we're just saying you don't have to be alone. You have another option."

She stared at their joined hands. That warmth from earlier slipped through her again. There had to be ground rules. Her hand had to stay out of his. It was simple. She'd have to avoid him. Stay out of his way. Then she wouldn't have to worry about keeping her guard up. It was a big farmhouse. With lots of other people around. She could do it. Rules in place, she gave in. "A real bed does sound enticing and so does a really hot shower."

"We have both at the farmhouse." He grinned.

"We'll stay." She pulled her hand free. "But I'm only staying until the air conditioning is fixed in the camper."

"Got it," Grant said. "But fair warning, Gran Claire used to tell her guests: one night in our farmhouse and you won't ever want to leave."

"That won't be a problem. My only gear is on-the-go," she assured him. *But if you asked me to stay, I might...*

"I've got that same gear too," he said.

Translation: *I won't ever ask you to stay.* Maggie secured that Do Not Disturb sign back over heart. After all, she excelled at casual relationships, friend zones and uncomplicated departures. The same as her city doctor.

Their goodbye, when it came, would be effortless. That was what they both wanted.

And Maggie saw no reason why they shouldn't both get exactly what they wanted.

CHAPTER ELEVEN

GRANT NEEDED SPACE. For the second time that day, a woman was the cause.

That afternoon, his mother had texted to inform Grant that she'd flown back to New York. There was a work situation that required her personal attention. She hadn't included a return date. Or a request to reschedule dinner. No apology. No "see you soon."

Grant should have expected nothing else from Lilian Sloan. That he was even marginally disappointed was ridiculous. That he'd let Lilian Sloan get to him again was maddening. And proof that letting someone in, even a fraction, only caused unnecessary pain.

After his mother's text, Grant had escaped to the Feisty Owl, wanting to be alone. To get his head right before he went home. His brothers had been spared a Lilian Sloan run-in and for that he was grateful. He intended to pretend his mother hadn't dropped into his exam room, stirred up his world, then disappeared not forty-eight hours later.

But he hadn't found the solitude he'd sought at the Owl. And a run-in with Kelsey Orr led to an impromptu dinner with Maggie.

Now Grant couldn't pretend he hadn't held Maggie's hand. Or that he didn't want to take her hand again and draw her even closer. Like into his arms.

And the feeling wasn't subsiding. Despite having spent the last sixty minutes loading Maggie's camper and hitching it to Ryan's truck. Despite no accidental brushes of their arms. No more words spoken other than directions on where to store the folding chairs and table.

But Maggie and Grant were only in Three Springs for a short while. Both soon would be gone. And getting to know her, well, Grant wasn't looking for a friend. He was more than comfortable on his own. Besides, being alone wasn't a problem that required a fix.

That left only one recourse for Grant. He needed to widen the space between Maggie and himself. Until he couldn't recall the sparkle in her gaze or hear her sweet laugh. Until she was back in the not-quite-friend zone, where Grant could walk away from her and pretend he felt nothing for his cowgirl.

Ryan stepped around the back of the trailer. "Looks like everything is set."

"That's good." Grant checked the lock on the storage bay on the side of the camper. "There's no more room."

"It's a puzzle every time we pack her up." Maggie walked over and patted the trailer. "But somehow we always manage to fit it all back in."

"Let's get rolling." Ryan pulled out his truck keys. "There's homemade chocolate cake, courtesy of Tess, at the house and I got a text from Grandpa that the cards are being shuffled. Teams have been decided. They're waiting on us to get home."

"I should probably…" Grant started.

"Brush up on your card skills on the drive home." Ryan aimed his car keys at Grant as if ready to pop holes in any of Grant's excuses for not joining his family. "We're partners, Grant, and I don't feel like losing tonight. Mags, you're with Grandpa Sam."

Maggie grinned. "I'll ride with you, Ryan, and you can explain the game to me."

Ryan opened his mouth as if to argue.

"That's a good idea," Grant said, cutting his brother off and reaching in his pocket for his own keys. He'd wanted space. He was taking it now. "Ryan, you play more cards than me anyway. You'll have insider tips for Maggie on how to win, I'm sure."

Grant spent the drive to his family's property telling himself that Maggie was just a guest. He would pack up his interest in Maggie and keep his distance. The farmhouse was filled with people to entertain her. Give her whatever she needed. Grant didn't have to be the one watching over her. Checking on her. Hospitality wasn't his strength, anyway. He'd leave that to his family.

Pleased that his plan was solid, Grant parked outside the four-car garage and watched another familiar truck pull in beside his.

Kelsey cut the engine and climbed out of the vintage truck. Then she joined him near the tailgate, carrying a cloth shopping bag. She grinned, yet her words were cool. "Dr. Sloan, I only asked you to bring dinner to Mags. Not bring her back to your home."

"The invitation came from Ryan." Grant pointed to where Ryan guided the camper into the empty space beside the garage. "And technically Ryan brought Maggie home."

Ryan's headlights clicked off. The front doors opened. Maggie hopped out of the passenger seat. All blond hair, soft skin, and entirely too much appeal. She waved. Her laughter was like a hit of adrenaline spiking his awareness, locking Grant's attention on her.

"It's interesting, though," Kelsey mused beside Grant.

More of Maggie's laughter spilled free into the night, powering up that appeal. His brother joined Maggie and the pair walked toward them. Grant couldn't look away from his cowgirl. "What is?"

"That you're the first person my sister looked for when she got out of the truck," Kelsey said.

Not as interesting as the fact that Grant wanted to take Maggie's hand, lead her away from the farmhouse and linger outside. Under the full moon. With just her. "You should know that Maggie and I share the same philosophy on dating."

"What's that exactly?" Curiosity swirled around Kelsey's words.

"We don't date," Grant stated. And it wasn't something he planned to change. Not even for a cowgirl that intrigued him more than any other woman he'd ever met.

Maggie hugged her sister. "Grant and Ryan offered us real mattresses in their guest rooms, hot showers in the guest bathrooms and working air conditioning."

"That's certainly hard to resist." Kelsey arched an eyebrow at Grant as if she too noted that her sister had called him by his first name, not Dr. Sloan.

Grant liked the lack of formality a bit too much. Would've considered it progress had he been interested in pursuing more with Maggie than the not-quite-friends status.

Maggie walked beside her sister toward the back porch and poked the cloth bag hanging from her sister's good shoulder. "Kelsey, what's in the bag?"

"Aprons and several shirts. Some of the staff asked me to pretty them up after I worked on an Owl apron over dinner." Kelsey nudged her elbow into her sister's side. "You know this means another craft store run. I need more supplies."

Maggie didn't appear or sound even remotely excited about the prospect of a craft store excursion. She said, "I've been telling Kelsey to open an online store and sell her wares."

"Always good to have another income stream," Ryan said.

Kelsey chuckled and patted the over-full bag. "This is just a fun hobby."

"Still, a paying customer base would be helpful right now seeing as we're probably going to need a new air conditioner," Maggie said.

"That's why we have the emergency fund, Mags," Kelsey followed her sister up the porch steps.

"It's just we've been dipping into that fund more and more recently." Maggie's voice sounded strained.

"I'm sure you'll figure it out, Mags." Kelsey wrapped her good arm around Maggie's waist and squeezed her sister. "You always do."

Maggie's smile was now strained too. Too stiff. Not that her happiness or lack of it was Grant's responsibility. Still, he preferred to see her upbeat and cheerful. Now he had a foolish urge to help make things right for her. Instead, he stepped around her and her sister to get to the back door.

"If it's a job you want, Mags, then you should go work with Grant," Ryan said, all too cheerful and reasonable.

Grant stopped in the middle of the porch and slowly turned back around. That was a bad idea. Everything was wrong with his brother's suggestion. Working with Maggie put her close to Grant all day. He frowned at his brother.

"What?" Ryan considered Grant. His gaze sharpened, his words were clear and convincing. "You need a competent temporary receptionist at your clinic until Dr. Toro returns to hire a permanent one. You told me that yesterday."

"When does Dr. Toro return again?" Kelsey's

voice was mild, as if she didn't have an opinion one way or the other.

As for Maggie, she gaped at her sister as if she had too many opinions and wasn't quite certain where to start.

"Dr. Toro is scheduled to be back in his clinic in two weeks," Grant said carefully and intentionally. His family had been referring to Dr. Toro's clinic as Grant's since Grant had agreed to fill in for his mentor. No matter how many times Grant had corrected them, they just kept on. So, too, did Grant. His clinic was in California, and everyone needed to remember that.

"We are here for the next ten days so the timing fits our schedule really well." Kelsey still wore the same bright smile she'd arrived with. "Maggie could fill in as your receptionist until we leave."

Maggie chewed on her lower lip and remained silent.

"It shouldn't be a problem." Kelsey's gaze collided with Grant's. One of her eyebrows twitched. She continued, "It's not like you two are dating or anything. So, it's all perfectly professional."

Grant nodded. Business only. It would be a strictly professional arrangement. Because there were no vacancies in Grant's personal life. At least, not any he was inclined to fill.

"You can't go the rest of the summer without air conditioning in the camper, Mags." Ryan tugged Maggie's ponytail playfully. "You and Grant can even carpool together."

Working. Living. Now carpooling too. Grant couldn't be the only one thinking that was too much. A bridge too far. He had limits. Boundaries. A perfectly solid self-imposed, keep-his-distance-from-Maggie plan. That was now steadily veering off course. Grant coughed and covered his mouth with the back of his hand.

Maggie's gaze skipped around the porch but never connected with Grant's.

"It makes sense," Ryan continued. "You can't deny the logic, Grant. Neither can you, Mags."

Yes, it made sense. They all knew it. What didn't make sense was Grant's racing heart. Or his sudden nerves. He cleared his throat. "Maggie, you've been quiet. What do you think?"

What looked like a crease of uncertainty marred Maggie's brow. "Well, I… "

Grant stalled. Unsure if he wanted her to accept or not. He searched for another solution and found none.

The door opened. Grandpa Sam stepped out

and motioned to them. "Well, come on then. Get a move on. The cards are dealt. Bets have been decided. All we need now are our players." Grandpa Sam pointed at them. "That's you four if I haven't made myself clear enough."

"Grandpa." Ryan walked over to their grandfather and propped the door open. "Grant is going to hire Maggie to work at his office. What do you think about that?"

"Best decision he could make," Grandpa Sam said with a satisfied smile. Then he frowned at Grant. "After that time-zone fiasco, Boone and I have overheard people discussing the clinic for the past few days while eating at the Owl. It wasn't compliments, either."

Grant ground his teeth. The locals would move on eventually. It was only a short-term problem. Same as his interest in Maggie. One would be solved by a qualified temp. And the other by denial. Plain and simple.

"Welcome to our home. We're glad to have you both stay." Grandpa Sam lifted his hat to acknowledge the sisters. Then he grinned and held his arm out for Maggie. "Come on, partner. Let's go show my grandsons how to win at cards."

CHAPTER TWELVE

IT WAS SEVERAL more hours before the card game ended and the house fully quieted for the night. Even then, Grant had remained in Carter's office with a medical journal for company. Just to be certain everyone was in bed. Where they were supposed to be.

Hearing only silence, Grant headed upstairs.

At the end of the hallway, the bathroom door swung open. And what do you know? Not everyone was where they should have been, after all.

Maggie paused in the doorway, wearing a Chance Blackwell concert t-shirt, cotton shorts and holding her toothbrush.

Grant should really mind more. Instead, he took in her freshly washed face. Her bare feet. And the way her hair, bundled in a loose bun, looked ready for his fingers to tumble it all free.

Yeah, he should mind. He should stick to his plan to put distance between them.

Maggie watched him. Her voice was as mellow as the light streaming from the bathroom. "You know that you don't have to hire me. You were backed into a corner earlier tonight."

"Not really." As if he'd ever let that happen. He crossed his arms over his chest to keep from reaching for her. Proving he was still following his plan. "Can you turn on a computer?"

She nodded.

"Answer a phone," he asked, "without hanging up on the caller on hold?"

She nodded again. "I worked every summer at the local inn when I was in high school and then for a year after I graduated. The inn also had the only sit-down restaurant, so I took reservations for both."

One corner of Grant's mouth tipped up. "You're hired."

"I promise you won't notice I'm there."

Too late for that. He'd notice Maggie in a crowded stadium.

"And I won't get in your way, either," she rushed on. Her bun finally gave up and collapsed. Her blond hair fell past her shoulders.

For the first time in a long time, Grant was transfixed. Completely transfixed by one adorably sweet cowgirl. He stepped into her space. Waited for her to lift her gaze to his. Waited until he had her full attention. "Maggie."

Her voice was barely more than a whisper. "Yeah?"

He let his gaze travel over her face, slowly. As if he was prepared to stand there all night and just take it all in. Her lips opened. His gaze slid back to hers. Leaning in, he inhaled the vanilla scent of her soap and murmured, "You're already in my way, Maggie."

She blinked. Her grip flexed on the toothbrush she still clutched. A beat later, her eyebrows lifted toward her forehead. Her smile broke free, radiant and all for him. She chuckled. "Right. You're waiting for the bathroom."

Grant nodded. He would wait all night to see her smile at him like that again.

"It's all yours." She slipped around him without brushing against him. No accidental touch of their hands. Nothing.

Before Grant corrected that oversight, he forced himself to get back to his original idea. "Hey, Maggie."

She turned around in the doorway of the guest bedroom.

He pointed to a closed door down the hallway. "If you need anything, Ryan is next door."

Her gaze searched his. "Will I have to inflate a mattress in here?"

He shook his head. "No."

"Then I won't need anything." She reached for the door handle and not him.

It should feel right. Not all wrong, as it did. "Sleep well, Maggie."

With that, Grant skipped the bathroom and headed downstairs, not stopping until he was on the porch. Inhaling several deep breaths, he tried to clear his head. Then he collapsed on one of the patio chairs and rested his feet on the wrought-iron coffee table.

Grandpa Sam stepped outside, holding a bowl of ice cream and a spoon. "Tried counting sheep, but they're hungry and wanted some Rocky Road. What's keeping you up?"

"How do you know there's something on my mind?" Grant asked.

"You've always done your deepest thinking outdoors." Sam settled into the chair beside Grant and stacked his booted feet on the coffee table. "Since that first summer you came to stay with us, in fact."

Back then, Grant had been wishing on stars. Wishing for his parents to come get him and take him back to his old life.

"Whenever your grandmother couldn't find you in bed, she'd send me out to look for you." Sam waved his spoon in the direction of the stables. "Usually found you up in the loft in the stable barn."

Because the loft put a very young, very naive Grant closer to those stars. Made him believe those stars were almost within reach. And his wishes would come true. "I've always done my best thinking at night."

"That's because your brothers were too loud and rowdy during the daytime." Sam scooped out a big bite of ice cream. "Always inserting their opinions into everyone's business. They still are, I suppose."

Grant chuckled. "I can't disagree."

"You've always been one to come to your decisions on your own," Sam mused. "Before letting the others weigh in."

Also true. Grant waited. He knew too that his grandfather had a point and he'd get there in his own good time. His grandpa would call the wait the power of patience.

Sam's spoon scraped against his bowl. "Everything moving forward with your job in California?"

"I have a video call tomorrow," Grant said. "It's the last of the formal process. An offer letter should follow soon after that."

Sam wiped a napkin over his mouth. "Then it must be a woman keeping you up. They sure can disrupt a man's mind and his sleep."

Grant wouldn't allow a woman to do that to him. Not even the intriguing cowgirl sleeping across the hall from him. His grandfather would take whatever Grant said about Maggie and spin it into a matchmaking opportunity. Grant chose an entirely different direction. "Do you think my mother regrets her choices?"

"What's brought this about?" Sam tossed his napkin into his empty bowl and set it on his lap. "Can't recall the last time you wanted to talk about your mother."

"Guess I thought I'd hear from her when I got into medical school. Or when I graduated." Or even when he'd been accepted into one of the most elite fellowships in the nation. After all, he was following in her illustrious footsteps. But he'd gotten only silence.

Until two days ago. He should be happy that there was silence again. Grant stared at the sky. Glad for the clouds concealing the stars. His nights for wishing had long passed anyway.

"When it comes to your mother, I can't say for sure what she thinks." Sam smoothed his fingers over his beard. "Or even why she made the choices she did. I suppose she thought she was making the best decision in the moment."

Lilian Sloan hadn't only left her children— she'd burdened her parents with five young boys. Grant still didn't know if his mom had even asked her parents or just expected they'd step up because they were that type of people—honest, loving and always willing to do anything for family. Grant tipped his head toward his grandpa. "Do you regret the choices she made?"

Sam reached over and clasped Grant's arm. His gaze was steady. His words fierce with affection. "I can tell you I don't regret one minute I've been given with you and your brothers."

"What about the time Ryan and I convinced the twins that you wanted them to do all our chores too?" As far as schemes went, it was one of the better ones Ryan and Grant had devised. It was even more thrilling when the twins had bought in to their argument. "Then Ryan and I snuck off to the pond to swim."

Grant grinned at the memory. It'd all been one spectacular day on the rope swing with Ryan until their grandpa had arrived at the pond. Ryan and Grant had ended up doing the whole house's chores for a month. The worst part, though, had been they'd both lost rope swing privileges for two months—the rest of the summer, essentially.

"Can't say you boys didn't keep me on my toes. And your grandma on hers." Sam chuckled and patted Grant's arm. "Still, I have no regrets. And we all came out okay, didn't we?"

"Better than okay." Grant covered his grandpa's weathered hand with his own. His grandparents hadn't just stepped up. They'd stepped in with the love and stability the boys had needed. He owed his grandparents so much. "It's all because of you and Gran."

"Your gran deserves most of the credit." His grandpa's smile turned wistful. Affection was thick in his words as it always was whenever he spoke of his Claire. Theirs had been the love of a lifetime.

Grant kept his hand over his grandfather's and searched the sky again. "Gran would want us to forgive our mother."

His grandpa placed his free hand on his chest. "Your gran would want you to do what feels right in your heart. Nothing more. Nothing less."

Best be careful, Grant. That quick mind of yours will talk you out of listening to your heart. And sometimes what your heart is saying is all you need to hear. Grant's heart had stopped trying to be heard years ago. And that had suited Grant perfectly well for a long time. He shifted in the chair.

"I'm gonna head on to bed." His grandfather squeezed Grant's arm one last time. Then, holding his empty bowl, Sam stood up. "Don't forget what else your gran used to tell you."

"What's that?" Grant asked. His grandmother had a catalogue of advice that she quoted from often. A saying for every situation, big or small.

Sam pointed at the night sky. "If you spend too much time wishing…"

"You miss out on living," Grant finished for him.

Sam grinned. "Knew you'd remember. Now I'll leave you to your thoughts."

Grant watched his grandfather until he was safely back inside the farmhouse. He lingered for several minutes, his gaze fixed on the sky before heading indoors.

He wasn't wishing tonight. Tonight, he was remembering. Remembering everything he'd rather forget. Like how much he still missed Gran Claire even after so much time. And just how far he was from ever forgiving his mother.

Grant shut the back door on the pain and the past. He slipped off his boots and padded in his socks into the kitchen.

Not so silently. Because he startled Maggie. The water from the glass she clutched splashed onto her t-shirt. She pressed her other hand over her heart. "Did they teach you to move that quietly in medical school?"

"I learned stealth mode as a kid." Grant tried not to smile. He tore off a paper towel and handed it to her. "Sorry. Didn't mean to scare you."

"I came down for some water." Maggie wiped at her chin. "I sleep next to the refrigerator in the camper so nighttime raids are always within easy reach."

She was within easy reach now. But what would holding onto Maggie get him? Temporary comfort, sure. Or worse, a not-so-temporary urge to hold her again. For longer. Grant walked to the refrigerator and opened the doors. "I'm sure we can do better than water for a nighttime kitchen raid."

"You didn't eat enough at dinner?" Maggie leaned her hip against the island.

Grant set Tess's homemade triple-layer chocolate cake with marshmallow filling on the counter. He cut a thick slice, then handed Maggie a fork. "There's something special about a midnight snack."

Maggie scooped up a bite of cake. "That makes you feel like you're getting away with something really good."

"Exactly." Grant cut his fork through the cake. "I always liked sneaking down here around this time because I didn't have to worry about sharing."

"Did you do a lot of midnight snacking as a kid?" Amusement was clear from her words.

He would've snuck down more if Maggie had been waiting in the kitchen. He shrugged, focusing his attention back to the cake and away from his cowgirl. "A couple times a week. Whenever Gran Claire made my favorite foods."

"What about your brothers?" she asked.

"Also when Gran Claire cooked their favorites." Grant chuckled and eased into the memories. So many good ones with his brothers. In this house. Out on the ranch. "My brothers and I ran into each other in the kitchen whenever Gran cooked meatballs and spaghetti, fried chicken, or her turtle ice cream pie. When we got a little loud, Grandpa would come out and order us back to bed. But not before we all got to finish off the leftovers with him."

Maggie covered her laughter with her hand.

"Those dishes are still family favorites," Grant said. "What about you? What's your favorite food?"

"I would fight you for the last piece of this cake. Or the last piece of any kind of chocolate." Maggie waved her fork as if preparing to fend him off. "And I wouldn't feel the least bit bad about it."

Grant grinned. "I'll keep that in mind."

"Keep what in mind?" Ryan walked into the kitchen and ran a hand through his hair, messing it up even more.

Maggie set her fork on the counter and picked up her water glass.

Ryan frowned at their empty cake plate. "Grant, you always were the worst one at sharing."

He still was. For example, right now, Grant didn't want to share his time with Maggie. Not with anyone. And wasn't that a revelation. Grant rinsed the cake plate in the sink and turned around.

"Now that you're staying here with us, Mags, we can start season three of the *Black Rose Guardians* series." Ryan rubbed his hands together. Anticipation evident on his face. "I think we should watch episode one now. Come on, Mags. You know you want to."

Grant wanted to order his brother back to bed and away from *Mags*. What was wrong with him? This was exactly what he expected. Mags and his brother—the logical choice for each other.

Maggie glanced at Grant and grinned. "Ryan and I discovered our mutual adoration for all things *Black Rose Guardians* last year after a particularly bad weekend of competition."

And Grant was quickly discovering there was nothing agreeable about seeing his brother with Maggie. Nothing at all.

"We don't mention that weekend. Ever."

Ryan walked into the pantry and returned with several chip bags. "But after binge-watching our TV show, we decided we must watch it at night for the full experience."

"And your brother gets scared, so he needs to watch it with someone," Maggie teased.

"Not cool, Mustang Mags. But you're not totally wrong." Ryan opened a bag of popcorn. "Grant, are you in? We have double-cheddar popcorn and sour-cream-and-onion chips. And we know it's a work night, so we won't stay up too late. Right, Mags?"

Maggie laughed. "Two episodes at the most."

"I think I'll let you two have this," Grant said.

Maggie stared at him. "Are you sure you don't want to join us?"

No. Grant nodded.

What he wanted was a good night's sleep and to prepare for his upcoming interview.

What he wished for…well, that wasn't important. And about as fleeting as a shooting star.

Besides, the life he was building didn't include kitchen rendezvous and late-night meetups with pretty cowgirls like Maggie. The same as Maggie's life didn't include city stopovers with closed-off doctors like him.

He didn't need more facts to know a future was impossible for them.

Grant left Maggie and Ryan to their TV show and headed upstairs to his room.

Now all he had to do was accept the impossible.

CHAPTER THIRTEEN

THE NEXT MORNING, with five miles notched into the soles of her running shoes and dawn lighting the sky, Maggie started to feel like herself again. She'd spent a restless night thinking round and round about Grant and kisses.

Grant had almost kissed her in the hallway outside the bathroom last night. Worse, Maggie had almost kissed him back. And suddenly kissing her doctor had been all she could think about. Not even her favorite TV show had distracted her. At the first peek of dawn, Maggie had hightailed it out of the farmhouse for a long, head-clearing run.

There was nothing for it now. She simply couldn't be within hand-holding distance or kissing range of Grant, either at the farmhouse or the clinic. And she'd keep herself busy. Being busy would surely block all her misplaced ideas, especially the impractical ones about city docs and free-spirited cowgirls. Midnight kisses and unrealistic futures.

She slowed to a jog, pulled out her earbuds,

then veered toward the stables. Busy started now. With her horses and an early morning house call from Dr. Paige Bishop. Then it was a shower and her first day of office temping.

Inside the stable, a mare with a reddish-brown coat and thick chestnut-colored mane peeked her head over a stall door. Maggie grinned and greeted the mare. "Good morning, Cleo. I don't have much time, but I can put a fancier style in your mane real fast."

The friendly mare nuzzled Maggie's shoulder. A familiar nicker came from the far end of the stables before Tango's head popped over the stall door. Maggie called out, "Tango, Kelsey will turn you out when it's not so hot. For now, you need to chill in here."

A little later, the stable door opened and slammed shut. Maggie peered out of Lady Dasher's stall and waved to Dr. Paige Bishop. "I'm down here."

"Hi, Maggie. Thanks for meeting me so early. I've got new medicine I want to give Lady Dasher." Paige greeted Cleo, ran her fingers over the double Dutch braid in the mare's mane and complimented the horse on her stylish updo. "Maggie, did you do this? How did you do this? I love it."

"Just some braids." And an excuse for avoiding the farmhouse and breakfast and a possible run-in with Grant. She worked a brush through Lady Dasher's mane.

"If it's okay with you I'd like to text pictures of Cleo's braids to my stepdaughter." Paige walked into Lady Dasher's stall and set her housecall vet-kit down. Right away, she rubbed her hand over the mare's back, greeting her. "Riley is nine. She and her friends have decided they want to enter a junior miss rodeo contest. But first they need to practice. Riley is working on her riding skills as well as learning how to fully care for her horse."

"Sure thing." Maggie smiled at Paige's excitement and obvious affection for her stepdaughter. Paige lit up whenever she talked about her husband or Riley. That was love—the true, lasting forever kind. Maggie had never aspired to fall in love again. Once had left enough of an impression to convince Maggie that she wasn't missing anything. She had a career she adored. And there was her sister and father too. Yet, listening to Paige, seeing Kelsey practically glow after her unofficial date with Chef Nolan last night, well, Maggie started to wonder. Started to reconsider.

Nothing good came from getting sidetracked now. There was her sister to think about. Their precarious financial situation. Securing that automatic bid to nationals. The sisters' potential sponsorship. Maggie had chosen to put her family first years ago, and there was no turning back. She sectioned off a part of the mare's thick black mane.

"Riley loves it. Thanks." Paige clutched her phone in both hands. Hope filled her face. "She wants to know if you can teach her."

"Happy to." Maggie worked a braid into the mane and leaned into the idea of teaching Riley and welcoming another diversion. "I could show her how to weave ribbons or flowers into her horse's mane and tail. When she does enter the junior miss rodeo contest, you could style her hair to match. If you think she might like that."

"Are you kidding? She's going to want that." Paige's eyebrows pulled together as she swiped at her phone again.

"Everything okay?" Maggie peered at Paige over the mare's muscular back.

"I'm getting lectured over text." Paige flashed her phone screen at Maggie. Amusement danced in her gaze. "And reminded of who you and your sister are. Even though Riley has talked about you nonstop since I told her Lady Dasher is my patient. Riley's entire text is in all caps too."

Maggie chuckled. "Who are we?"

"Only the best girl ropers ever. Like ever,

Mama Paige. That's a direct quote." Paige read from her phone, then eyed Maggie. "She wants to know if you're as pretty in person as you are in the pictures she's seen on the internet."

"Prettier." That confident declaration came from behind Maggie.

She spun around to find Grant leaning his arms on the stable door. Just her luck. She was sweaty, flushed, and in need of a shower. While her city doc was completely put together and entirely too handsome. Worse, that nervous flutter was back, flickering up into her chest.

"Hey, Grant." Paige returned her attention to her phone. "I totally agree with you about Maggie. She's pretty in pictures and in person."

"Thanks," Maggie managed. Her fingers made quick work of the braid. If only she could be quick about containing her reaction to Grant. If only he hadn't called her pretty again.

"Maggie." Paige ran her hand over the mare's neck. "Riley is pleading with me. And well, she's really hard to resist. Right, Grant?"

"Riley is definitely a force to be reckoned with." The warmth in Grant's expression was also captured in his words. "Adorable and determined all in one package, like someone else I know. Hard to resist, for sure."

Maggie gazed at Grant. As he watched her, his fingers tapped a restless beat against his lower lip. Surely, he wasn't thinking about their almost kiss. The one that couldn't happen. The one she had no right anticipating. Maggie's fingers tangled in her horse's mane. She corrected her mistake and concentrated on her new friend Paige.

"Maggie, would you consider giving Riley some pointers on her riding and horsemanship? Anything that might help her prepare for the junior miss rodeo contest." Paige examined Lady Dasher's eye and praised the mare's healing. Then she said, "Riley is convinced you know more about the rodeo than anyone. I bet she'll listen to every word you tell her."

Maggie chuckled. "I'm free tomorrow after work."

"Riley will be at her best friend's house for a playdate and sleepover." Paige dropped her light into her vet-kit and picked up the bag handles. "That means it's Friday date night for Evan and me," she said, her delight evident "It will be candles on a private table tucked in the corner of The Spiced Beehive Bistro. Good food. And my husband all to myself. If you can't tell, I'm really looking forward to it."

A date night. With Grant. Having her doctor all to herself. Maggie pressed pause on that road to nowhere, swallowed and avoided looking at him.

"Is Riley coming over for the partner challenge on Saturday?" Grant asked.

"Riley wouldn't miss it." Paige set her vet-kit outside the stall and chuckled. "Riley and her dad are already discussing which steers to bring for the challenge. I'm not sure who is more excited, Evan or Riley."

"If you bring Riley over early, she can help us warm up the horses." Maggie finished the braid, secured it, and followed Paige out of the stall. "I could give her some tips then."

"Thank you. You may have just leveled me up to super cool Mama Paige status in Riley's eyes. You've made my day." Paige walked out with Maggie and Grant. In the driveway, she hugged Maggie, added a few last-minute instructions for the mare's care between now and her next visit, and climbed into her truck. "I'm off to the Bakers' farm. One of their alpacas has a tooth issue. You both know how to reach me."

With a wave through her open truck window, the veterinarian left the farm. And before Maggie found herself alone with her doctor, Ryan appeared on the back porch.

"Grant, we still have time for that run before

you need to leave for work." Ryan jogged over to them. "Mags, want to join us?"

Maggie wiped her forehead. "I ran earlier."

"Why didn't you wake us up?" Ryan stretched his arms over his head. "Then you wouldn't have had to run alone."

"It's fine." Maggie kept her attention on Ryan, motioned toward the stables. "Paige met me early. I wanted to check on Lady Dasher before I left." She ran her palms over her running shorts. "Now I better go get dressed for work."

"Don't forget to eat." Grant touched her arm, drawing her gaze to his. "And drink some water. You look like you need it."

His words sounded like a clinical assessment. But the tender concern in his eyes was anything but detached and professional. Maggie tightened her ponytail and brushed more sweat off her neck.

"Wow." Ryan punched his brother's shoulder lightly. "Little brother, you must win over everyone with a bedside manner like that."

"What?" Grant held out both hands. Determination crossed his face. "Maggie wasn't jogging or walking earlier, Ryan. I saw her. She was seriously running and would no doubt have left us in her dust. Athletes need to fuel their bodies correctly for the best performance."

"Grant. Stop talking." Ryan dragged his

palms over his face, then glanced at Maggie. "I'll work on him, Mags. Teach him how to cause a woman to swoon."

That was definitely not necessary. Her city doc already tipped her off-balance enough.

"When have you ever caused a woman to, what was the word? Swoon." Grant nudged his elbow into Ryan's side and started jogging backward. One corner of his mouth tipped into a grin. "Oh, was it with Natalie Wymer? No. You accidentally tripped Natalie in the hallway when you stepped on her shoelaces with your big cowboy boots in middle school."

Ryan groaned and shook his head.

"Maybe it was Juliana Pruitt." Grant chuckled, snapped his fingers, and continued his shuffle. "No. Juliana tackled you in PE during flag football. Do you remember that, Ry-Ry? I can still picture it so clearly. Does that mean *you* swooned, big brother?"

"See you, Mags. I have to give the good doctor a memory lesson or two." Ryan turned his baseball hat around on his head and took off after his brother.

Maggie watched the two brothers playfully shove each other on the dirt road. The breeze blew their laughter, unrestrained and animated, back to her. And Maggie realized she enjoyed the sound of her city doc's richly textured laugh. A lot.

But finding more things to like about her doc wasn't necessary.

It was, however, necessary to remember her relationship with Dr. Grant Sloan was a working one only.

After all, he was her best friend's brother. And her sister's doctor. And those were certainly enough violations to the dating code.

Now, Dr. Grant Sloan was also Maggie's boss. Maggie didn't need another reason to convince her that falling for her city doc was a bad idea. *A very bad idea.*

Still, the only fall Maggie was willing to risk was one from Lady Dasher. She was quite certain falling in the arena would cause less damage than falling for her way-too-intriguing doctor turned boss.

CHAPTER FOURTEEN

TWO PATIENT VISITS and one successful interview complete, Grant was certain he could maintain both a professional distance and business appropriate rapport with Maggie. Especially if he kept to the exam rooms and Dr. Toro's private office. And if he did not give in to his ridiculous inclination to drift up to the front reception area to check on Maggie. Or to find out why she was laughing. Or who was making her laugh.

Grant frowned. He had a full caseload of patients to care for. Not a cowgirl to entertain.

Besides, Dr. Toro's nurses and medical assistants had been extremely welcoming and provided Maggie with an entire team who could answer her questions and offer assistance. A team that was much more qualified than Grant, as he'd only been at the clinic about a week longer than Maggie.

Grant scanned the chart for the patient in exam room three, knocked, then stepped inside to introduce himself to fifteen-year-old Brynlee Brenton and her father, Charlie Brenton.

"Would it be okay with you, Dr. Sloan, if Ms. Orr came in?" Charlie rested his elbows on his blue jean–covered knees and turned his faded cowboy hat in his hands. "We'd sort of like to hear Ms. Orr's opinion on things."

Maggie. They wanted Maggie. Not Dr. Toro. Grant adjusted the knot on his tie. Suddenly feeling slightly out of place for no good reason.

Brynlee sat on the exam table, her left leg stretched out, her injured ankle resting on a pillow. Pain shadowed her tight expression. Yet, a quiet awe filled her words. "Maggie Orr is one of my idols. I can't believe she's here. Like *here* here."

Neither could Grant. His cowgirl had gone from his patient's sister to a houseguest to an employee in less than a week. And Grant's interest in his cowgirl had gone from considerately polite to acutely aware in less time than that.

"Let me get Ms. Orr." Grant stepped into the hallway and asked nurse Aiden to send Maggie to exam room three.

Minutes later, Maggie swept in. Her muted-red flowery sundress floated around her brown cowboy boots. Compassion lit her face. She was a blend of summer, cheer, and grace. She paused to ensure the teenager's comfort, then took a seat beside Charlie Brenton at the rancher's request.

"I was about to go over the results of Brynlee's MRI and x-rays." Grant leaned into his clinical side, where he excelled. Where he belonged. He wasn't meant for strolling in the sunshine and dancing under the stars. Even if his cowgirl brought to mind all that and more. Grant cleared his throat. "Mr. Brenton requested that you be here, Ms. Orr."

"Brynlee was telling me about rolling her ankle when she slipped on her dismount at practice last night." Maggie patted Brynlee's arm. "I've landed wrong on my dismount too. I know how much it hurts."

Brynlee fiddled with the bandage wrapped around her ankle and never looked away from Maggie.

Grant pulled the x-ray images up on the computer and turned the screen for everyone to view. "Brynlee, your ankle and foot bones are intact. However, you do have a moderate ankle sprain."

"But nothing is broken." Charlie looked to Maggie as if he required confirmation. "She can walk now, can't she? And ride? We've got livestock to take to the auction house."

Maggie's eyebrows furrowed, then she glanced

at Grant. "Not until the swelling and inflammation subsides, right, Dr. Sloan?"

"An ankle sprain like Brynlee's can take four weeks to heal. Her recovery needs to include ice, rest, compression, and keeping her ankle elevated, as well as physical therapy," Grant explained. "Brynlee, we need to improve the stability and strength of your ankle joint."

"But I need to practice and help my dad," Brynlee pleaded with Maggie. "And I work at the ice cream shop. I'm saving up to buy a new saddle before school starts."

Charlie leaned closer to Maggie and whispered none to softly, "Does she really need to do that therapy stuff?"

Grant resisted the urge to raise his arm, point at himself and declare: doctor's orders.

Maggie's gaze collided with Grant's, then skipped to Mr. Brenton. She spoke quickly, but reassuringly as if she sensed Grant's exasperation. "Dr. Sloan's treatment plan will make sure Brynlee's ankle heals properly and stronger than before. My sister and I have both gone to physical therapists and haven't ever regretted the decision or the time we spent there."

Charlie Brenton scratched his cheek. His expression uncertain.

Grant jumped back into the conversation. "I'd also like Brynlee's riding boots and stirrups assessed for proper fit and alignment to eliminate stress and tension."

Charlie Brenton frowned at Grant's dress shoes.

"I always wrap our horse's legs for trailering and often for competition," Maggie said. Her smile kind. Her words empathetic. At the man's nod, Maggie continued, "A lace-up boot will help keep Brynlee's ankle from rolling again in the arena and from you having to make another visit here. My sister swears by her shock-absorbing stirrups."

"Dad, we need to get those. Please." Brynlee eyed her father.

"We'll look into it when we get home. I don't believe I have any more questions." Charlie Brenton flattened his hat on his head and stood. He smiled at Maggie "Thank you, Ms. Orr." He gave Grant a small nod. "Dr. Sloan."

Maggie rose and helped Brynlee with her crutches. "I'll print out Dr. Sloan's treatment plan. It'll have instructions for home care. And I'll call over to the physical therapy clinic to see about their first available appointment for Brynlee."

The trio exited the exam room, discussing Brynlee's different stirrup options. Grant dictated a patient summary for Brynlee's file and then headed for the front office. He checked the waiting room. Empty. Then braced his palms on the reception desk and eyed Maggie. "What just happened back there with my patient?"

"They don't trust you." Maggie lifted a pencil from the holder and wrote a note across a sticky pad. Then she looked up and tipped her head at him. "You need to lose the tie. And find some boots."

"I had an interview this morning." A very successful one, in fact. One that ended with the assurance that a formal offer letter and contract would be in his hands early next week. Grant should be celebrating. His future was practically set. Instead, he smoothed his palm over his tie as if Maggie aimed surgical scissors, not a pencil, at him. "And what's wrong with this tie? I've always liked it."

"I'm trying to help you." Maggie shook her head." You're dressed for the city, Dr. Sloan. To the Brentons' way of thinking, your mind is already on the West Coast." She leaned toward him as if imparting a profound secret. "People around here sense insincerity same as the cows can sense an approaching storm."

He'd given a medical diagnosis and his treatment recommendation. It wasn't about being sincere so much as it was about relaying the correct medical facts. Grant frowned at her. "Don't you have a front desk to manage?"

"I'd like to do that." Maggie exhaled, adding an exaggerated weariness to her words. Her expression remained impassive. "But my boss is disrupting me with his questionable wardrobe choices."

Grant pushed away from the reception desk. He had impeccable taste in clothing. Thanks to Gran Claire, who'd taken him shopping on more than one occasion. Gran Claire had explained the difference between cotton and linen and the importance of button-down collars. *If you want to be taken seriously by your peers and colleagues, you must first dress appropriately, Grant. You've only one first impression, use it wisely.*

When in Texas... He loosened his tie and tossed it on the visitor's chair in Dr. Toro's office. He also rolled the sleeves of his dress shirt to his elbows and released the top button at his neck. His boots were in his bedroom closet at the farmhouse. With nothing left to loosen up, he grabbed the chart for exam room one and met up-and-coming bull rider Jake Dean Wolfolk.

Twenty minutes later, Grant walked beside J.D. toward the front desk. The bull rider's limp was pronounced, but he never winced.

"We could use you on site, Doc." J.D. wiped his hand through his blond hair before setting his cowboy hat back in place. "Dr. Toro keeps threatening to retire every time he comes out to watch us ride."

"It'll be years before Dr. Toro retires," Grant said.

"But another set of trained and qualified eyes like yours in the arena would be good." J.D. selected a candy from a bowl Grant hadn't seen before. The cowboy peeled off the wrapper and popped the hard sweet into his mouth. "It'd save us some travel time to Belleridge too."

Soon enough the travel time to reach Grant would be even farther. With the fastest route being by air. Impractical for rodeo competitors hauling horses and gear like Maggie. Not that Maggie would be traveling to California for Grant. Or that he'd ever ask her to. Grant concentrated on his patient. "Remember ice and elevation every day, J.D. As often as you can manage."

"Got it, Doc." J.D. tapped his knuckles against the counter. "Mags, do us all a favor and convince Doc Sloan to join you at the arena."

"Afraid I don't have any influence over Dr. Sloan." Maggie handed the bull rider an appointment card. Her expression was neutral. Her words were optimistic. "But I'll put in a good word on behalf of all the competitors."

"See you in Amarillo, Mags." J.D. slipped the card in his front shirt pocket. "Call me if you need anything when you get to town."

"Will do." Maggie finished typing and called out, "Rest and elevation isn't code for binge eating either, J.D. Skip the double patty cheeseburger and loaded French fries in the drive-thru. The bull will thank you in a few weeks."

"You're cruel, Mags." J.D. pressed his hand against his stomach. "What am I supposed to eat?"

"Carrots and roasted cauliflower," Maggie replied.

"Doc, I changed my mind. You come down to the arena." J.D. aimed his sunglasses at Maggie. "And leave no-fun Mags at home."

Grant watched the sliding doors close, then grinned at Maggie. He should probably thank her for her suggestion to loosen his attire. Just removing his tie had instantly relaxed him. And his conversation with J.D. had been surprisingly easy. They'd quickly come to understand each other. He appreciated Maggie's words and frankness. "Did you hear that?"

"What?" Maggie's finger tapped on the computer keyboard.

"J.D. just called me fun." Grant added an extra dose of light teasing to his words.

"No, he called me no-fun Mags," she corrected him.

"It's the same thing." Grant picked up the clipboard with the afternoon schedule but kept his attention on Maggie. "Someone thinks I'm fun, even in my dress shirt and slacks. What do you think about that, no-fun Mags?"

"I think you have patients waiting, Dr. Skip-the-tie-and-wear-boots-next-time Sloan." Maggie handed him a folder. Still, there was a definite spark in her gaze. "This is for exam room two."

He scanned the patient appointments for the afternoon. He recognized the name of a bronc rider from conversations with Ryan. Then it was a possible torn ACL for a cheerleader from the university not an hour south of the clinic. And a shoulder strain for a nationally ranked swimmer. Hardly the patient load he'd expected to find in small town Belleridge. Yet, Grant couldn't say he was disappointed.

He might not ooze sincerity like Maggie, but Grant knew his purpose. That was to get all of his patients back to living their best lives. On their terms. Just like he lived his. He headed to exam room two.

It wasn't long before Grant's last patient headed out the main doors promising to drop off zucchini bread for the staff the following day. While the staff exited, too, Grant approached Maggie's desk. "I've got a few more clinical notes to dictate, then I think we can call it a day."

"Take your time," Maggie said. "I want to research junior miss rodeo contests. The phones were busy most of the afternoon and I never got a chance at lunch."

Maggie had proven to be more than capable as the clinic's receptionist. While Grant had proven less than capable of keeping away from her. He'd even taken to walking his patients out, escorting them all the way to the desk and Maggie. Something for him to work on tomorrow.

The main doors slid open. A pair of silver-haired retirees bustled through the entrance, their steps spry and their expressions shrewd. Grant quickly assessed the petite pair. No catch in their gait. Their arms swung and hands moved as they chatted spiritedly with each other.

Grant grinned, stepped into the waiting room and greeted the town's favorite sister act. "Hello, Breezy. Gayle. What brings you two by? You don't have appointments."

"Don't be thinking we've come to talk about replacements, knee or any kind, Doc Sloan." Breezy Baker's thin eyebrows flexed into her forehead. "We have important bowling league business to discuss with Maggie over there."

Gayle Baker shooed Grant toward the fill-in receptionist. "Doc! Will you get on with the introductions, so we can get on with our important bowling business?"

Grant ran through a quick introduction. In took less time for Maggie to fall under the Bakers' spell. The duo was instantaneously likable.

Formalities concluded, Gayle hurried around the wide desk, her tote bag bouncing against it. She bundled Maggie into her arms for an enthusiastic hug, then cradled Maggie's face in her palms. "Aren't you stunning, dear. With your blue eyes big as a baby doe's. Look, Breezy, isn't Maggie lovely?"

"Sure is." Breezy nudged her sister aside to get a better look at Maggie. Delight laced Breezy's clever gaze. "You must have your choice of cowboys on the circuit."

That observation didn't sit well with Grant. Most likely because he suspected it was true. But jealous wasn't something Grant ever aspired to be.

"Once upon a time, Breezy and I had our picks too." Gayle's laughter was as cheerful as the sunflowers painted on her overalls.

"We still do." Breezy pressed her fingers

against her cheeks as if to catch the cackle in her laugh.

"I don't know about having my pick." Maggie looked to Grant, then to the sisters. Her hands slipped into the pockets in her sundress. "But it hardly matters. I've decided that cowboys are just too much trouble. And I'm much better being on my own."

On that point, Maggie and Grant agreed. Wholeheartedly, in fact. Which made it strange that he felt slightly apologetic and almost regretful right now.

"Oh, you poor dear." Gayle wrapped her arm around Maggie's waist and squeezed. Her frown dipped into glum. "Got a bruised heart, I suppose. Cowboys always seem to forget to tread lightly."

"It's their boots." Breezy pursed her lips and studied Grant as if awaiting his apology.

Grant caught Maggie's grin before she smoothed her expression back to impartial. Grant stepped around the counter into full view of the lively retirees and pointed at his dress shoes. "Well, it's a good thing then that I don't wear boots."

Gayle sniffed and pushed her owl-round glasses up her nose. "Doesn't mean you know how to tread any softer, Grant Sloan."

"Sure doesn't. But we'll have to get back

to matters of the heart later, dears," Breezy announced. "Right now, we've got a bowling predicament. And, Maggie, your sister claims you can solve it for us."

Maggie gaped. "I'm not sure what Kelsey told you."

"We had a lovely lunch with her and Nolan at the Owl today," Gayle explained. "She's quite delightful."

"Your sister and Nolan make such a sweet pair." Breezy sighed into her clasped hands. "Couldn't have matched them better myself. Too bad about her shoulder, though."

"Otherwise, we would've recruited her to be on our bowling team tonight." Gayle rummaged inside the tote bag on her arm.

"But Kelsey claims you're a much better bowler than her anyway." Breezy beamed at Maggie. "That's why we need you, Maggie. We've got a winning streak to uphold."

"We're undefeated this season," Gayle exclaimed, then sobered. "But we lost Celia-Ann Guthrie. Her daughter, Nicole rolled her ankle something good at the park, chasing her two-year-old. Doc Sloan, you saw Nicole here earlier this week."

"She was the pregnant one," Breezy whispered as if he needed his memory jogged.

Grant nodded and tried to keep up. Maggie's gaze had narrowed slightly as if she was concentrating too.

"Doc Sloan put the poor mother-to-be in one of those cumbersome boots, then told Nicole to get a chair for her knee to wheel around on. How she gets upstairs to her children's rooms I don't know." Breezy looked momentarily perplexed as she paused to catch her breath.

Grant rubbed his forehead, exhausted for Breezy and Celia-Ann's daughter, Nicole.

Breezy rattled on, "Anyway, Celia-Ann is babysitting her grandkids on account of her son-in-law needing to go to Houston for a last-minute business meeting, and Nicole needing to rest and put her bad ankle on ice."

Gayle flung her arms out. Alarm widened her eyes. "Now we've lost Celia-Ann to her grandma duties and she's our ringer for league play tonight."

"We must have a ringer." Breezy watched Maggie. Hope shifted across her face.

"Just so I'm clear." Maggie held up her hand. "You want me to bowl with you for your league tonight?"

Gayle and Breezy glanced at each other. Their faces scrunched as if they weren't sure what had been unclear about their request.

Grant cleared his throat, ready to give Maggie an out.

"I'd love to be on your team." Maggie's smile stretched wide. "Although I have to warn you, I haven't bowled for a while."

"It's like riding a bike." Breezy all but ignored Maggie's warning. "One or two practice runs and it'll all come back to you."

"Kind of like dating," Gayle mused. "You go out on a few practice dates. Remember why it's fun and worthwhile, then you settle right back into the game."

"I'm happy to bowl." Maggie straightened the folders on the desk and avoided looking at Grant. "But dating and love aren't a game I ever intend to play again."

Love wasn't a game Grant wanted to play either. They had that in common too. Yet the insight left him more deflated than elated.

"It's best we leave your dating discord for another time, dear." Gayle's words were sympathetic. Then she tugged a metallic purple button-down shirt from her tote bag. "We need you to concentrate on winning."

"Can't have any discord in the alley. Makes the balls skid into the gutter. We certainly don't want that." Breezy took the purple shirt from her sister and handed it to Maggie. "Now here's your team shirt. Your sister already sparkled it up for you at lunch. Such a thoughtful girl."

Maggie hugged the shirt against her chest as if the sisters had given her a precious gift. With a flurry of hugs and see you tonights, the sisters departed.

Not long after, Grant drove out of the clinic parking lot and glanced at Maggie in the passenger seat of his truck. "Am I really taking you to bowling league?"

"Absolutely." Maggie smoothed her hands over the bowling shirt she put on over her sundress.

"Are you always like this?" Grant asked.

"Like what?" Maggie twisted the end of the shirt into a loose knot at her waist.

"So willing and ready to join in." She'd jumped right in at the office too. Blending in as if she'd always worked there. As if she'd always been friends with the staff. She was the same at the farmhouse. She just seemed to fit wherever she was. Even beside him right now.

"Are you always so standoffish?" she countered. "Or are you shy? You secretly want to bowl, but you're afraid no one will pick you for their team."

Grant swallowed his laugh. "I've never been called shy."

"That's what I thought," Maggie mused then she reached over and touched his arm. "Don't worry, Dr. Sloan, we'll find you a team."

Grant wanted to take her hand in his. Pick his own team. Pick Maggie.

But Grant had never been much of a team player. So, he kept his hands on the steering wheel and a tight grip on his heart.

CHAPTER FIFTEEN

MAGGIE KEPT HER hand on Grant's arm a beat past friendly and fleeting. She acknowledged the warmth of his skin. His strength. Considered holding on. As if she wanted to encourage whatever was between them. But to what end? An even more uncomfortable goodbye.

She pulled her arm away. She was alone with her doctor. For the first time all day. Didn't mean she couldn't keep to herself. Although, she wanted to know about his interview. And if he liked her being in the office as much as she'd enjoyed being there. Really, anything he wanted to share. But this wasn't the start of something. Sharing and handholding were reserved for next-level relationships.

Yet, the slow tempo of the country song about lazy mornings and stolen kisses only circled her back to Grant and the idea of leveling up things between them. The quiet inside the truck cab seemed to stretch in anticipation.

"I've been reading up on junior miss rodeo contests." Maggie fumbled with her cell phone and scattered the silence. "I think the hardest part is the speech. Hands down. I would've been terrified at nine years old to give a three-minute speech, knowing I was being judged."

Grant glanced at her. "Weren't you competing in the arena when you were that age?"

"That was me and my horse against a clock." Maggie swiped her finger across her phone screen. "Would you have gotten on stage for a speech about you, your horse and what the rodeo means to you when you were nine years old? Never mind making it fun and creative to display your personality in order to win over a panel of judges."

"When I was nine, my brothers and I were at the pond, climbing trees to find the strongest branch for our rope swing." He chuckled. "All we cared about was seeing who could swing the farthest over the water and make the biggest splash. Good times."

"Sounds like it." Maggie considered him. His smile was soft and relaxed as if he welcomed a really great, forgotten memory. That, she was learning, was his look whenever he talked about his family. He loved them. That much was obvious. Yet, he was leaving. And she was suddenly curious. "So, tell me, when did this whole brooding, I-go-it-alone thing start?"

"What thing is that?" Confusion crowded through his words.

"Well, every story you tell from your childhood starts with my brothers and I," she said. "Did you know that?" And whenever Grant spoke of his family, he lit up.

His mouth opened, then closed. His focus remained on the road.

Maggie continued, "But Tess had to beg you to come to breakfast with your family." When he opened his mouth again as if to argue, Maggie cut him off. "Don't deny it. I heard you and Tess on the porch the other morning."

"It's impolite to eavesdrop." There was no censure in his words.

"I wasn't eavesdropping. I was walking back to the house," Maggie said. "And you guys weren't exactly being quiet."

Grant flinched as if he was rewinding his conversation with Tess in his mind.

Maggie should stop. She saw the bowling alley sign up ahead. And this was none of her business. But his family was the kind she'd dreamed about as a kid—loud, loyal, and loving. Not to mention the farmhouse and the ranch. So much space. So much freedom. It was the kind of place where boots were planted. Yet, it was cut and run for her doctor. "Did something happen to set you off on your own path without your family?"

"Nothing happened." Grant pulled into the bowling alley and parked. Then he shrugged. "We all grew up. It happens in every family."

But growing up didn't mean growing apart. Maggie unbuckled, reached for her purse, and closed the conversation. He obviously knew what was best for him. She wasn't there to change his mind. Besides, her roots were shallow and no deeper than the pavement. Even if there was something about Three Springs that had her thinking more and more about home.

Grant cut the engine and grinned at her. "You can still back out."

"No way." Maggie opened her door and smiled over her shoulder at him. "Come on, Dr. Sloan, let me show you how much fun joining in can be."

"I'm just dropping you off," he said, yet he followed her inside.

Bowling shoes in hand, Maggie made her way over to lane eight and her teammates. Breezy introduced Maggie to Freida Hall, their fourth teammate.

"I make sure to do everything the same week after week." The former school teacher dabbed more bright red lipstick onto her lips then finger-combed her silver side-swept bangs into place. Freida added, "It's part of my secret to getting two consecutive strikes in a game."

Gayle linked her arm with Freida's. "We've time for a quick restroom break before play begins."

Maggie laced up her bowling shoes and watched the pair work the crowded bowling alley as if they were the hostesses of a formal gala. Stopping for hugs and quick exchanges every few steps.

"Grant, we're happy to bring Maggie back to the farmhouse later," Breezy offered. She wiped a polishing cloth over her silver-flecked purple-and-pink bowling ball.

"I think I'll stay." Grant stood with his arms crossed over his chest and his feet planted wide. He looked like an irritable bouncer. The one all the club goers went out of their way to avoid.

"You're staying?" Maggie scrambled off the bench toward him. "What happened to you not wanting to join in?"

He glanced at her. "It might be good if I'm here in case someone accidently trips over their bowling ball or something."

"If you're staying, you can't be so…" Maggie swirled her hands in front of him.

He arched an eyebrow at her. His gaze locked on her. "So what?"

"You know." Maggie stepped closer to him. "We talked about this in the car."

He didn't budge.

Maggie gripped his arms and tugged until he gave in and uncrossed them. Finally, he stuck his hands in the pockets of his dress pants and considered her. "Is this better?"

Much better. Now she wasn't tempted to grab a hold of his hand. She wrinkled her nose. "It's better, but now you're hovering."

"Hovering." His expression never changed and his voice became monotone.

"Yes. Hovering. And you're making me more nervous. I'm nervous already, Grant," she said. The slightest grin, secretive and private, shifted onto his face. His gaze dipped to her mouth. And her stomach fluttered. She added enticing to her list of things her city doc needed to stop being and said, "They're undefeated. I can't let these sweet ladies down. They're counting on me." She pointed at him. "So, you need to stop."

"Let me get this straight," he said, his voice pensive. "I look standoffish and I'm hovering. And if you don't bowl well tonight, it will be my fault."

"Exactly." Maggie smiled at him.

His eyes narrowed. "What exactly do you want me to do?"

Meet me for a midnight chocolate run. Show me who you are. Sweep me off my feet. Pick one. Pick me. But last night had been their first and only midnight meetup. And the rest wasn't what she should want. *If you love me, Maggie, you'll choose me over the rodeo.* Maggie had chosen. Now she chose again. Not to like her doctor any more than she already did. She flung her arm sideways. "Go mingle. Go talk to people. I think most of Three Springs is here."

Grant frowned. "I don't like small talk."

"Everyone likes small talk," Maggie argued. It was easy and simple. Required none of the hard stuff like career decisions or sharing feelings. Or any of the other uncomfortable stuff where hearts were on the line.

"Chitchat was never really my thing," Grant shook his head as if discarding the idea of mingling. "I prefer conversations that have a direction. A purpose."

Exasperating man. Maggie was beginning to think that was his goal—exasperating her. She lifted her gaze to the ceiling. "Grant."

"Maggie." He extended her name into two long, drawn-out syllables.

Yet, it was the invitation in his tone that pulled her attention back to him.

He leaned in and whispered, "Did you know that you're really cute when you're flustered?"

Maggie jumped back.

One corner of his mouth tipped up. His gaze was clear, affection-filled, and fixed on Maggie. "And I bet you're not nervous now."

She was a different kind of nervous now. The foolishly giddy kind that set her stomach on tumble. And made her want to take a risk. That involved hearts, heads, and heels. But that was a fall she might not recover from. "I'm not going to thank you."

"Fine." He shrugged. "But if you win, we will both know I was the reason."

Maggie shook her head. Her laughter refused to remain silent.

"Never thought I'd see my big brother in the bowling alley." Josh walked up and rapped his knuckles against Grant's shoulder. "Not after that blind date debacle in college."

Grant's chin dropped to his chest. "I cannot believe you brought that up."

Maggie's eyes widened. "What blind date?"

"He didn't tell you?" Josh rubbed his palms together. "Okay if I tell this one, big brother?"

Grant set his hands on his hips. "I don't think I can stop you without making a scene."

"That's what happened on his blind date." Josh laughed. "It could be like old times. You'd really have a reputation at the bowling alley then."

"Let's move this story along." Grant huffed. "Maggie tells me I need to go and mingle."

Maggie pushed playfully on Grant's shoulder. "You can go and mingle, Grant. Josh doesn't need you. I'm sure his memory about your blind date debacle is good."

"It's a very vivid memory," Josh added.

"Josh is coming with me when I mingle," Grant said.

"No, he isn't." Maggie stepped closer to Josh, ready to block him in case he was tempted to join his brother. "You won't mingle if you have Josh beside you."

"That's the point." Grant's eyebrows raised. "I like my brother. I like talking to him."

"Thanks, Grant. That's the nicest thing you've said to me in years." Josh shooed his brother away. "Now go on and mingle."

"You're supposed to be helping me out." Grant made a face at Josh. "Not encouraging Maggie. Tell Maggie it will be bad for me."

"Actually, I want to see this." Josh tapped his cowboy hat higher on his forehead as if to clear his view.

Grant pointed at his brother. "There will be payback for this."

Josh only grinned wider. "Do your best, Doc."

"My work here is finished anyway." Grant eyed Maggie. "You know where to find me if," he trailed off for a beat, then added, "Well, you know where to find me if you need me."

Warmth surged through Maggie, heating her cheeks.

He gave her another one of those sweet private grins and sauntered off. He stopped to charm the Baker sisters and Freida before moving down the lanes, shaking hands and bumping fists with almost everyone he met. He looked at ease and comfortable. And not the least bit standoffish.

"Maggie," Josh said. "I think you're really good for my brother."

Unfortunately, Maggie was starting to wonder if it wasn't mutual. But Maggie was *good* on her own. She glanced at Josh. "So, are you going to tell me about this blind date debacle?"

"I'd like to, but Grandpa Sam is flagging me down and you're about to start bowling." Josh waved at his grandfather and Sam's teammates. He started walking away but turned around. "Maggie, I can tell you this. Grant has one seriously big heart. Maybe the biggest in our whole family. He's just careful with it. That makes him reserved. But he knows how to have fun. How to love if given the chance."

If given the chance. Maggie's gaze fell on

Grant. He was surrounded by several men, his head tipped back. Laughter filled his face. He straightened and his gaze locked on Maggie. Held. And stayed that way while he spoke to the people around him.

There was the connection. That instant awareness. That flutter inside, not unwelcome. Not entirely inconvenient.

Still, Maggie worried. If she discovered her serious city doc had a fun side and a big heart, she might consider him everything she hadn't known she wanted.

Except she already knew what she wanted, didn't she?

CHAPTER SIXTEEN

TWO DAYS LATER, Grant felt like he was still riding Maggie's winning high from the bowling league on Thursday night. He'd ended the work week yesterday with one of the most enjoyable moments he could recall having at work in a long while. His patient visits had been interesting. Two of which were injuries that were far from basic and challenged Grant's skills and training. He would definitely be following up with Dr. Toro about those patients, if not several others too, after he left.

But it wasn't business on Grant's mind now. It was his cowgirl.

Maggie was on King with nine-year-old Riley Bishop seated in the saddle in front of her. Riley's pink boots complemented Maggie's bedazzled pink tank top. Both wore matching wide smiles and had their hair braided in the same intricate style. They'd been guiding the gelding around cones set up the length of the arena for almost an hour. After several passes,

Maggie had Grant rearrange the cones into a new pattern.

The pair had been inseparable since young Riley's arrival that morning. From cleaning out stalls to feeding the horses to braiding each mane in the stable barn, Riley absorbed Maggie's every word. Followed her every instruction. Grant hadn't been much better. He'd checked on them, helped when he could, and basically lingered nearby. Easier to hear their laughter and lend a hand if needed.

Maggie stopped King in the center of the arena and whispered something to Riley. The pair's focus was centered on something behind Grant.

Before he could turn around, a rope looped over Grant and tightened around his torso.

"That's how it's done, people," Caleb shouted, and his burst of laugher ricocheted around the arena.

Grant tipped his head at Maggie and Riley. "You two could've given me a warning," he said.

Riley's eyes lit up and she caught her giggle in her hands. Maggie simply threw her head back and spoke through her laughter. "Sorry. There wasn't really time." Then she smiled at his brother. "Caleb, that was pretty impressive."

"Thanks." Caleb came into Grant's view,

seated atop a stunning palomino quarter horse named Whiskey Moon.

"That was luck." Grant shimmied out of the rope, then eyed Caleb. "You'll need more than luck this afternoon, little brother."

Caleb leaned forward in his saddle. "Grant, you should be disqualified for sneaking in extra practice with Maggie and Riley."

"Even with private lessons, Grant is not going to win." Ryan strolled inside the arena, leading Mischief, his grullo mustang. "You shouldn't waste your worry on him."

"Seriously, it's me you all should be concerned about beating." Josh followed, trotting into the arena on Cyrus his Morgan horse, and tipped his hat in greeting to Maggie and Riley.

That launched the brothers into a good-natured debate about their skills right there in the center of the arena.

Roy and Sam strolled in next. Their boots kicking up dust, their cowboy hats pulled low. Their own laughter booming. Grandpa Sam rested his arms on the metal railing, propped his boot on the lower rung, and let out a shrill whistle. The same sound that used to stop the five brothers in their boots wherever they were on the farm.

Grant turned around. So did his brothers.

Maggie helped Riley dismount and the pair moved over to Grant's grandfather and uncle.

Grandpa Sam hollered. "Don't know why some of you are mounted up already. The partner pick challenge hasn't even begun yet."

Uncle Roy tapped his silver curls and shook his head. "You boys haven't heard what we've got in store."

"We're going to rope steer." Caleb swung out of his saddle and set his hands on his hips. "The steer Evan brought over from his ranch. We get three tries each. And the fastest time overall wins. Just like always."

"And then Maggie will have a roping partner to practice with," Ryan said. "Like we all agreed to at breakfast the other morning."

"Anyone can rope a steer." Grandpa Sam dismissed the thought with a swipe of his arm through the air. "And practice steers? They're no match for you boys."

"Got that right." Uncle Roy rested his hands on his bronze belt buckle and swayed back and forth in his boots.

"Where's Grandpa going with this?" Josh muttered.

Grant shrugged and kept quiet.

"This is about Maggie and finding her the best partner," Grandpa Sam announced and motioned Maggie and Riley closer.

Though there was nothing sly in his grandfather's gaze, Grant became more alert. Not trusting that his matchmaking minded grandfather hadn't intentionally left out the word: practice. This was supposed to be about finding Maggie's best *practice* partner. Right?

His gaze shifted to Maggie. *Her best partner.* It wasn't him. She hadn't been wrong when she'd called it his go-it-alone thing in the truck the other evening. Except the more time Grant was around Maggie, the more he began to reevaluate having a partner. Yet, there wasn't a scenario where his cowgirl and he ended up together without one of them giving up something. And then, it was only a matter of time before the inevitable resentment set in. Best to keep to what he knew.

Grandpa Sam announced, "To be the perfect partner for Maggie, you have to prove you have the skills to be a top-notch roper."

"Sam and I researched ropers." A gleeful note framed Uncle Roy's words.

Too gleeful. Grant frowned. His grandpa and uncle were definitely up to something. His brothers shifted and widened their stances next to Grant.

Uncle Roy patted his head. "We collected what we found. Then put our heads together and came up with five challenges to test your skills."

Carter suddenly came into the arena, along with Evan Bishop, Riley's dad. Carter and Evan were pushing a large dry erase board Grant had never seen the likes of outside his high school classrooms. Carter and Evan had been friends since grade school. Evan was practically another brother to Grant. As such, Grant knew his tells and Carter's. The two friends were trying their hardest not to bust out laughing. Their faces kept pinching and they avoided looking anywhere but the ground. Finally, they rolled the dry erase board to a stop near Grandpa Sam and Uncle Roy.

Grandpa Sam's teeth flashed behind his grin. He rubbed his palms together. "It's time to show 'em what we came up with."

Evan and Carter swung the board around, revealing the details of the challenge. And gave up the effort to stifle their own laughter.

"Does that seriously say catch a goldfish?" Surprise tinged Caleb's words.

"Yeah." Grant scratched his chin. He studied the neat block print covering the entire board and tried to ignore Carter's rambling about how good the afternoon was going to be. And Evan's muttering about how he couldn't wait.

How they both had their phones already set to video.

"Number four says balance beam while holding a chicken." Josh sounded as incredulous as his twin. "I am reading that correctly, aren't I?"

"Hey, stop jumping ahead." Grandpa Sam frowned and waved his hands at them. "We'll get to each one of the challenges in good time. But first, here's the overview. You'll earn points for where you finish in each of the five events. Highest point earner overall wins."

"First up is cornhole." Uncle Roy waggled his eyebrows. "But this isn't your kid's version. You gotta toss belt buckles, not bean bags. Only counts if the belt buckle drops clean through the hole."

"Belt buckle cornhole." Ryan massaged the back of his neck, then ran his hand up and down over his face as if nothing made sense. "What does this have to do with roping?"

"Hand-eye coordination." Grandpa Sam wiggled his fingers. Uncle Roy tapped the corner of his eye. Grandpa Sam added, "It's a good skill for roping and life. If you don't have good hand-eye coordination, you won't be able to see the good ones or catch 'em either."

Grant glanced at Maggie. She was chuckling to herself. But her gaze sparked and gave her away.

She leaned toward him. Her voice was pitched low and only for him. "What was it you told me at breakfast, Dr. Sloan? Oh, that's right. Just go with it."

So, he had. So, he would. Grant rubbed his palms together and grinned. "Count me in, Grandpa. I can catch goldfish and take on whatever else you have planned."

Grant's brothers quickly followed his lead and jumped right in.

Ryan won belt buckle cornhole. The brothers decided that was fitting. After all, their bronc-riding brother had quite the collection of belt buckles.

Kelsey slipped in, followed by more friends, and the arena started to fill. First Paige, Riley, and Riley's mom, Ilene Bishop, turned up. Then Paige and Tess's cousin, Abby, and her husband, Wes, with their two-year-old daughter. Soon after, the Baker sisters appeared with Boone, his grandfather's best friend. Grandpa Sam kept close to Maggie and handled the introductions with each new arrival. It wasn't long before Maggie was surrounded on the metal bleachers by Grant's family and friends. And something about her sitting there, chatting easily and openly with everyone, looked and felt right.

Next up was hay bale tower topple. The hay bales had been stacked three wide and seven tall. And like the children's game, with each turn a hay bale needed to be strategically removed. Whoever removed the most hay bales without the tower collapsing won.

According to their grandfather, this challenge was all about having a sound strategy. That mattered in the arena and in life. But they also needed to recognize when their next move might not be the best one.

Grant leaned his arms against the railing and watched Caleb take his turn at the massive hay bale tower.

Grant currently sat in first place. But Caleb was closing in quickly. If his tower held through three more hay bales, Caleb would knock Grant to second place. Caleb reached for one and Grant stopped him, calling out, "Too unstable. Go up and to the right."

At some point after the belt buckle cornhole, but before the hay bale challenge, the brothers had moved from their usual good-natured ribbing and teasing to strategizing and offering tips and advice to one another. Caleb heeded Grant's suggestion. Four bales later, Caleb's tower toppled, yet he took first place.

"That's how it's done." Caleb walked over and fist-bumped Grant. Then his brother moved off to strategize with his twin.

Carter tallied the points on the dry erase board.

Grandpa Sam stood and announced the next challenge. "Gotta catch three fish from the trough in the fastest time."

"How could this possibly be related to roping?" Ryan considered the giant water trough and the dozen or so goldfish swimming in the water.

"Roping is all about a clean catch," Grandpa Sam explained. "A good header knows you only have three clean catch options, or you're penalized. Simple."

Ryan had his boots off and his jeans rolled up when the buzzer sounded. He jumped right into the trough as he did most things in life. Water splashed everywhere, yet he kept coming up empty. But he never gave up. Just continued splashing around the trough.

Grant offered advice, but his laughter muffled his words. Around him, his brothers were bent over, clutching their stomachs. And on, Ryan searched. Until Carter called time and wiped the tears from his eyes.

Caleb went next and attempted a hand-scooping approach. But every time he lifted his cupped hands from the water, the goldfish wiggled free. At the buzzer, he successfully held one plump goldfish. Josh spent several minutes pacing in front of the trough. He'd always been one to overanalyze and map things out in his mind first. Like his twin, Josh went for the hand-cupping and fared slightly better with two fish.

A tug on Grant's t-shirt pulled his attention away from the action. He glanced down to find Riley watching him intently. Her braids were still perfectly intact and her sweet smile still in place.

Grant crouched to the girl's level. "Hey, Riley. Did you need something?"

Riley pressed her hand against her cheek, and whispered, "Doc Grant, Ms. Maggie wants me to tell you to catch the fish with your shirt pocket."

Grant worked to keep his smile contained and his attention on Riley. He whispered back, "Do you think that will work?"

Riley nodded. She pointed at his shirt. "You got a big pocket right there on your shirt. Better pick the little ones, though. Just in case. You don't wanna squish them."

"I think you might be right, Riley." Grant kept his voice extra soft. "Now can you do me a favor and thank Ms. Maggie for me?"

"You got it, Doc Grant." Riley wrapped her arms around him.

He caught the young girl easily, welcoming her surprise hug. She released him and spun around, a burst of lollipop pink from her tank top to her jeans to her matching pink boots. She skipped back to the bench where Maggie sat between his uncle and grandfather. Then she climbed up into Maggie's lap.

Grant watched Maggie's arms curve around Riley's waist. The pair chatted and laughed together. And Grant smiled as if he was sitting beside them. As if he too was wrapped up in their joy.

For his turn at the trough, Grant slipped his shirt over his head and wrapped it around his hand and up his arm. The open pocket rested in his palm. He glanced at Carter and nodded. Carter started the clock. Grant scooped up four fish in the fastest time. The fish returned unharmed to the trough and eventually he joined his brothers.

"Grandpa," Caleb shouted. "Grant should be disqualified for catching fish with his shirt."

"Grant's time stands," Grandpa Sam declared and then chuckled. "All I told you was to catch three fish the fastest and the cleanest. I never said you could only use your hands. Good ropers pay attention to the details."

Ryan groaned beside Grant and wrung more water from his jeans, drawing out another laugh from Grant and the others.

Grant's gaze landed on Maggie. He touched the rim of his cowboy hat and barely dipped his chin in gratitude. Maggie smiled and tapped the brim of hers in return.

"Good ropers catch steer, not fish." Caleb jabbed his elbow into Grant's side. "I'm coming for you on the next one, Doc."

At the start of the balance beam challenge that would showcase their agility, Riley returned. Another tug on his t-shirt. More whispered advice. And another quick hug before she raced back to Maggie. Thanks to Maggie, Grant managed to spin in the required ten circles without getting too dizzy. Then complete the balance beam without dropping his live chicken. Grant finished and fist-bumped with Josh. "Careful of the chicken. She's a squirrely one."

"Watch this," Josh said. "You inspired me on the fish challenge." He grinned and stepped up for his turn. He completed his rotations, accepted the chicken, and promptly tucked his feathered friend into the front of his shirt. Then he skimmed across the balance beam in record time for first place.

It all came down to the last event: axe throwing with your nondominant hand. Top competitors knew roping required the use of both hands. One to throw and one to guide the horse. Ryan and Grant were tied for the lead. Whoever won axe throwing won the entire challenge.

Riley skipped into the arena again. This time she slipped her hand into Grant's and said, "Doc Grant, Ms. Maggie wishes you good luck."

Grant kept Riley's hand in his and crouched down beside her. "Well, Riley. Got any advice for me?"

Riley's nose wrinkled. "I'm right-handed, Doc Grant. And when I try to tell my left hand to do something, it doesn't listen too well."

Grant nodded as if he suffered from the same problem. "What's your dad tell you before your soccer games?"

"Just do my best." Riley beamed at Grant. "And that's what I do."

"Then I'll do that too." Grant squeezed her hand and stood up.

Riley returned to her place on Maggie's lap. And Carter did a quick run-through of the standings and scores.

Riley cheered with all she had when Carter announced Grant was tied for the lead. The one-sided grin Maggie aimed at Grant was like his own personal dose of sunshine. Maggie was surrounded by his friends and family as if she'd always been one of them. As if she'd always belonged. Her smile as bright as Riley's laughter. He was taken in. Completely enchanted.

And having fun.

More fun than he'd had in a long, long time. He'd missed this. Being with his brothers and friends. Relaxed. Happy. Nothing to prove. He'd missed his family. That truth burst inside him. It was more unsettling. He hadn't come home to fall back into his old life. He'd left all that behind him, readily and willingly, years ago.

Now he was only a visitor. A guest. This wasn't the life he wanted. Or ever envisioned. Grant rubbed his neck as if that impending goodbye to his family and friends was already caught in his throat. He had his future planned out and it was in California. The career he wanted waited there. But the woman he wanted…

Grant's gaze skipped to Maggie and held. *No.* Falling for a woman wasn't part of his agenda. His work already fulfilled him. His career was enough. He was good with that. More than good. He shoved away from the railing, his boots grinding into the dirt, but doubt trailed him like a dust cloud.

Still, there was nothing else to do. He had to shut it down. All of it. Now. Before things like his heart started to demand to be heard. That would only lead to more pain. That was why it was better not to feel at all.

Grant picked up an axe in his left hand and tested the weight.

"You're up, bro." Ryan bumped his shoulder against Grant's. "This is it. You and me. Winner takes all. Don't choke and don't use too much strength. This one is all about finesse."

Yeah, and it was all about doing it badly. With just enough finesse that it looked accidental, not intentional. Grant let the axe fly through the air. It landed on target just outside the last ring.

Caleb checked the axe's location and hollered, "So close. Looks like Ryan is going to take it."

Carter tallied the last scores, confirmed Caleb's assessment, then declared Ryan the winner of the first Partner Pick Competition. Cheers and applause filled the enclosed arena.

Ryan never paused. Never celebrated. Instead, he came at Grant like an agitated steer. Carter joined him. Josh and Caleb seemed to quickly catch on to the impending confrontation. The twins spun away and captured the attention of the onlookers as if they'd been tapped for crowd control.

Grant stood his ground. He'd known it would've been too much to expect his brothers to let it pass. To let him lose graciously. To let him retreat as he wanted. But when had his brothers ever made anything easy?

"You threw it!" Ryan pulled himself up just before the toes of his boots touched Grant's. But his accusation dropped like an anvil between them. Ryan continued, "You could've hit that target with your eyes closed. You've always been the best at darts. You still hold all the records at the house."

Grant also held more than one dart record at several bars near his alma mater in Austin. He'd spent most of his undergraduate days throwing darts and making wagers to pay bar tabs and meal tickets. He'd gotten so good, he'd started playing with his left hand in an effort to even the odds.

"It's those steady hands." Carter's gaze narrowed on Grant. "Good hand-eye coordination makes Grant excellent at darts, axes, and surgery."

"I guess today wasn't my day." Grant stonewalled.

Ryan's jaw clenched and unclenched, his stare

hardened. "Not good enough, little brother. Try again."

"That's all I've got," Grant told them, lifting d his arms as if to show there was nothing else. "Not my day to win. That's all there is to it."

Carter ran the back of his hand over his mouth as if catching his initial curt response. "You do know who you're talking to right now, correct?"

Yes. Unfortunately. Aside from their grandfather, Carter and Ryan knew Grant the best. Grant tipped up his chin. "Can't you just leave it alone?"

"If we'd planned to do that, we wouldn't be standing here now," Carter countered.

Grant ground his teeth together. "It's not that serious. The best man won. Let it go."

Ryan yanked off his cowboy hat and tugged at his hair. Confusion flashed across his face. "What is wrong with you?"

Nope. Not going there either. Over his brother's shoulder, Maggie held an animated exchange with Caleb and Josh. Her blond braids swung as she darted around the twins. Her smile dropped as soon as her gaze locked on Grant and his two brothers. Grant warned them, "We've got company."

Carter and Ryan both twisted around. And Grant escaped, hightailing it for the side door.

Sure, it wasn't his finest moment. But Grant was in preservation mode. He'd done what he had to. What was right. Not even Maggie, his favorite cowgirl, was going to change his mind. He refused to allow it.

And if he had to avoid her to accomplish that, so be it.

CHAPTER SEVENTEEN

"GRANT." MAGGIE'S VOICE came from behind him and sounded more than irritated.

He'd run, but not fast enough. Grant squeezed his eyes shut and slowed. The bunkhouse was only a short jog away. The farmhouse not much farther beyond that. Now he was between the pasture, the paddock, and a displeased cowgirl. Out in the open with nowhere to hide. Grant turned and discovered Maggie closer than he'd like.

"You threw it, didn't you?" Maggie accused him. All indignant and enchanting. "Ryan was right."

If Grant had thought his brothers were a force, they had nothing on this particular wisp of a cowgirl. He crossed his arms over his chest, firmed his stance. "Does it matter?"

Maggie crossed her arms over her chest and notched her chin several clicks higher, leveling her cool gaze on his. "Why would you do that?"

"Ryan is the better choice. He has the experience. Knows how to best help you." He leaned forward until their arms brushed. One more inch and their lips would brush too. He held himself perfectly still and carefully shifted his focus away from her mouth. His words sounded sour in his mouth. "Ryan is the logical choice. In every way that matters."

"This isn't about simply being my practice partner, is it?" Maggie edged closer as if daring him to pull away.

Grant pressed his arms against his sides until the urge to sweep Maggie off her feet passed. She was making him selfish. Short-sighted. Making him want to forget why he couldn't have her. Why they'd never work. Still, he wanted to hold her. Kiss her. No matter the consequences. But this was about more than Grant and his selfish ways. Maggie was more important. Not hurting Maggie was vital. And that kept him in check.

"News flash, Doc." Maggie's eyes danced. Her tone resolute. "The choice is mine to make. I decide who is best for me."

"So, tell me?" He matched her beat for beat. Challenge for challenge. How could he not? She was magnificent. And if he'd been in the mindset for falling, he would've fallen for her now. "Tell me, Maggie, who would you choose?"

A tremor worked over her bottom lip. And

he knew. She felt it too. Whatever it was between them. Grant lost his breath and forgot his words. *Walk away. Run.*

"Are you scared I'll pick you, Doc?" Her gaze, intense and incredibly candid, lifted to his, locking him in place. The quiet confidence in her words speared right into his chest. A direct hit. But she wasn't through. "Or are you more terrified I won't?"

"Maggie." Grant lost himself then. Lost himself in the moment. In her. He framed her face in his hands. "Maggie, I'm not scared of you. Not at all."

She reached up, curled her fingers around his wrists, but never pulled his arms away. If anything, she was like an anchor, holding him right where she wanted him.

No. He wasn't scared of her, but he was scared that she'd imprinted herself on him so deeply he'd never forget her. And despite that fact, he leaned forward.

She met him halfway. Their lips collided. Nothing shy or hesitant about their kiss. Nothing awkward or demanding. It was breath-stealing and entrancing. So much more than he could have ever expected.

Finally, Grant's brain sounded a warning, and so he slowed the kiss, released her, and edged away. Now he knew there wasn't a place far enough where he'd ever forget his cowgirl.

Maggie exhaled and stuffed her hands in the pockets of her jeans. "Maybe it's best if I don't fill in at your clinic anymore."

"Why stop? I need help. You need a job." And he wasn't ready for their goodbye. He was getting more selfish by the minute. Still, he kept on. "It's a professional arrangement."

"Right." Her fingers touched her mouth before she used her arm to motion between them. "And that kiss just now?"

"Can't happen again." Shouldn't have happened period. Yet, he wanted to kiss her again.

Right here. Until all the reasons shouting at him that it was a bad idea fell away. Until it became only about him and her. Not about city versus ranch. Or careers. Or life goals. Not about impasses and difficult situations. Or sacrifices that could never be asked. Grant set his hands on his hips and stared at the ground as if he'd suddenly lost his way after all.

Maggie cleared her throat. "So, it looks like we agree."

"On what?" Grant searched her face.

She gave nothing away. Simply met his gaze, without flinching. Without regret. As if she'd mastered emotional detachment too. Finally, she said, "We agree we'd never choose each other."

But that kiss defied logic. Told an entirely different story. "Then what are we?"

"It seems we are back to where we started," Maggie said. She spoke softly, her words confident and sure. "Just passing through each other's lives."

"Then it's settled." And there was nothing left to discuss. Exactly as he'd wanted. They'd come full circle. Except he wasn't sure he wanted to be back at the beginning now. "You should go and enjoy dinner. The tent's all set up."

"What about you?" she asked.

He'd lost his appetite when he'd given up Maggie. "I'm going to take advantage of the house being empty and grab a shower."

"Okay." She just stood there.

So did he. Neither one moved as if they weren't certain where to go next. Or perhaps that was only Grant.

Confusion flashed across her face. Just a brief hit before she blurted, "Did I do something wrong?"

"No." She was quite likely the most perfect person he'd ever met. He shook his head. "You didn't do anything. I did."

She looked surprised. "What was that?"

"I came home." With that, Grant turned and walked away.

Three Springs was nothing like what he wanted. The same was true for a relationship. Relationships had expectations like opening up and giving things like his heart. As if he'd ever do that.

His specialty was fixing things that were broken. But a broken heart was beyond even his expertise.

CHAPTER EIGHTEEN

FIFTEEN MINUTES.

That was how long Kelsey was giving her sister to show up to the BBQ that had been arranged for after the Partner Pick Competition. Everyone was mingling under the large tent the brothers had installed beside the arena. Everyone except for Kelsey's little sister and Dr. Sloan.

Maggie had taken off after Grant once Ryan had been declared the winner. They'd both slipped out a side door of the arena. Kelsey checked her watch. Time was up.

She stood to go find her sister, but Ryan and Josh dropped onto the bench across from her.

"Kelsey, we need to run something by you." Ryan set a clipboard on the picnic table. "My brother and I talked about it, and we came up with a better practice plan for Maggie."

But I have plans for Maggie. I have dreams for Maggie. And there are things I promised her. Kelsey sat back down.

"Between Ryan's contacts and mine, Maggie

has access to several top-notch practice facilities in the area." Josh grinned at Kelsey, then tapped his finger on the clipboard. "We can get her there. Practice with her. Help her train."

But she's mine. My responsibility. When their mother had walked out, Kelsey had stepped in. Kelsey had read to Maggie when thunderstorms had scared her awake. Kelsey had held Maggie's hand every first day of school and walked her home every day after. *I'm the one who is always there for her.* Now the entire Sloan family was treating Maggie and even Kelsey as their own. Not that she didn't appreciate it, but...

"We've arranged everything." Ryan snatched a carrot from the plate of vegetables Kelsey had brought with her. Ryan added, "We put it all together on this schedule. We're each taking a day to be there for Maggie, so she has what she needs to be ready for Amarillo."

Maggie has what she needs with me. We're building something on our own. Something special. Kelsey leaned forward and bumped her sling against the table, reminding her of her injury. She was nowhere near a hundred percent. Again. *Good things came to those who waited, right?* Her gaze fell on Nolan at the smoker. Her heart skipped a beat. But that too must wait. She had a little sister to take care of.

Kelsey slid the clipboard closer and scanned the schedule. One name was missing. "What about Grant?"

"Maggie and Grant are at the clinic working together all day." Josh set his hat on the bench and rearranged his wavy hair. "We figured a break might be good."

Josh Sloan was the quietest of the brothers, but Kelsey had quickly realized he was the most observant. Kelsey tipped her head at him and couldn't resist teasing the twin. "Doesn't Grant like to be around my sister?"

Josh's eyebrows knit together as if he was holding his breath, then he looked at Ryan.

"That's not Grant's problem." Ryan aimed a carrot stick at Kelsey and arched an eyebrow at her. "We both know what the problem is."

The problem was twofold. Maggie liked Grant. And Kelsey suspected Grant liked her little sister. But Kelsey always protected Maggie. She had to look out for her now. "It won't work."

"They're both too stubborn," Ryan frowned. "Way too set in their ways."

Kelsey wanted her sister to find love someday. Only she wanted it to be the right love and on Maggie's terms. Same as Kelsey wanted love. Someday. In the future. When she knew her little sister was set and secure. Kelsey's gaze connected with Nolan's. He gave her one of his half-grins. The kind that made her sigh. But today wasn't someday. Kelsey looked at Ryan. "It won't work between them. Grant is moving to the city. Maggie will be on the road."

"There are rodeos in California," Ryan argued.

Kelsey frowned at him. "So, Maggie has to go to Grant then?" And once again have love on someone else's terms.

"There are these things called planes and trains." Ryan crunched on a carrot and considered Kelsey. "Grant knows how to travel too."

"But it's long distance, Ryan." Kelsey avoided looking at Nolan. Still, she heard his boisterous laugh. Wanted in on the joke. Wanted to be near him. But she was leaving soon too. Call it bad timing. "How many long-distance relationships have we seen work out over the years we've been on the circuit?"

Ryan wiped his hands together, then crossed his arms over his chest. He looked and sounded inflexible. "I'm just saying that distance shouldn't be some excuse if it's the right person."

Kelsey touched the amethyst wrap bracelet Nolan had given her. He'd claimed it was for positive energy and healing. Then later confessed he saw it while running errands, thought of Kelsey, and hoped she might like it. She'd yet to take it off. Kelsey eyed Ryan. "How do you know if you've found the right person?"

Ryan quickly raised both hands and leaned back as if wanting to distance himself from Kelsey and her question. "Don't ask me."

Josh chuckled and dropped his hand on Ryan's shoulder. "My big brother believes if he isn't looking for the right person, she won't find him. Then he can avoid all this messy relationship stuff."

"You should talk." Ryan tossed a carrot stick at Josh. "Josh was married for less than six months. That was more than five years ago. Since then, he's been on maybe three first dates. Never a second. I don't know much, but I know that's not how you find your person."

Kelsey wasn't looking to find her person either. She touched the bracelet on her wrist. Heard Nolan's laugh drift around her again.

"This isn't about me." Josh settled his hat back on his head. "But for the record, I thought I met the right one. Turned out I was wrong. Incredibly wrong. Then I realized how much I really don't like being wrong."

Perhaps Kelsey's feelings were wrong. Her career was upside down. Her life too. Nolan was just a steady center in the chaos. A crush was safer, easier to handle than the decisions

Maggie and Kelsey needed to make. "Maybe we are wrong about Maggie and Grant."

"We need to be wrong." Discontent crossed Ryan's face and was clear in his words. "Because both Maggie and Grant getting hurt doesn't sit well with me."

Josh nodded, looking equally as unhappy.

Kelsey didn't want to hurt Nolan either. Or get hurt herself. This was what happened when they got distracted. Lost focus. Feelings and emotions had no place in the arena. It was about winning jackpots, not winning hearts. Someday she could think about love and all that. But this wasn't someday. Kelsey tugged the practice schedule from the clipboard. "I'm going to find Maggie. She'll want to see this."

Sam stepped over to the table. "Kelsey, mind if I join you? I seem to have a misplaced grandson."

Kelsey folded the schedule, tucked it into the back pocket of her jeans, then smiled at the older cowboy. Sam was one of her favorite reasons for being at the farmhouse. He was always ready with a quick bit of motivation or an entertaining story. Same as his brother, Roy. She was going to miss the cowboy pair when she and Maggie left. "Sure. Maggie might know where your grandson is."

"Lead the way." Sam offered Kelsey his arm.

"We're headed to the stables." Kelsey linked her arm around Sam's and matched his pace. "I'm sure you know the fastest way."

"There's more than one way to the stables. None of them right or wrong." Sam adjusted his bolo tie and slanted his gaze toward her. "But they all eventually take you where you were meant to be."

Kelsey nodded and walked beside Sam. Evening had settled over the farm. The night's choir was warming up. The sounds usually soothed Kelsey. Not tonight. The stable came into view and Kelsey asked, "Sam. How do you know you're in the right place?"

They stepped through the large, open sliding doors. At the far end of the stable barn, Kelsey saw a flash of Maggie's blond hair.

"It's simple, really." Sam tipped his head toward the last stall in the barn. "You know you're in the right place when you find what you were looking for."

And there was the root of Kelsey's problem. "What if I'm not sure what I'm looking for anymore?"

"That is when my Claire would have said, it's time for a reset." Sam squeezed Kelsey's arm "Course Claire's reset often involved a glass of her favorite wine and a good book."

Kelsey chuckled.

Sam gazed at Kelsey. His words were all too wise. "Sounds like you might need a reset."

"My body is already taking a break." Kelsey touched her arm sling.

"It's your mind that may need that reset. Sit for a spell. Hush your thoughts and hear your heart," Sam explained. "Claire always claimed that was easier to do outside, with her toes dipped in the pond and a book in her hand. Maybe for you it's a gourmet meal on a candlelit table."

Nolan. But Kelsey's heart was full already. With her sister. There wasn't any more room. Not since their mother had left and Maggie had become Kelsey's responsibility. Kelsey moved with Sam toward the last stall. "Maggie. I told Sam we'd find you in here."

"It was time for Lady Dasher's eye medicine." Maggie stepped out of the stall, latched the gate, then brushed her hands over her jeans.

Nice cover, little sister. And the mare wasn't the only one fighting an eye issue. Maggie had been crying. Kelsey covered her own unhappiness with a small grin. "The food is almost ready, Mags. And Nolan will be upset if you don't try his newest honey BBQ sauce."

"Then we should head over." Maggie reached out and touched Sam's shoulder. "Sam,

I haven't thanked you properly for all you've done for my sister and me."

"I'm the grateful one." Sam took Maggie's hand in his. "You brought all five of my grandsons together. It's been quite a while since that happened. I'm not afraid to admit seeing them having so much fun made my heart swell today."

"It was certainly an entertaining afternoon." Maggie's smile failed to reach her eyes.

"It certainly won't be one we forget any time soon," Kelsey added. Although the wobble in Maggie's smile had Kelsey believing Maggie wanted nothing more than to put the entire day behind her.

"It was unexpected, that's for sure. I find there can be joy in that, but it might require changing perspective." Sam stroked his fingers through his white beard. His voice was mild, but the cunning in his gaze was not. "I should go find my grandson and remind him of his manners. His Gran Claire taught him to be a better host than this."

"You'll find Grant at the farmhouse," Maggie offered. "He mentioned something about taking a shower while the place was empty."

Sam nodded, touched the brim of his hat and strolled out the open doors.

Kelsey wrapped her good arm around Maggie's waist. "You want to talk about what happened with Grant?"

Maggie stiffened. "There's nothing to say."

"Mags," Kelsey started.

"We should go and eat." Maggie took Kelsey's hand and gently tugged her toward the open doors. "Nolan will be looking for you. You don't want to keep him waiting."

But her sister came first. Kelsey looked at Maggie. Saw the resolve in her gaze and the set of her chin. Her little sister wasn't ready to talk. Kelsey would be patient. She knew how to wait her little sister out. "You can press pause on this conversation, Mags, for now. But we will talk about what happened."

"I'm okay, Kels. Really, I am." Maggie squeezed Kelsey's hand. "I'm committed to us. To our team. Like I always have been. That's all that matters."

That was all that should matter. That was all it had been about for the sisters for more years than Kelsey would have expected. But now there was something else in play. Kelsey felt it. Knew Maggie did too. But it all came down to what mattered most. That was Maggie.

Back at the BBQ, Kelsey watched Grant return from the farmhouse. Gone was his cowboy hat, boots, and jeans. He wore a button-down shirt and pressed pants. Dr. Sloan had returned. His hooded gaze landed on Maggie and held as if caught by some unseen hook.

Yes. Dr. Sloan had caught himself a cowgirl. Yet, he couldn't see that he was a cowboy too. And always would be.

Kelsey hoped Dr. Sloan would figure this out before he completely broke her little sister's heart. Either way, she'd be there to pick up the pieces. After all, that's what big sisters did.

CHAPTER NINETEEN

A SEVEN-MILE run after sunrise. *Check.*

Stalls cleaned. *Check.*

Horses exercised. *Check.*

Camper tidied. *Check.*

Now the lunch hour was fast approaching, and Maggie was quickly running out of items on her to-do list. What she wasn't running out of—highlights from yesterday. With one particular moment set on repeat.

Her kiss with Grant. It had been bold. Amazing. Over too soon.

And not happening again. They'd both agreed. That was as it should be. If she kissed Grant a second time, she might be tempted to flip that sign on her heart from *do not disturb* to *ready for love.*

Maggie had been ready for love once before. She'd bought into love's promises. Believed love conquered all. Believed love was the solution. She'd been eager to sign love's contract. Then she'd read the fine print. Discovered there were conditions for love that required blind loyalty and no questions asked. Those Maggie hadn't been willing to accept. And she'd walked away.

Same as she'd walked away from Grant yesterday. She could fall for her doctor. Yet, she feared having to prove her love. Feared failing. Because Maggie, as she was, hadn't ever been enough. *If you love me, Maggie, you will*...everyone close to Maggie, from her father to her mother to her ex, had used that line on Maggie more than once. Everyone except her sister.

Now there was Grant. But a solid future wasn't founded on chemistry or one kiss. No matter how incredibly right the kiss had felt. Besides, that forever kind of love required trusting someone else with her heart. Someone like her city doc. But that was a risk too far. So, friends-only was all they'd ever be.

Maggie wiped down the last section of counter space in the camper. Then she stored the cleaning supplies, realigned her priorities and headed outside.

"Good. I found you." Kelsey was approaching, her sunglasses and rhinestone bedazzled sling reflected the sunlight. An urgency filled her words. "It's all-hands-on-deck."

"What's going on?" Maggie swept off her straw cowboy hat and wiped at her forehead.

"We need to head into downtown," Kelsey

said. "There's a movie night in the square. Tess's cousin Abby needs help setting up and Nolan needs assistance with the food prep. Their scheduled staff called in with family emergencies and illness."

"Let me get cleaned up and I'll be right out," Maggie said.

"You're fine as you are," Kelsey said. "Come on."

Maggie glanced at her frayed jean shorts and faded tank top. "I've been cleaning all morning."

"And you'll be setting up in the heat." Kelsey tugged on Maggie's arm. "We need to go. Everyone is waiting."

"Fine." Maggie gathered her hair together into a low ponytail and settled her straw cowboy hat on her head, then trailed after her sister.

Ryan was behind the wheel of his truck, the engine already running. Maggie didn't see Grant. Wondered if he'd come up with a valid excuse to get out of movie night setup. It hardly seemed like something he'd want to participate in. Not that she was avoiding him or anything. More like steering clear of.

Sam waved from the front seat of Ryan's truck. "Come on, you two. There's room in the back."

Maggie opened the passenger door and her gaze landed on Grant sitting on the far side of the bench seat. The brim of his baseball hat didn't dull the weight of his stare. Maggie swallowed around her sudden nerves.

"Hurry up." Kelsey poked Maggie from behind. "It's hot out here and you're letting the cold air out."

Maggie scooted onto the bench seat. Reminded herself Grant and she were friends only. By mutual agreement. And that her nerves were utterly unnecessary. And quite absurd. She sat inches from Grant. Far enough away to avoid any accidental contact.

Caleb stuck his head in the open doorway and grinned wide. "Move it on over. I'm riding with you guys."

Kelsey nudged her hip against Maggie's, forcing Maggie into direct contact with Grant. And rattling Maggie's nerves.

"We have more vehicles." Grant's words were bland. Still, he lifted his arm up onto the back of the bench seat behind Maggie.

And Maggie found herself settling quite nicely right into her doctor's side. If only they hadn't also agreed they were back at the beginning. Maggie could've leaned into him fully and rested her head on his shoulder. Shared his space as if getting closer to each other was their goal.

"Carter's truck is already down there. Josh's too." Sam waved his hand and buckled his seat belt. "That's enough. We need to leave parking spaces for everyone else."

"There's plenty of room back here." Caleb shut the truck door and stretched his arms out as if making himself comfortable. "And it's more fun to ride together."

Ryan peered into the back seat. "But Grant doesn't have fun. He's a doctor now, remember?"

"I was having fun before you interrupted a minute ago," Grant argued.

Caleb leaned forward and gaped at Grant. "You were in Carter's office reading one of your medical journals."

"It was an article on chronic refractory pain after joint replacement." Grant's fingers brushed against Maggie's bare shoulder. His words were cool.

His touch anything but. Maggie's breath caught. A featherlight caress. There and gone. She kept her focus fixed on the front windshield and the view outside.

Grant added, "Very fascinating article."

"You're proving our point, Grant." Caleb settled back against the seat.

Ryan glanced in the rearview mirror. "What

was the last thing you did strictly for fun, Grant?"

"And it needs to be before yesterday," Caleb added.

"I can't remember." Grant's fingers brushed across Maggie's shoulder again.

Once. Twice. Those butterflies stirred in Maggie's stomach.

Ryan shook his head as if disappointed and turned onto the main road that led into downtown.

"Grant was in medical school, Ryan. Then he had a residency and a fellowship." Maggie jumped into the conversation. Better than melting underneath Grant's absent-minded caress. She added, "I can't imagine Grant has had a lot of free time."

"Fair point," Ryan allowed. "But there still needs to be a little time for fun. Right, Grandpa?"

"Claire always told me: we can't make more time, Sam. But we can have fun and make more memories." Sam shifted to look behind him. A wise gleam in his gaze. "So that's what we did. Had fun. Made memories. Each day. Nothing big, mind you. Simple moments we collected."

Maggie had moments with Grant. Ones she'd remember when the fun was difficult to find.

Caleb leaned around Kelsey again and

grinned. "Grant, how do you add bits of fun to your day?"

Grant lifted his arm and straightened beside Maggie.

He was pulling away. That should satisfy, not frustrate Maggie. She argued, "Grant sees patients back-to-back at the clinic. It's not like he has time for a quick pick-up game of basketball at lunch."

"Mags, stop defending our brother," Ryan chided.

"Seriously, Mags." Kelsey lowered her sunglasses and looked at Maggie over the frames. "When was the last time you had fun?"

Yesterday with Grant. At the bowling alley the other night. With Grant. At the clinic. With Grant. Maggie swished her hand through the air. "Why does this matter?"

"Maggie and I are both okay, even without the fun factor." Grant's arm curved around Maggie's shoulders again. "We're dedicated to jobs we like and achieving our goals. There's nothing wrong with that."

There was also nothing wrong with how she fit inside Grant's hold.

"Well, it's clear." Sam patted the center console as if calling a meeting to order.

"What's that?" Grant's words were hesitant.

"It's clear that you and Maggie need to have

more fun." Sam leaned on the console and eyed them. Then he pointed at Maggie and Grant. "Together. You both could use it."

Maggie resisted the urge to shake her head. What they could use was more space. More room between them. Then Maggie would remember those boundaries. That friend zone.

"I agree." Ryan grinned in the rearview mirror. "You two should do something together tonight."

"Go night swimming in the pond," Caleb suggested.

"That I can tell you from experience is quite enjoyable." Sam chuckled. "Nothing like swimming under the stars. Almost as fun as dancing outside under a full moon."

No dancing. Not with Grant. And not under the stars and moon. Then Maggie would think about romance and kisses and all the things a friend wasn't supposed to consider. Maggie shifted on the bench seat, but there was no way to avoid Grant. "I can't."

Ryan watched her in the rearview mirror. One eyebrow arched. "Is it movie night you don't want to miss?"

"No. I have plans." Plans she hadn't told Grant about. Not that it should be a big deal. Maggie looked briefly at Grant then again at

Ryan. "I sort of have to cook lunch for the staff at the clinic tomorrow."

Grant balked beside her. "What?"

"Every Monday someone brings lunch for the entire staff," Maggie explained. "It's a long-standing tradition that began the first year Dr. Toro opened the clinic. Dr. Toro believes it starts the week off on a positive note for the staff."

"Nothing wrong with that." Sam eyed Grant. "Why aren't you making lunch?"

"I didn't know it was a thing," Grant countered.

"What were you doing last Monday at the clinic?" Caleb asked.

"I've worked through lunch every day since I got there." Grant ran a hand over his face.

"But it's a tradition," Ryan argued.

"It's not my tradition or my staff," Grant countered.

"But you're there now." Sam's eyebrows pinched together. He considered Grant. "It's important that the staff knows you care too, Grant."

It was more important that Maggie got Grant off the hook. "This is my fault. I like to join in. I have a problem when it comes to joining in. Ask Kelsey."

Kelsey nodded beside Maggie. "You do tend

to get involved in things every place we stop for longer than a weekend."

"I can handle lunch," Maggie added. "Tess is helping with dessert. And Tess told me I could use the kitchen in the empty apartment behind the Feisty Owl."

"Why would you use that kitchen?" Ryan frowned at her.

"The farmhouse has a bigger kitchen," Sam stated.

But Grant was at the farmhouse and Maggie had the whole steering clear thing she was testing out. "It's no problem."

"Here's what we're going to do." Sam's words were firm and final. "Grant, you can take Maggie to the grocery store. Then head back to the farmhouse and cook for your Monday luncheon."

Ryan pulled into the parking lot beside the Owl, cut the engine, and tossed his keys to Grant. "If you don't have enough fun doing that, you can head out to the pond for a night swim afterward."

Maggie ran her palms over her legs and searched for a way out. "What about setting up for movie night?"

"We've got that covered." Caleb sounded all too pleased and hopped out of the truck. "We'll be fine without you guys."

But would Maggie be fine alone with Grant? She was about to find out.

"Looks like they are determined to see that we have fun," Grant said from the driver's seat a few minutes later. He adjusted the truck mirrors and glanced at Maggie. His smile easy, his words casual. "What exactly are we making for lunch?"

"A trio of salads. Caprese tortellini salad, chicken salad on croissants and fruit salad." Maggie buckled her seat belt and followed Grant's lead. Proving she'd meant to keep her word and not talk about what happened yesterday. After all, there was nothing left to say. If only she would stop thinking about their kiss, then she'd be all set. "With cookies and cream brownies for dessert."

"That sounds like a lot." Grant drove toward the grocery store. "Maybe we leave the brownies at the farmhouse."

And risk a midnight chocolate run-in with Grant. No way. "I already told the staff what I was bringing. Can't disappoint them." As for her own disappointment, that she'd deal with.

They opted for a divide-and-conquer approach inside the busy grocery store and split the shopping list. Back at the farmhouse, they agreed on an upbeat country music playlist while Maggie cooked, and Grant chopped.

The conversation hovered around the recipes, where to find mixing bowls, and seasonings. It was anything, but awkward. Anything but uncomfortable. And over too soon.

"Looks like we're done." Maggie stored the salads in the refrigerator and dried her hands on a towel. "I think I'll head out and give Lady Dasher her medicine."

Grant nodded and stuck his hands in the pockets of his shorts. "I'll be in the office if you need me."

What if I needed to tell you I was wrong? I don't want to be back at the beginning. I want to be back at... Maggie escaped outside before she forgot herself and asked about that night swim. Or that dance. Or anything that would keep him beside her longer. A while later, Maggie heard the stable door open and close.

Grant appeared outside Lady Dasher's stall, holding two cocktail glasses and a half-grin. "Bourbon smash. Figured my brother owns a distillery, we might as well make use of his whiskey."

"I like the way you think, Dr. Sloan." Maggie latched the stall gate, accepted the glass, and tapped it against his. Then sipped, tasting the fresh lemon, mint, and honey.

"I also made use of Tess's garden." Grant

grinned then eyed her. "I do know how to have fun, Maggie."

Maggie considered him. He looked too earnest as if it was important she understood that about him.

"You were right about medical school. There's also the patients and surgeries." Grant waved his hands as if juggling all his responsibilities. "Now there's interviews. A new job. A relocation."

Obligations. How Maggie understood those all too well. "When will you make time for fun?"

He sipped his drink, his eyes narrowed briefly before he asked, "Can I show you something?"

"Will it be fun?" The tease threaded through Maggie's words before she could stop it.

"It's where I went as a kid." His gaze lit up. "Where I wished. Where I dreamed. Sometimes even where I slept."

Now she was way too curious. "Sure. Lead the way."

He turned and headed past the tack room, not outside. Maggie followed him up the stairs to the loft. The wide, rolling doors were closed. Grant walked around the hay bale stacks, guiding her to the last dormer window. He opened the wide shutter-style windows easily, letting the night in. Then he leaned his arm against the windowsill and considered her. "What would you do if not roping?"

"Breakaway." Her reply came quick. Instantly. Maggie frowned into her cocktail glass.

"But that's still the rodeo." One of his eyebrows arched.

Surely, he'd expected a different reply. *Rodeo is not a real career, Maggie.* She lifted her chin.

Grant only smiled. "More people should have the passion and dedication you do, Maggie. It's admirable."

His compliment set Maggie back. Her career had cost her a chance at a different life once before. She tried hard not to sound flustered at his words. "What about you? If not medicine, then what?"

"Race car driver," he declared and lifted his glass in a toast to her. "Definitely."

"You aren't serious." She gaped at him.

"But I am, and I can prove it." He handed her his cocktail glass, then used his foot to brush aside the hay. Next, he lifted a board in the floor, laughed, and reached inside. He set half a dozen toy cars on the floor and what looked like racetrack pieces. "This was my hideout when I was a little kid. These are my race cars that I used to dream about driving one day."

Maggie peered over his shoulder and looked inside the cubby hole. "What is that still in there?"

"Telescope. From my Gran Claire." Grant picked it up, stood and pointed it toward the open window. "I used to spend hours up here looking at the stars. Wishing on them."

Maggie stepped over to the window and lifted her gaze to the sky. "There are so many stars tonight. It feels like you could almost touch them from here."

"That's what I thought as a kid." He moved beside her and took his glass back. His fingers brushed against hers.

Too brief. Maggie tightened her grip on her glass and those wishes in her heart. "What about now?"

"Now it's about reaching for the practical and the obtainable." He sipped his drink. His gaze moved toward the sky. "It's about making things happen for myself."

There was a thread of reluctance in his words. Or perhaps that was only Maggie hoping. But she'd followed her heart before and still ended up alone. Grant had it right. It was up to her to make things happen for herself. And love would only interfere.

Still, she stayed where she was with her arms resting on the windowsill and her gaze lifted to the sky. And if she edged closer to Grant until their shoulders connected that was her secret.

Because wishes in the heart could be silenced, but not always ignored.

CHAPTER TWENTY

MONDAY MORNING, Grant had back-to-back patient appointments and one case that required surgery at Belleridge Regional Hospital. Thankfully, the hospital staff had an operating room available for Grant and his patient that afternoon. Now Grant had time to stop in at the office luncheon before he headed to the hospital to change and prep.

The breakroom was full of people. The salad bowls almost empty. The brownies down to the last row. But Grant's gaze skipped straight to Maggie. Same as it always did whenever he knew she was in a room. And when he couldn't see her, he was thinking about her. He'd never before given a friend so much mental space. So much significance. Of course, he'd never had a friend quite like Maggie.

"I wasn't sure if you'd make it or not. Figured you should eat before your surgery." Maggie walked over and handed him a tin foil–covered plate. "You can take it to go."

He wanted to take her hand and go. Go into

his office and test out his theory that their second kiss would be even better than the first. But Maggie and kisses could not be part of the same conversation. *Ever.* Grant didn't need a friend, but that didn't mean he couldn't act like one. Grant tipped his head toward two empty seats at the corner table. "I think I'll eat here."

"Just so you know." Maggie's grin flashed. "If you sit, you have to play. Staff rules."

"Play?" Grant scanned the room. The staff watched him. Several nodded and smiled.

"Trivia night practice, Dr. Sloan." Aiden tapped the screen on his notepad. Aiden was a favorite among the staff and the patients. He was a skilled nurse and excelled at patient care. And was apparently the trivia team coach. Aiden added, "Wednesday night is team trivia night at the Feisty Owl. We have to win this week. We lost to Evenson Family Dentistry last week."

Groans and grumbles drifted around the room.

"Today's theme is science. I haven't been much help." Maggie headed to the empty table, then called out, "I asked Aiden to change to pop culture, but he refused."

"We've got a science weakness, Maggie. That means we need to practice that subject," Aiden claimed and lifted his eyebrows at Maggie. "But you still have to join us Wednesday night, Maggie. We need your enthusiasm."

The staff laughed, offered their agreement and more encouragement.

"Here we go." Aiden brushed his hands on his scrubs and read from his notepad screen. "Remember, the theme is science. Here's the question: An unlit match has what kind of energy?"

Silence settled around the room. Several people shrugged. Heads shook. Grant swallowed a bite of his croissant, then said, "Chemical energy."

"Correct." Aiden announced and swiped his finger across his screen. "The eye catches what color first?"

Several of the staff offered suggestions. Grant polished off his sandwich and said, "Yellow."

"Dr. Sloan for the win." Aiden laughed, then looked at Grant directly. "Dr. Sloan, these are for you. What element is named after the Greek word for green?"

"Chlorine," Grant replied.

"Nice." Excitement lit Aiden's face. "What is the shape of the Milky Way?"

"Spiral." Grant grinned and speared tortellini on his fork.

Aiden nodded and asked, "Coldest temperature ever recorded on earth?"

"128.6 degrees Fahrenheit." Grant wiped his napkin across his mouth and tossed it on his plate.

"Right," Aiden said. The staff cheered.

Maggie leaned toward him and whispered, "Show-off. Is there anything you're not good at?"

Grant glanced at her. His gaze dipped to her mouth and lifted again. Yeah, he wasn't particularly good at the whole friend thing. Not when it came to Maggie.

"That settles it. Dr. Sloan, we need you and Maggie on Wednesday for trivia night." Aiden closed his notepad. His words were equal parts hope and plea. "Please tell us you'll be there."

Trivia night. With Maggie. Grant took in the expectant faces of the staff. Then he looked at Maggie and realized his error too late. She arched an eyebrow as if challenging him. But it was the happy in her blue eyes that stole his breath. That was all he wanted—to see Maggie happy. One more night together. Hard to refuse that. "I think we can make it Wednesday."

"Nice. Watch out, Evenson Dentistry." Aiden closed his notepad and slipped it into a backpack. "Suppose that means it's time to get back to work."

The staff thanked Maggie and Grant for lunch and dispersed into the clinic. Maggie handed him a piece of brownie on a napkin. "Do I wish you good luck before a surgery? Or just tell you that I know you'll be great."

"I hope I don't have to rely on luck alone for any surgery." Grant walked into the hallway as he took a bite of the brownie. "But I appreciate the confidence boost."

"Then go be great, Dr. Sloan." Maggie smiled and headed toward the front desk. "I'll be here when you get back."

I'll be here. Those were the words Grant needed. He smiled the entire walk from the clinic to the hospital. Then when he thanked the skilled OR team for their assistance. And again, when he informed his patient's family the surgery was successful and he expected a full recovery without limitations.

Then it was back to the clinic and Maggie. Grant found himself grinning from the inside out. Unable to slow his quick pace or stall the anticipation rushing through him. His feelings for Maggie were all wrong. After all, he was still riding the adrenaline rush of a successful surgery. Of doing what he loved—helping people heal. At least, that was what he told himself.

He wished his staff a good evening in the parking lot and headed inside. Considered asking Maggie to dinner. As friends, of course.

His phone vibrated. Grant swiped the phone screen and lost his smile.

Only a few feet away from Maggie, he veered left and headed into Dr. Toro's private office for a moment alone. He dropped his phone on the desk and sat in the tall leather chair. Once again, Dr. Lilian Sloan had impeccable timing.

His mother had returned to town. Again. She was staying at the historic Amber Garden Inn in Belleridge. She still wanted to have dinner. Still expected him to keep his word to be there. She'd even made reservations at Four Fiddlers Tavern. Both the tavern and inn were within walking distance of the clinic. She'd made it convenient for Grant. She wasn't asking to meet at the family farmhouse in Three Springs. Or anywhere in Three Springs for that matter. Looked like the time had come to face his past.

Maggie appeared in the open doorway. Concern dominated her face and stole her smile. "You look like a man with secrets you don't want to share."

Grant leaned back in the comfortable chair and took in Maggie. Pretty on the outside, beautiful on the inside. It was her kindness. Her compassion. A million little things that drew him to her. He asked, "What does a person look like if they want to share their secrets?"

"I suppose that depends on if it's a good or bad secret." She stepped further into the room and kept her gaze on him as if trying to read his mood.

Grant wanted to guide her around the desk and into his lap. Where he could just hold her. Hold her until his world settled. Until he believed in things like love again. But love hadn't brought his mom home all those years ago. Hadn't healed those wounds either. Love hurt. "Aren't all secrets the same?"

"A good secret would be that I hid extra cookies and cream brownies in a desk drawer with two forks for us." Maggie tipped her head, her eyebrows arched. "A bad secret would be that I already ate them."

"I wish it was as simple as brownies and who ate them all." Or as simple as a boy liking a girl. Grant scrubbed his palms over his face. "Would you take a walk with me?"

"Now?" Surprise flashed in her gaze.

He nodded. "Just around downtown Belleridge." *Just until I find my way again.*

She eyed him for a moment. "Sure."

Outside, Grant inhaled the evening air and stuck his hands in his pockets. He'd rather have Maggie's hand in his. But this wasn't about furthering their connection. It was about finding his balance again.

"Tell me something, Maggie." *Then maybe I won't want to kiss you. To see if that settled all the restless places inside me.* Grant kept his distance from her on the sidewalk and his words to a polite low-key chat. "Tell me how you got into the rodeo? Why you chose roping."

"Kelsey tells the story about how she sat down at dinner one night with my dad and me and proudly announced that she and I were going to become a famous roping team." Maggie took a sip from the water bottle she'd grabbed from the breakroom on their way out. Then she took a longer drink as if washing away the dust from the memory. "Team Orr began that night."

"Did it not really happen that way?" Grant asked.

"Yes, it did." She combed her fingers through her hair as if putting herself and her thoughts together. Her shoulder bumped against his. "But that's not the real reason I got into rodeo."

Grant tucked his elbows into his sides. He wanted to hold her, but he wanted to know her more. "What was the reason?"

"Simple." Maggie stopped and considered him. The plastic water bottle crinkled in her grip. The creases around her eyes deepened as if wanting to guard her truths. "I wanted my father's attention."

He heard the ache in her voice. Watched her wince slightly. "Something tells me nothing about that was simple at all."

"You really are a good listener. Your patients must appreciate that." Maggie shrugged. Yet, there was nothing loose to her words. "I suppose it's not too complicated. Kelsey can talk fashion with our mom for hours on end. They have that in common. On the flip side, Kelsey is also our dad's favorite. She was before the divorce, and after that nothing changed."

And where had that left Maggie? There was no bitterness in her words. Just acceptance. Still, Grant saw the hurt in Maggie's round eyes. And Maggie hurting, in the past or now, didn't sit well with Grant. However, he wasn't about to examine that too closely.

"The rodeo is in my dad's blood. He rode bulls, did well until my grandfather passed away and he had to return home to help my grandmother run the family ranch." Maggie started walking again as if the memories bothered her less in motion. "After my mom left us, Kelsey and I went to the rodeo with my dad a lot. Almost every weekend while my mom was getting settled into her new life in the city."

Grant reached for a quaint, happy image. A young, excited Maggie holding her dad's hand at the rodeo. It would've eased the inevitable pain of her parents' divorce. But he sensed that was an illusion.

"Our dad hardly noticed Kelsey and me sitting up in the stands. He filled in as a pickup rider or helped in the chutes or wherever they needed him on the floor," Maggie continued. Her words straightforward. "I figured out that what mattered—who mattered—to my dad was inside the arena strapped to a bull or bucking bronc. So, I started learning breakaway. Barrel racing. Goat tying. Whatever they would allow an eight-year-old girl to do in an arena."

"And you got your dad's attention." When she should've already had it. Maggie should've been her dad's whole world. Grant frowned. He knew a thing or two about parents and unmet expectations.

Still, he'd never felt as if he had to fight for his grandparents' attention growing up. There never seemed to be anything more important to his grandparents than Grant and his brothers. That, he realized now, was a gift. One he wished Maggie had experienced.

"I had my dad's attention, and his approval came that night at the dinner table." Maggie's smile was small and her words melancholy. "After Kelsey's team roping comment, Dad was thrilled. Kelsey was excited. All I could think was that my big sister chose me to be her teammate. I couldn't turn that down."

"And your dad was proud of you," Grant guessed.

"Yes, he was," Maggie said. "I suppose he is in his own way now too."

"Do you ever wonder if what you do will ever be enough for him?" he asked.

She stared at him as if he'd revealed an even darker worry. A deeper secret.

"Before you answer, let me tell you my own truth." Grant stopped in front of a toy store and stared at the spaceship built out of plastic building blocks in the window. He and his brothers had built entire towns out of their plastic bricks. To Gran Claire's endless amazement and praise. He had his grandparents' love, that was for sure. It should've been all he'd ever need. "I went into medicine to get my mom's attention."

Maggie met his gaze in the reflection of the shop window. "Your mom?"

"You sound surprised." Grant turned away from the toy store. "Isn't that every kid's wish? To be their parent's pride and joy?"

"It's just Ryan never talks about your parents." Her words were soft and restrained as if she didn't want to pry. Or overstep. "Ryan told me that your parents are divorced like mine. I got the impression your mom wasn't around."

"She's not." Until now. Grant frowned. "There's a good reason Ryan doesn't talk about our parents. None of us do, really. Talking about our parents tends to open old wounds that we'd rather not deal with."

Maggie glanced at him. "Can I ask what happened?"

"Our mother left us at our grandparents' farm when we were kids and never came back." Grant's arm bumped against hers. He straightened and pushed his shoulders back. Better to brace himself for the memory. "She and our father got divorced that same summer. Dad went on to a new life that didn't include us. Then our mother went to medical school and became one of the leading heart surgeons in the nation."

Maggie frowned, shook her head, then said, "I'm impressed, even though I don't want to be."

"Mom didn't come back. Not once," he continued. His words controlled and quiet.

"I'm sorry." Sincerity oozed from Maggie.

"It's fine." *I'm fine*. Grant ran a hand over his head, down the back of his neck. "It's in the past. Over and done, as they say. We've moved on." That should've ended his confession. But

Grant's truths weren't done being spilled on the sidewalk. With Maggie. "Or at least I thought I had moved on. Until my mother pretended to be a patient and showed up at the clinic last week."

Shock slowed Maggie's steps and her words. "You didn't know she was there?"

"Not until I walked into exam room four." Grant stared at the sidewalk as if he feared tripping over his confessions. "She has called a few times over the past month or so. But I deleted the messages."

"Did you talk in the exam room?" Maggie asked.

"No, not really. She wanted to meet for dinner. I agreed." Grant jammed his hands in his pockets. "I haven't told my grandfather or my brothers."

"Why not?" Maggie asked. "Don't you want them with you? I think I'd want Kelsey with me. You shouldn't have to face her alone."

Alone. That was where Grant was most comfortable. Except when he was with Maggie. "I don't want them to get hurt. My mother already canceled once. She had to fly back to New York for business."

Maggie nodded.

He flashed his phone screen at Maggie.

"Then she texted me this afternoon on my way back from surgery."

Maggie tipped her head and studied him. "What did she say?"

"She made dinner reservations for us this Wednesday." Grant returned his phone to his pocket. Yet, his hands fluttered around in front of him. But he was a surgeon. He always knew what to do with his hands. His words spilled out, "It's funny. I would've given anything for an hour with my mom growing up. Now I'm angry she's here. Even more angry that there is this sliver of hope that I finally have her attention."

Maggie stepped closer and reached for his hand. And Grant settled, from the inside out. Right there on the sidewalk in the middle of downtown.

"What gets me is that I still care." He stared at their joined hands. His words sounded bewildered even to him. "I shouldn't still care."

She didn't link her fingers around his. But kept her grip light, loose. As if ensuring it was easy for either of them to break free from. "Just because you ignore your feelings doesn't mean they aren't still there."

"But I'm the least emotional of my brothers." Grant's gaze searched hers. One adjustment and he would have their palms pressed together. Their fingers intertwined. "Always have been unemotional. I prefer it that way."

"Or perhaps you're simply the best at hiding your emotions." Maggie watched him.

"Doesn't matter. I vowed years ago my mom wouldn't get to me ever again." He squeezed her hand. His voice resolved. Detached, unlike his hand in hers. "I'm certain I can handle one dinner with her."

What he was less certain of was how he was ever going to let Maggie go.

"You don't have to go alone," Maggie said. "I could—"

Grant shook his head and stopped her. "I've already dragged you too far into my family drama. I'll handle it." For himself. And his brothers. "We should probably head home. Caleb is trying out his new pizza oven tonight and we promised not to miss dinner."

Maggie considered him, then nodded.

They walked back to the clinic. Silent and lost in their own thoughts. Only he kept her hand tucked in his. Because he wasn't ready to let go yet.

CHAPTER TWENTY-ONE

DUSK COVERED THE sky when Grant walked inside Four Fiddlers Tavern on Wednesday evening. He'd changed from his scrubs back into his business wear and still felt that pinch of anger toward Lilian Sloan. But he'd given his word to his mother he'd show for dinner. And if nothing else, he wanted to prove he kept his promises.

He greeted the hostess and gave her his last name. She led him through the bar, past the booths and out onto a private patio. A gentleman sat with his back to Grant, facing the outdoor fountain. But Grant didn't need to see his face to know who it was. He stopped the hostess, told her he saw his party and slipped around her to get to the table for four.

"Grandpa." Grant gripped the back of an empty chair and eyed his grandfather. "You've been holding out."

Sam straightened in his chair as if he understood he still held a position as head of the Sloan family. As such he answered to no one.

"Same can be said of you, Grant Alexander Sloan."

Translation: *you should've confided in me. Your grandfather of all people.* Grant pulled out the chair and slid into it feeling like a boy again, disliking the disappointment on his grandfather's face.

"Your mother wasn't certain you'd show." Sam stroked his fingers through his beard and tipped his chin at Grant. "But I reminded her that I raised my grandsons to only give their word when they meant to keep it."

"I wasn't sure I could show," Grant confessed and folded his hands on top of the plastic menu. Under the table, his legs shook as if warming up for a quick retreat. Showing, after all, was not the same staying.

Sam nodded and stared into his cocktail glass. "You're entitled to do what best suits you, Grant. There's no right or wrong to your feelings or how you react."

"Have you forgiven her then?" Grant asked.

Sam's eyes widened. "I haven't seen her yet. Don't even know if that's what brought her here after all these years."

"How long have you been talking to her?" Grant smoothed his fingers over a water glass, rubbing away the condensation. Both his fingertips and words were cool.

"Got a call about a month ago," Sam confessed and took a long sip of his whiskey. "I didn't recognize the number, so I didn't pick up. Then she left a message."

"So, you called her back." Unlike Grant. He'd hit the delete button without listening to the messages.

"Not then, I didn't call back." Sam swirled the large ice cube in his whiskey glass, slowly and precisely. Same as his words sounded. "I waited for her to call again. Figured if she called a second time, the first time wasn't a mistake."

His grandpa was being cautious too. Grant relaxed slightly. "Why call her back at all?"

"She's my only daughter," Sam said simply. A weariness settled over his thin shoulders. "She's family too."

"But she didn't leave just us. She left you and Gran Claire as well." Disapproval roughened Grant's voice. He flattened his palms on the table, inhaled, and strove to keep calm. "What does she want now?"

"Can't say exactly." Sam looked at him. "That's the truth. She hasn't told me much other than she wanted to talk to you and me."

Grant's leg shook more. He scratched his cheek. "What did you tell her?"

"That it wasn't going to be as easy as a phone call." His grandpa looked grim. "I guess she figured that out because she sure got creative pretending to be a patient to get to you."

Creative was one word. Desperate was another one that rolled through the back of Grant's mind and refused to go away. He eyed his grandfather. "You're disappointed I didn't call her back."

"Don't go telling me how I feel," Sam argued.

Grant wanted someone to tell him how he felt. He wanted to run and remain where he was. He blamed that little kid inside him still looking for his mother's attention. Her affection. Her approval. That little kid who still hoped. But he'd grown up. He knew better now. He checked his watch. "Maybe she changed her mind."

"That would certainly give us a direction to go, wouldn't it?" Sam stared into his whiskey glass again. "Sure wish your Gran Claire was here. She was always better at handling this kind of stuff than I ever was."

Grant blinked and studied his grandfather. Saw the lines of sadness and hurt fanning around his eyes. The doubt framing his mouth. Grant reached over and set his hand on his grandfather's arm. "We can leave, Grandpa. If that's what you want."

"I've come this far." His grandfather patted Grant's hand and looked Grant in the eye. "I intend to sit and listen. See this through."

"What if I can't?" Grant pulled his arm away and tugged on his ear.

"That is not a decision I can make for you," his grandpa said. "But whatever you choose, you have my support. Never doubt that."

Grant exhaled and glanced across the outdoor patio. Lilian Sloan had finally arrived. His mother tucked a pair of fashionable sunglasses into her purse and made her way toward their table. Her chin length hair swayed sharply against her jawline. She wore another perfectly tailored burgundy suit and walked with strict purpose. As if she believed wasting time, even a minute, was a severe offense.

Grant shifted his attention to his grandfather. "She's here. Looks like we have a direction."

Sam sat up in the chair and adjusted his bolo tie.

Lilian Sloan stepped up to the table, dropped her designer purse on a chair, and focused on her father. She touched her pearl earring, then her throat, then said, "Dad."

Sam cleared his throat and pushed himself up from his chair. He reached out and took Lilian's hand. "Lilly-bee, it's been too long."

Her chin quivered. That was the first crack in his mother's veneer that Grant had seen. He crossed his arms over his chest and refused to be moved.

"Let's sit." Lilian released her father's hand and motioned to the table. Then she took a chair across from Grant, but beside Grandpa Sam. Her gaze shifted from his grandfather to Grant. "Thank you for coming. There's a lot I want to say to you both."

Grant pressed his arms against his chest. Tried to still the emotions flaring up inside him. Now he wished Gran Claire was there. Or Maggie. She would've settled him. Taken his hand and anchored him as he looked into a past he'd thought he'd left behind. He only ever looked forward for a reason.

Lilian tucked her hair behind her ear and eyed Grant. "I don't know quite where to start."

Grant had an idea. An apology. A very long overdue apology. Or an explanation why her family wasn't enough to stick around for. Or a reason why she never kept her promises to come back. He stayed silent and still.

"I have always loved you and your brothers, Grant," Lilian said. Her words sounded matter of fact, almost clinical. "Always I have loved my sons. That I can guarantee."

Grant's throat closed. Silence descended around the table. Pensive and stifling. And Grant realized he knew better. His mother wasn't there because she was proud of him. Or because she was sorry. She hadn't even offered an apology for being late. Lilian Sloan was there for herself. And her own agenda. As usual.

Grant pressed his palms against the table and stood up. He focused on his grandfather. "I'm sorry, Grandpa. I cannot do this."

His grandfather nodded. One slow dip of his chin. Understanding flared in his grandpa's solemn gaze. It was all the acknowledgment Grant required.

He turned and walked away. Straight out of the restaurant. Straight to his truck. Where he sat, alone with his troubles. Yet, solutions were hard to come by.

Finally, he got out his phone. Noted he had a text from the hiring director at Silverlining TeamMed. His official offer letter was in his email inbox. He'd walked away from his past just now. Here, his future in California was ready for him. And for the first time in years, Grant hesitated and stalled in the present.

He opened his text app and sent a message to Maggie. On my way home. Tell me you'll be there.

Her reply came quick. Are you okay?

No. Not even a little. He answered. I just really need to see you.

I'll be here. Drive safe.

CHAPTER TWENTY-TWO

MAGGIE WAITED ON the back porch of the farmhouse with her phone pressed against her chest. Her thoughts circled around Grant. He was supposed to be at dinner with his mother. But he was coming home to Maggie.

I just really need to see you.

Maggie clutched her phone tighter. She needed to see Grant. Needed to know she was overreacting. That she was reading too much into one text.

Finally, Grant's truck pulled into the driveway and parked. He stepped out and turned toward her. He looked weary. Lost. Their gazes collided over the truck bed. His deflated. Hers worried. She hadn't been wrong.

Maggie didn't hesitate. She crashed through those friendship boundaries, rushed to him, and wrapped him in her embrace. Then held on. As if a cowgirl like her could give a city doc like him all he would ever need. His arms curved around her waist, and he gathered her closer to him. And Maggie was exactly where she wanted to be.

"I couldn't sit there, Maggie. I couldn't do it." He pulled away and kept her hand in his. Remorse circled his words. His lips pressed into a deep frown. "She started with how she always loved me and my brothers. I'm no expert on love, but abandoning your kids is a strange way to show it."

Maggie watched his jaw tense. His only tell that he was hurting. And she suddenly hurt too. For him. For the boy he'd been. The man he was.

"She came here for herself." Grant ran his hand over his head, shifting the short strands in every direction. "She has an agenda, Maggie. I don't want any part of it. Besides, shouldn't she be asking for my forgiveness?"

Maggie nodded. Yet, she wasn't quite certain how any of it was supposed to work. She knew only that Grant was hurting. Wanted to believe Lilian Sloan might be too. But Maggie wasn't his family. She was just…

"You look really nice." His gaze trailed over Maggie, seeming to take in her sundress and sandals in one sweep. "You're dressed for trivia night. That's tonight. We're supposed to be there." He smoothed his hand down the front of his dress shirt as if collecting himself. "I should change. We should go."

"Grant." Maggie set her palm on his cheek,

drawing his focus back to her, keeping him in place. "You don't have to go to trivia night."

"But you were looking forward to it. I heard you talking to Tess about it this morning." He curved his fingers around hers. "You should still go."

But she wanted to stay. With him. "What are you going to do?"

"Haven't figured that out yet." He shrugged. "I'll be fine."

"I know you will." Maggie squeezed his hands. There was a gentle insistence in her words. "But you don't have to be alone. Remember you told me that? Now I'm saying it to you."

"I'd like you to stay." He released her hands as if proving he was more than willing to let her go. "But I won't ask you to."

"You don't have to. I've already made up my mind." He mattered. More than a trivia night. More than he should. But for one night, Maggie was pushing that all aside. Tonight, she wanted to be there. For Grant. As a friend. As more. Whatever so long as she was with him. She smiled, hoping it encouraged him. "Now we just need to decide how we're going to spend our evening."

"I might not be good company." His words were a warning and an out.

"We can talk or not. I'll leave that entirely up to you." Maggie turned toward the house. "Or we can just be."

"Just be," he repeated and fell in step beside her.

Just be together. Maggie gestured to the house and headed up the porch stairs. "You know. Chill. Count the stars. Take a night swim. So many options."

Grant touched her arm, stopping her on the porch. "Did you say night swim?"

"That's what your grandfather told us to do when he talked about us having fun." Maggie watched him. The lost look in his eyes was clearing. Interest flared. Suddenly, Maggie felt lighter herself. "Have you been night swimming?"

"I have." A grin shifted across his mouth. "What about you?"

"True story," she started. His full smile was all the push she needed to know she'd made the right choice to stay. "I've never been night swimming."

"Well, now we know how we're spending our evening." He held open the back door. His smile flashed in his eyes. "Let's change and head to the pond."

After a quick change into her swimsuit, Maggie texted the twins and persuaded Josh and Caleb to join Dr. Toro's trivia team in her place and Grant's. She nudged aside the twinge of guilt over feigning not feeling well. It was for a good cause. That cause being Grant.

Maggie returned to the kitchen and found Grant already there. She watched him add several containers to a cooler on the island. "What's all that?"

"If this is your first night swim, we have to go about it the right way." Grant closed the lid on the cooler. "Drinks and snacks are a must."

"Would there be chocolate inside that cooler, by chance?" She grinned at him, pleased he seemed to be back to himself again.

"For you." Grant's deep voice surrounded her. His piercing gaze trapped hers. "Always."

Out at the family pond, Maggie learned Sam and Claire had recited their vows there. And the Sloan brothers and their friends had spent endless summer days jumping from the rope swing. Grant lit a fire in the firepit, for ambiance he claimed, not warmth. Their summer night was warm all on its own.

Maggie showed Grant how to *just be*. Their inner tubes clipped together, they floated in the water, counted lightning bug sightings, and listened to nature's nighttime chorus. The conversation flowed from favorite movies to worst dates back to other favorites. Maggie let

Grant lead, never pressed. Never pried. But she learned Sam had been at dinner too and the conversation hadn't gotten far before Grant had walked out.

Now they were sitting on a blanket. The contents of the cooler spread out between them. Somehow, the conversation had gotten back around to Maggie and the rodeo.

"I can't believe nothing has come between you and your sister since you started roping together." Grant stretched out on his back and tucked his hands behind his head. "That's really impressive."

Maybe it was the shelter of the night. Or perhaps that Grant had trusted her with his own secrets. Whatever it was, Maggie rested her elbows on her raised knees and shared a bit more of herself. "Someone tried to come between us once."

"Another roper tried to steal you away for their team, didn't they?" Grant teased.

"No. It was my ex-fiancé." Water dripped from her damp hair, trailing down her arms and back, leaving a chill behind. "Although, can I call him my fiancé if he never actually proposed? It doesn't matter. It's not important. I chose my sister. My team."

"What happened?" Grant rolled onto his

side, faced her, and propped his head in his hand. "If you don't mind me asking."

"I fell in love." Maggie stared blankly out at the water. "Or I thought it was love like the kind I imagine Sam and your Gran Claire shared. The unbreakable, unwavering kind." The kind that seemed to only be reserved for other people. She'd been fine with that. Until recently. She tipped her head toward Grant. "You know what I mean?"

"Yeah." Grant nodded. His expression was thoughtful. "I've seen that kind of love."

But had he ever felt it? Ever been betrayed by it. Maggie smoothed her hands over her wet hair, squeezed out more water. But the discontent remained. "My ex told me all the things I wanted to hear. Gave me all the right words and I believed him. Believed in us. If you have true love, you can conquer anything, right?"

"That's what I'm told." A subtle skepticism wove around his words.

"Well, for the record, it's not true," Maggie said.

A shadow crossed Grant's face as if he wanted her to defend the power of love.

"My ex told me he'd marry me, but I had to give up the rodeo. Find myself a real career." Maggie felt the tremor in her chin. The memory, even long past, still stung. How could she have gotten it all so horribly wrong? She swallowed and added, "And if I truly loved him, I wouldn't hesitate to leave my family to build our own." *Give it all up, Maggie. For us. It'll be better than you can imagine. You trust me, don't you?*

Grant's eyebrows lowered. "Where did your ex want to build this new life together?"

"The city where he was going to law school." Maggie picked several grapes from the plastic container. Her movements rigid like her tone. "He was willing to live in the suburbs. No farther. That was proof of how much he loved me."

Grant looked confused. "But your ex had to know your passion for the rodeo."

"We always talked about leaving our hometown." Maggie's mouth twisted around the sweet grapes. "But we never talked about what that meant to us. How it looked. I suppose we never really talked about the important details."

His gaze shifted toward the pond. His words sounded careful. "Did you want your ex to go with you on the circuit?"

"Kelsey and I had only just started tossing around the idea," Maggie explained. "We were winning at the local level and wanting to prove ourselves at bigger events. Our dad was encouraging us to go."

"You had the chance to do what your father never did." His words were all too perceptive.

"Kelsey and my dad put together this big plan for our roping success that would take us across the country. I told my ex all about it." She'd been so excited. Couldn't wait to share it with him. He'd been less than thrilled. Far from supportive. Maggie looked at Grant. "I guess I thought I could have it all. A husband. A home. A career in the rodeo."

"But something had to give." Grant's words were flat. Resigned.

"Yeah. My ex ended things." Maggie stretched out her legs as if she could push away the painful parts of her past. "Kelsey had the camper packed the next day. She told me there was no room for my broken heart and to leave it behind. I had to focus because it was up to us to make our own dreams come true."

"Would you do it all again?" He sounded mildly curious.

"Go after my dreams? Definitely. I'd do all that again." She tipped her head toward him and gave him a wry smile. "Maybe I should've told you about my awkward first kiss with Jason Cote instead. It would've been funny and certainly more entertaining than exes and lost love."

"I don't want to talk about exes or first kisses." He sat up and closed the distance between them in one quick move. "But I very much want to talk about second kisses."

Maggie's pulse picked up. "That's not a conversation we should be having."

"Except it's pretty much all I've been thinking about since I saw you on the porch tonight." His gaze warmed.

Maggie opened her mouth.

"Actually, that's not true." He caught the water droplets on her neck with his fingertips. His touch gentle, his words undeniably clear. "I've been thinking about kissing you ever since our first one."

So had she. But she'd been a fool before. Letting her heart lead. Falling into a kiss and an illusion. This time she knew the facts. Her doctor was leaving. Their time together was always only ever temporary. Their goodbye inevitable. Yet, she wanted that second kiss. With Grant. Wanted to feel chosen, even if only for this one moment. "But we agreed."

"We still agree." He reached up, tucked her damp hair behind both her ears.

His hands lingered on either side of her face. The lightest of holds. The moment became fragile. Maggie's words were already breathless. "Second kisses are a really bad idea."

Because if I kiss you now, you'll know exactly how I feel about you. And that was a secret her heart intended to keep. After all, she still very much planned to have that uncomplicated goodbye.

His gaze traveled over her face as if memorizing her. "We should head back to the farmhouse."

"Yes, we should leave right now." They both moved. Closer to each other. Maggie held his stare. "There are some things that are better left unsaid anyway."

"I don't plan on saying anything." He leaned in.

"Me, either." Maggie met him then.

For a kiss that spoke to hearts. And promised things like love and forever.

It was a kiss that made the impossible seem possible.

BACK AT THE FARMHOUSE, Grant unloaded the cooler from the UTV, took Maggie's hand in his free one and walked up the porch steps. His mellow mood evaporated the instant he saw his grandfather sitting in a chair on the porch.

Maggie squeezed his hand, then slipped the cooler from his grip. "I'm going to head inside and take a shower." She stopped beside his grandfather's chair, set her hand on Sam's shoulder, but their exchange was too soft for Grant to hear.

Once the back door closed, his grandfather peered at him. Something like delight flashed in his grin. "See you two finally took my advice and went for that night swim after all. How was it?"

"Everything I needed." And more. Grant sat in the chair next to his grandfather and stared up at the crescent moon.

It was a night of highs and lows. At the center had been Maggie. Now he knew why his grandfather had wanted Gran Claire with him at the restaurant earlier. His grandfather wasn't wrong. There was something about a woman—the right one. Not that Grant was the right guy. Not for Maggie.

"Maggie is special, Grant." Satisfaction smoothed over his grandfather's face. "Your Gran Claire would tell you Maggie is a treasure like the kind you find at the end of a rainbow."

"But you can't chase a rainbow, Grandpa." Grant folded his arms over his chest and pressed his back into the seat cushion. "It always keeps moving out of reach."

"Could be you're already standing at the

end of your rainbow," his grandpa suggested. "Could be you just need to stand still long enough to see it."

What Grant had seen was the hurt deep in Maggie's gaze when she'd spoken about her ex. Her only fault had been falling in love with the wrong guy. Maggie deserved better. But not Grant. He was just a guy who'd only ever given things like rainbows and love nothing more than a passing glance.

Besides, rainbows disappeared without the right conditions. Even if Maggie was the right person, the timing was all wrong. For him. For her too. That was all he needed to know. He propped his feet on the coffee table. "Are you going to call a family meeting so that we can tell everyone about our dinner guest tonight?"

"You didn't have dinner with your mother. I did." His grandfather eyed him. His face neutral. His words matter of fact. "You have nothing to tell."

"What about you?" Grant asked. "Aren't you going to tell them?"

"Not just yet." His grandfather's fingers tapped on the armrests of his chair.

"Why not?"

"We've all got to figure out what's best for ourselves when it comes to your mother," his grandfather said. "And I suspect each of your brothers is going to have their own specific re-action to the news of Lilian's return."

Grant shook his head. His brothers claimed he was the most unemotional among them. Yet, even Grant hadn't been able to keep it together for one meal with their mother. "I don't think it's going to be good when they find out."

Sam chuckled softly. "I never even consid-ered it would be."

"Do you know why my mother called me and not Carter?" It made sense for Lilian Sloan to start with her oldest son. Carter had always stepped up to take care of things as the old-est sibling.

Sam shifted and looked at Grant. His eyes narrowed as if he was choosing his words care-fully. "I suppose Lilian thought you might be the one who could understand her."

"Because I'm the most like her." Grant dropped his head back on the chair and frowned at the sky. "Well, I don't understand, Grandpa. I don't understand turning your back on family like she did."

"You're moving to California." His grandfa-ther's words were soft yet prickly all the same. "Some might claim you're doing the very same thing."

"What I'm doing is entirely different." And not up for discussion. *Never be too scared to go after your best life, Grant. What if it's beyond Three Springs, Gran Claire? Then be fearless and spread your wings wide.* Grant pushed out of the chair and paced around the porch. "What now?"

"Now we sleep on it." His grandfather stood and crossed over to Grant. He set his hand on Grant's shoulder. "I've found that things often look different in the bright light of the morning. Sometimes that's all I need to change my perspective."

Grant wasn't looking to change his perspective or his path. All he wanted was closure. To put his past in the past and step into his future unburdened.

A light lit a window on the second floor of the farmhouse. The guestroom. Maggie's room.

He wanted to run inside and kiss her goodnight. Then he wanted to meet her in the hallway at dawn and kiss her good morning. And spend all the hours in between with her. Yet, their time together was slipping away. Quickly coming to an end.

And Grant suddenly found himself right back where he'd started the evening. Restless. Unsteady. Unsure.

He knew there was nothing about Maggie he wanted to put in the past.

And his future looked too much like the vision her ex had imagined for them. The parallels were undeniable, even if Grant wouldn't ever ask Maggie to give up her roping career. Yet beyond the rodeo, Maggie belonged on a place like his family's property. Surrounded by horses and family and wide open sky. Not in a high rise in the city center with a doctor who spent more time in the operating room than at home.

He wanted so much more for Maggie. Wanted her to be happy. And that meant letting her go. Stepping aside. Even if it meant he'd never be the same.

CHAPTER TWENTY-THREE

"HEY, KELSEY."

Kelsey glanced up from her rhinestone embroidery and took in Dr. Sloan, wearing dress pants and a silk tie. He looked solemn and clinical even without his white doctor's coat. "Dr. Sloan. Have a seat. Or if you prefer, head out onto the dance floor. I'm sure Maggie would like that."

Her sister, along with the Sloan twins, were line dancing their way through another set of lively country songs. They'd been sliding their boots across the Feisty Owl's outdoor dancefloor for almost an hour now. Ryan had even joined in until he'd gotten pulled into a dart game with Tess and Carter inside. Tonight was about celebrating before Maggie and Kelsey left in the morning for Amarillo and the Stagecoach Pro Buckle Series rodeo.

"I think I'll sit it out tonight." Dr. Sloan dropped into the chair beside Kelsey, set his glass of amber beer on the table, then pointed at his polished leather dress shoes. "Wrong shoes."

And wrong night. It wasn't Grant, her little sister's boyfriend—if Kelsey could call him that—sitting next to her. It was cool and reserved Dr. Sloan.

As such, he didn't waste any time getting to his point. "Kelsey, you should know that I received a progress report from your physical therapist today."

Kelsey's fingers never paused in setting her next stitch. She kept the needle and her words moving. "You aren't going to change your surgery recommendation, are you?"

"I can't." Dr. Sloan straightened his tie and picked up his beer. "I won't, especially not after reading the report."

Kelsey nodded and continued weaving her needle in and out of the fabric. "Do you love my sister, Dr. Sloan?" At the sudden stillness beside her, Kelsey looked up and considered the always composed doctor. "Let's pretend, Dr. Sloan, that you do love Maggie."

Dr. Sloan never flinched. Simply dipped his chin slightly and cradled his glass in both hands. His gaze and expression unreadable.

"For the record, you'd be foolish not to love Maggie," Kelsey continued. "My little sister is the best this world has to offer. And she deserves all the good she can handle and more."

He took a deep sip of his beer, then cleared his throat. "I don't disagree."

Kelsey's smile was small and gone quickly. "I haven't been the ideal partner, Dr. Sloan. I've been injured more than healthy. But I'm determined to give Maggie the best that I can." Kelsey stuck her needle in the fabric and focused fully on the well-meaning doctor. "You see. I love my sister and I gave her my word." So many years ago. Yet, Kelsey still meant to keep it.

Dr. Sloan simply nodded.

"If you loved her, Dr. Sloan, wouldn't you do the same?" Kelsey motioned toward the outdoor dance floor where Maggie tossed her head back and laughed. She held onto Josh as if she couldn't quite catch her breath. Kelsey eyed Dr. Sloan. He too watched the dance floor. And looked as if he couldn't catch his breath, either. Kelsey kept her words even and calm. "Wouldn't you do everything in your power to make Maggie happy, even if it caused you some discomfort?"

"Your pain is more than some discomfort, Kelsey." His perceptive gaze moved from the dance floor back to Kelsey. "We both know that."

"I understand the risks." Kelsey lifted her chin. "I accept those risks."

Dr. Sloan drank some of his beer and paused, as if weighing her words. "When do you put yourself first, Kelsey?"

"When I'm certain my little sister is taken care of." *And I'm not convinced you will do that, Dr. Sloan.*

"Maggie wouldn't want you to do this," he argued. "You should talk to her, Kelsey. She's your teammate and your sister. She'd want to know."

"You should talk to Maggie as well, Dr. Sloan." Kelsey pressed her finger against the tip of her needle. Felt the smallest sting. If only the truth didn't hurt worse. "You should tell Maggie that you love her before it's too late."

"Even if I did love your sister," he said. "It's already too late." He was too contained. So very stoic.

"That's why I have to fight, Dr. Sloan." Kelsey heard the insistent urgency in her own words.

"Why is that?" he asked.

"Because someone has to fight for Maggie." She shifted her gaze over Dr. Sloan's shoulder and smiled wide at the trio coming toward them. "Well, I thought you guys were going to dance all night."

The twins laughed and sat in the chairs across from Kelsey and relaxed.

"That's a workout for sure." Maggie flopped into the chair next to Grant and fanned her face. "You both look a little too serious over here. We thought we'd check in."

"Hopefully, we interrupted something good." Caleb grinned and rubbed his hands together. "I could use some exciting town gossip. It's been slow around here recently."

"You'll have to get your gossip inside at the bar." Dr. Sloan pointed toward the open archway. "Along with all our friends and neighbors."

Caleb frowned at his older brother and turned toward Kelsey. His expression eager.

"No gossip here, I'm afraid. Dr. Sloan and I were just arguing about rhinestones." Kelsey set her embroidery aside and picked up her cocktail glass. She spoke over the rim. "I want to put a rhinestone heart on Dr. Sloan's scrubs. But he's afraid to wear his heart on his sleeve."

"It's not that at all." Dr. Sloan toasted her with his beer. "It's just that I'm not a heart surgeon. I wouldn't want to give someone the wrong impression."

"What's the wrong impression?" Caleb teased. "That you have a heart?"

"Exactly." Grant sipped his beer and sat back.

Oh, Dr. Sloan had a heart. He could deny it

all he wanted. Same as her little sister denied hers. Now it was just a matter of who broke the other's heart first.

Before Kelsey could worry too much, strong arms wrapped around her from behind. The softest kiss landed on her cheek. The words, *hello beautiful*, were whispered into her ear. *Nolan*. Kelsey linked her fingers with her chef's and held on while he moved to perch on the armrest of her chair. Their joined hands he tucked against his leg.

"Good timing, Chef." Caleb patted his stomach. "I could use some food. Dancing makes me hungry."

"I'm not taking orders. Or cooking right now." Nolan stood and tugged Kelsey gently out of her chair. "But I am taking this lovely cowgirl away for a bit. She owes me a slow dance or three."

"Is that right?" Kelsey asked and followed Nolan to the dance floor.

He wrapped her in his arms, careful of her injured shoulder as was his way, and fell into a slow two-step. His smile was close-lipped and private and only for her. "Just for the record, this is a dance, not a date. I didn't want there to be any confusion."

"I never thought it was a date." Kelsey

shifted until she could press her cheek against his shoulder.

And just for the record, she pulled her own heart off her sleeve. Because, like Dr. Sloan, she didn't want to give anyone the wrong impression.

"I SAW THE light on." *I was looking for you.* Maggie stood in the doorway of Carter's office, holding a glass of water and searching for the exact moment she'd started to lose Grant. Tonight at the Owl? Last night, after they had shared secrets and kissed at the pond? Or perhaps it was before that.

Grant set his notepad computer on the side table and touched his watch. "I was reading, and lost track of time."

And he wasn't looking for you, Maggie. She should leave. Instead, she walked into the room.

"It's late." He shifted, moving his feet from the ottoman to the floor. "I would've thought all the dancing from earlier tonight wiped you out. You okay?"

"I'm good." She'd have been better if Grant had danced with her. Held her as tenderly as Nolan had embraced Kelsey on the dance floor. Or maybe if Grant had taken her hand on the drive home, rather than evaded her questions about his conversation with Kelsey. She knew it had been about more than rhinestones. Or perhaps if he'd kissed her goodnight. Anything that didn't make Maggie feel like there was only one word left to say between them. Goodbye. "I'm restless. Nervous. Mostly excited to compete this weekend."

"You love it." His gaze and smile were tender. Yet he was closed-off, already unreachable even in the chair only a couple of feet away from her.

"So much." Maggie sipped her water, then stalled. She'd never been good at the hard conversations. "I don't mind the travel or the new places. And I adore the community. They give me that sense of the familiar. A sense of security, despite being in another new town and another new arena."

Grant nodded and stayed where he was.

Too far away. "Now the air conditioning in the camper is working again. Thanks to Josh's friend." Maggie chuckled. Yet, she also wanted to cry. "So now the nights will be bearable." *As long as I don't think about you.*

"Sounds like you have everything you need," he said.

Except you. I don't have you, do I? She supposed she never really did. But when they'd kissed at the pond, she'd started to think. Hope, really.

Maggie touched a frame with a picture of the Sloan brothers as kids. Thought maybe if she listened hard enough, she'd hear their collective laughter. Feel their joy. Only the continuous tick of the wall clock interrupted the quiet. A reminder that dawn was coming. So was that goodbye? It was time to stop stalling. "I should probably get to bed. There's a lot to do in the morning so Kelsey and I can get on the road to Amarillo early."

"I need to do the same." Grant stood and stuck his hands in the pockets of his sweatpants. "I've got two surgeries tomorrow."

Maggie eyed him, reached for a smile she wasn't feeling. "You'll do great."

"As will you," he returned.

She nodded, unable to push a goodnight or a goodbye past her suddenly tight throat She headed toward the door. Tomorrow, she'd find the words.

Grant called out, "Maggie."

His voice was soft. Achingly soft. Or perhaps that was just Maggie aching already. It was supposed to be simple. Easy. They were worlds apart. She turned and bit her bottom lip to stop the tremor.

"Maggie," he said again. "If I… "

Yes. I want you at the rodeo. I want you in my life. Tell me I can have it all. With you. Maggie held her breath.

"If I don't see you in the morning, text me to let me know you got there safely," he said.

"Sure. Night, Grant." Maggie fled.

CHAPTER TWENTY-FOUR

"FEELS GOOD TO be in the saddle again, Mags."
Kelsey guided Tango beside Maggie and
smiled. "Lady Dasher is grinning. She's feeling good too. It's going to be a great weekend,
Mags. I just know it."

Maggie knew Lady Dasher was back to
being herself. Paige had cleared the mare yesterday, declaring no signs of a lingering eye
infection. Now Kelsey and Maggie were returning from an hour-long, late afternoon
ride through the vacant pastures bordering
the campground and arena hosting the Stagecoach Pro Buckle Series. All was well with
Lady Dasher. As for Maggie's big sister, that
was not so clear.

Kelsey urged Tango into a fast trot, pulling
ahead of Maggie. The campsite was within
view and full of familiar competitors. All
preparing to vie for the jackpot and the automatic bid to the world championships. Maggie needed things to be great. All four steers
roped. No penalties. No disqualifications.

Advancement to the next round. Then repeat. Until the final round when the sisters needed nothing less than their best.

She watched Kelsey up ahead. Her sister had been upbeat and positive since breakfast. Rainbows and sunshine all around. As for Maggie, she wasn't even a ray of sunshine. She hadn't seen Grant that morning. Wanted to convince herself that was for the best. As it was, that goodbye had still been lodged in her throat when she'd woken up. Not seeing Grant had left Maggie feeling more sour than sunshiny.

Maggie frowned. That was nothing she could take into the competition tomorrow. She had a job to do. And if her heart was bruised, so be it. She could worry about that later. Or never. She was where she wanted to be. Where she'd chosen to be. Her city doc had chosen somewhere else. Those were the facts. And if she hurt, well, she'd have to get over that too.

Kelsey turned in her saddle and hollered, "Get a move on. I'm hungry."

Maggie urged Lady Dasher to trot faster. Time to focus on what was, not what might have been.

An explosion like fireworks blasted through the air, the disturbing sound echoing from across the pasture. Maggie jolted and brought

Lady Dasher to a quick stop. Her heart pounding, she calmed her horse.

Up ahead, Tango spooked. He reared up wildly. Kelsey's left arm flailed. Her sister's scream filled the air as her body flew sideways out of the saddle.

Maggie leapt off Lady Dasher. She was running before her boots hit the dirt. Kelsey landed hard on her right side. Maggie's own shout pierced the air. She ran faster and dropped to her knees beside her sister's limp form. Kelsey's name fell from her lips, over and over.

The thud of boots sounded. People rushed toward her. Maggie called for someone to find Ryan. Ryan Sloan. Then she moved her hands lightly over Kelsey's body. Terrified to move her. Terrified that her sister wasn't moving.

But her sister was breathing. The rise and fall of Kelsey's chest barely calmed Maggie. "Open your eyes, Kels."

Maggie looked up. Saw Ryan through her tears. He was sprinting, a phone pressed against his ear, then he was kneeling on the other side of Kelsey. His look of alarm must have mirrored her own. "Mags, what happened?"

"There was an explosion or something." Maggie held Kelsey's hand. Her cheek was scraped and the cut on her forehead bled. Her eyes still weren't open.

Ryan frowned. "Truck backfired in the parking lot."

Maggie nodded, even though nothing made sense. "Tango bolted. Kelsey fell." She stiffened. "The horses. We need to get the horses."

Ryan grabbed her arm. His touch reassuring. "Mags, J.D. has the horses. They're fine. He'll get the veterinarian on staff to assess Tango."

Kelsey needed to be assessed too. She finally groaned, then cursed under her breath.

"Kelsey!" Maggie pleaded. She pressed the sleeve of her shirt against the cut on Kelsey's forehead. "Tell me where it hurts the most."

"My pride." Kelsey squinted at Maggie. Her voice cracked. "Hurts. All over."

"You need a doctor." They needed to get to the hospital. Now.

"No." Kelsey's eyes sprang open. She inhaled. Exhaled. Pinched her eyes closed. "Just. Give. Me." She inhaled and added, "A minute." Exhaled and said, "To. Catch. My. Breath."

"You're bleeding." Maggie lifted the sleeve of her shirt to show Kelsey proof.

"Just a scratch." Kelsey rolled onto her back and dabbed lightly at her face. "Bruised. But I'm okay."

"Kelsey, at least let me carry you back to the camper." Ryan set his hand on Kelsey's good arm. "You can get cleaned up. Rest."

"I can walk." Kelsey wiggled her legs to prove they worked. She pushed herself up onto her left elbow. No sooner had she propped herself up than she paled and collapsed against Ryan. Only one word escaped in a long, shaky shudder. "Shoulder."

Ryan never hesitated. He scooped Kelsey into his arms, stood and headed for the campground. His voice had lost all its usual carefree charm. "Kelsey Orr, you need a doctor."

Maggie kept pace with Ryan. "Kelsey, you need to go to the hospital."

"Ryan Sloan, listen up." Kelsey fisted his shirt in her fingers. Her jaw was clenched. Her words forced. Her face blanched. "I need ice. Rest. No hospital. Got it?"

Ryan glanced at Maggie.

"Oh, we got it, big sister." Maggie pressed Kelsey's head against Ryan's chest. "Now stop talking. And let us take care of you for once."

Twenty minutes later, Maggie and Ryan had Kelsey propped up in her bed with pillows and only her boots off. An ice pack was positioned over her right shoulder. Bandages covered the cuts on her face.

Yet, Maggie wasn't in the running for winning any award for good bedside manner. She stood with her arms crossed over her chest and gaped at her uncooperative patient. Forcing herself to sound calm, although it was the last thing she was feeling, she said, "Kelsey. We need to go to the ER. You need an x-ray. Or maybe something more."

Kelsey shook her head. "I'm good right here. The ice is helping."

"Move your arm then," Maggie challenged. If she sounded mean, so be it. She had to get through to her stubborn sister. And she knew deep inside that Kelsey couldn't talk her way out of her shoulder injury. Not this time.

Kelsey narrowed her eyes at Maggie and wiggled her fingers. "See. It's fine."

Maggie's exasperation ratcheted up a notch. Ryan stood in the doorway, hands on his hips. Concern set deep into his face. "Ryan, please tell my sister that she needs to go to the hospital."

"Ryan. Stay out of this." Kelsey's words were curt through her clenched teeth. "I'll go to the doctor on Monday, after we compete tomorrow."

Maggie wanted to blame the pain for her sister's ill-conceived ideas. Frustration and fear curled through her. "Ryan, talk to her, please, while I get another bag of ice."

Out in the kitchen, Maggie squeezed the edge of the small counter and worked to collect herself. She should have known her sister wasn't ready to ride. If she hadn't been distracted thinking about Grant, Maggie might have noticed her sister sitting so stiffly in the saddle. Or that she'd only gripped the reins with one hand. That even without the arm sling, Kelsey had favored her right side the entire day.

"Mags." Ryan's voice was gentle.

"I shouldn't have let her ride." Maggie strengthened her grip. If she held on tight enough, she might find her own balance again.

"I don't think you could've stopped her." Ryan stepped closer and set his hand on Maggie's shoulder. "She's determined to ride tomorrow."

Maggie lowered her head. "We can't compete."

"You're assuming." Ryan squeezed her shoulder. "We won't know without a doctor."

"She won't go to the hospital." Maggie gave up on finding her balance and shoved away from the kitchen counter.

"It doesn't matter." Ryan leaned back against the wall and eyed her. His tone was gentle. "I called Grant. He's on his way."

Grant. Maggie straightened. "Why did you do that?"

"Grant is a doctor." He pointed toward the closed bedroom door. "Kelsey's doctor, in fact."

Not anymore. Same as Grant wasn't anything to Maggie anymore, either. "You didn't have to bother him. The hospital isn't that far from here."

"I'd have called Grant even if we went to the hospital." Ryan watched her, his eyebrows pulled together slightly. "Grant would want to know. He'd want to be here. I'm surprised he wasn't your first call."

Grant couldn't be her first call. He wasn't her "in case of emergency". Or her shoulder to lean on. He wasn't her person. "He had surgeries and patients to see in the clinic. He doesn't need to worry about us too."

"My brother gets to choose who he worries about." Ryan filled another plastic bag with ice and handed it to Maggie. "And, like it or not, Grant will be here within the hour. I'm going to find more ice."

Ryan slipped outside. Maggie walked into the bedroom and changed the ice bags on Kelsey's shoulder.

"Can you sit with me, please?" Kelsey's grin was close-lipped, she was obviously in a lot of pain. "I don't want to argue."

"Me, either." Maggie climbed onto the bed beside her sister and took Kelsey's hand in her own.

Kelsey turned the volume up on the TV,

where one of their favorite cooking shows was playing.

Maggie settled in and waited for her doctor. Waited for Grant to arrive and tell her everything really was going to be okay.

Several hours later, Maggie was outside waiting for Grant to finish talking to her sister. He'd only just arrived with Nolan about thirty minutes ago. Needing fresh air and space, she had escaped for a bit, leaving Nolan inside, sitting on the couch. She leaned her arms on the top railing of the portable corral and searched the sky for a star to wish on. Dusk hadn't yet given way to night. It was too early for wishes.

"Maggie."

Maggie steeled herself and turned around to face her doctor. She knew from one look at him, his expression guarded, his gaze anything but, that the time for wishes was long past. Still, she had to hear it. Had to know. "How bad is it?"

"Kelsey needs surgery." He stepped closer. His words full of discontent. Frustration filled in the rest. "She can't compete tomorrow."

Or ever? Maggie clamped her mouth shut and pulled back the thought. That would be more than she wanted to know now. More than she could handle at the moment.

"Kelsey will be in good hands with Dr. Toro."

He stuck his hands in the back pockets of his jeans and tucked his elbows into his sides. "Kelsey likes Dr. Toro. Trusts him. That's good."

Grant was too far away from Maggie. That wasn't good. She wanted him to hold her, and that was worse. Time to prove to herself she could stand on her own. That she was on her own. She cleared her throat. "You won't be here for the surgery, will you?"

One small shake of his head. "I'm heading to California."

So soon? Maggie widened her stance. Locked her knees. "Then you got the formal offer?"

There was the smallest wince around his eyes. There and gone. "Last Wednesday."

When he'd walked out on his mother at dinner. When he'd kissed Maggie breathless at the pond. Their kiss hadn't been the start of something. It'd been the end. Maggie's mind spun. "When were you going to tell me?"

"I have been telling you," he said.

Right. Once again, she'd fallen for the illusion that things might work out. That they might find a way. Against the odds. Foolish Maggie. And it seemed she wasn't quite done being the fool. "Maybe I could go to the city."

Again, he shook his head. His expression even more remote than his tone. "The city isn't for you, Maggie."

Maggie caught her breath as if she stood too close to the edge of a cliff. She shivered, despite the humid summer night. "The city or you?"

"Both." The word cracked like broken glass in the chasm between them.

He didn't want her. He wanted to get to his future. The one in California. The one that didn't include her. Maggie brushed the dust off her shorts as if putting herself back together. As if that mattered when her entire world was crumbling.

"Don't you see, Maggie? You're busy living the dreams other people created for you, instead of your own." His gaze was startlingly cool and unflinching. His words straightforward. Frank. And far from complimentary. "If you came to California, you'd simply be living my dream. Not yours."

"What about you?" she charged.

"Me?" He pulled back.

"You aren't finding out who you are in California, Grant." Maggie's accusation snapped through the night air. "You are simply running from who you could be here."

He rubbed his fingers over his bottom lip as if attempting to wipe away his words before he spoke them out loud. "Who am I here, exactly?"

"You're more than your medical degree

here." She wanted to believe he'd been happy too. With her. The cold sank deeper into her. She started to ache. "But go on to California. You can hide in your career and guard your heart. After all, those medical books won't ever hurt you."

"At least I'm not exhausting myself trying to earn my family's love," he countered. "It's not your dad's approval you want, Maggie. It's his love. It's why you've stayed as Kelsey's roping partner for so long. It made you important to them and that makes you worthy of their love."

Maggie wrapped her arms around her stomach. Nothing stopped the bone-chilling ache inside her. "At least I have *their* love."

"Is that what you want? My love?" He yanked his hands out of his pockets as if showing her he had nothing left to give. "You already have that."

Maggie stilled. She searched his face. "What are you saying?"

"I love you, Maggie," he said simply.

It was everything. It was nothing. She found love. And still she lost. She hugged herself tighter. Held herself together. Her words whisper quiet. "You can't say that."

"Because I'm leaving?" His words were diluted in logic.

Without me. She nodded.

"But it was never about love." He ran his hands through his hair, then leveled his gaze on her. His words and expression imploring her to understand. "I love you, Maggie. But I can't, nor will I, ask you to put your life second. You were meant to be put first."

He refused to give her a choice. Made the choice for her. "And what about you?" *What if I loved you too*? The words got stuck in her tight, tear-filled throat.

He stepped back. His expression darkened. "I never wanted love."

Or your words. Or you. Because her kind of love wasn't ever enough. *You really are a fool, Maggie.* She fought back her tears. Love wouldn't break her. Not again. Not this time. It was anger, not anguish, in her words. It had to be. "Then I guess this is it. This is goodbye."

Except she didn't move. Neither did he.

Silence descended around them like a dust storm. Thick and suffocating and heart breaking.

But it was long past time Maggie stopped getting in her doctor's way and got out of it instead.

Finally, she found the strength to step around him without shaking. Without trembling. Without pleading for him to just let her love him.

On the camper stairs, she gripped the door

handle, steadied herself and found her words. "Good luck in California, Dr. Sloan. I hope it's everything you dreamed it would be."

CHAPTER TWENTY-FIVE

DREAMS. GRANT HAD stopped dreaming years and years ago. Success was built on hard choices and dedication, not wishes and stars. And it always came down to the execution. Being able to take the steps necessary to advance. To reach the goal. Those steps weren't always easy or simple. Often, they meant leaving things behind.

Grant pressed his palm against his chest. The farther he got from Maggie's camper, the more he felt like he was leaving his future behind. But he wasn't one to second-guess his decisions. This was right for Maggie. She would realize that soon. And if he hurt, that was hardly important. He yanked open the door to Ryan's camper and walked inside.

His brother jumped up from the couch. "What happened?"

"Kelsey needs surgery. Sooner rather than later." Grant paced in the compact kitchen, but it was too small to do more than bump into the counter then the table. "Maggie will withdraw in the morning." At least Kelsey was going to tell her to.

"Maggie can't withdraw." Ryan moved into the already too tight for one person kitchen. "The sponsors are here. They need to see her ride."

"Maggie has no partner." Grant braced his arms against the counter and leaned back as if searching for more space. "Unless you know someone."

"I'm looking at someone." Ryan pointed at him in case Grant misunderstood.

No. Grant had just told his cowgirl he loved her, then walked away. *Walked. Away.* Left the best woman he'd ever known behind. Because the opportunity of a lifetime waited in another state. And because he never wanted to hold her back. "Stop looking at me. I'm not qualified."

"You can rope, Grant." Ryan straightened to his full height and set his hands on his hips, expanding his space as if to better make his point. "I saw you and Maggie practicing together last week in the arena."

"On a plastic steer head," Grant argued. "Not a live steer." Like the ones Maggie roped for a living.

"You roped all through high school," Ryan countered. "It's like riding a bike. It'll all come back once you get in the box."

It wasn't like riding a bike. Besides, there was more at stake than Grant's pride. "I competed fifteen years ago. I was a kid. For fun." And to be with his brothers.

"You can do this for Maggie." Determination and a plea filtered through Ryan's words. "You need to do this for her."

"I need to shower." He'd barely changed out of his scrubs after surgery when he got Ryan's call about Kelsey's fall. Instead of heading home, he'd stopped at the Feisty Owl to grab Nolan and then drove straight to Amarillo. Grant ran his hand over his head. "Besides, Maggie won't want me as her partner. Not now."

"What did you do?" Ryan's frown settled deep. He studied Grant closer.

"Nothing." Grant kept his arms at his sides as if he had nothing to hide. "Maggie's got her life. I've got mine. It wasn't ever supposed to be anything. We both knew that."

Ryan's shoulders dropped. "Please tell me you didn't say that to her."

Grant shook his head. What he told her was worse. The words he gave Maggie were ones that were hard to come back from. He'd meant them. He loved Maggie. But he had to let her go.

Ryan braced an arm across the bathroom door and blocked Grant from entering. "What did you tell Maggie exactly?"

"Leave it alone, Ryan," Grant urged, then added, "Please."

"I can't." Ryan frowned. "Maggie is my friend. You're my brother."

"You can't fix this," Grant said.

Ryan peered at him. His eyes narrowed. "Do you love Maggie?"

"Why does everyone keep asking me that?" Grant dragged his palms over his face.

"You do. Wow. Never thought. Wow." Ryan slapped him on the shoulder. "That's all that really matters."

"Except it doesn't matter, Ryan." Grant flung one arm out, then motioned over his head. "I live on one coast. She lives in a camper."

"It can work," Ryan argued.

"Really? How's that look?" Grant set his hands on his hips. "Phone calls and weekends. Except weekends Maggie competes. And I'm with patients or in the OR on weekdays. Maybe we text during the day. Chat over video in the evenings. That's not a relationship." At least not the kind he would want with Maggie.

With Maggie he'd want to be present. For her. With her. He'd want to be there if she needed him. Not a phone call and a flight away. He would want to be close enough that he could get to her. Like he had tonight.

"But it can't just end between you two." Ryan

ran the back of his hand over his mouth. His frown returned. "It's not supposed to work like that."

"It's all I've got," Grant said.

"Then at least give Maggie a shot, Grant," Ryan urged. "Ride as her partner tomorrow. If she can secure the automatic bid as a heeler to the championships, it'll buy her time to find a new partner."

If you love her, Dr. Sloan, wouldn't you do everything in your power to make Maggie happy? Kelsey had been willing to do whatever it took for her sister. Heck, Kelsey was still trying, even as injured as she was. If he loved Maggie… Grant crossed his arms over his chest and sighed. "Who do we talk to?"

Ryan pumped his fist in the air. "Let's go see J.D. His uncle runs the show around here."

"J.D. Wolfolk?" Grant asked. At his brother's nod, Grant said, "I saw J.D. last week at the clinic."

"I know. He told me." Ryan grinned at him. "Sang your praises, too, by the way. Better get your roping arm warmed up, Doc. J.D. will get you in the arena with Maggie."

THE NEXT MORNING, Grant sat atop Moonshine in the outdoor warmup arena, wound his rope in his hands, and watched Maggie lead Lady Dasher toward him.

Inside the gate, her gaze landed on him fully. Her eyes widened before her eyebrows slammed together. "Grant. What are you doing?"

At least she hadn't called him Dr. Sloan. Most likely because he was in jeans, a plaid shirt, and a cowboy hat. Still, he considered it a small success. "I'm your roping partner." When she opened her mouth, he rushed on, "I won't be as fast as you're used to with Kelsey. But I can promise clean catches on all four steers. We just need to take it one go-round at a time."

"You can't." She knocked her cowboy hat higher on her head and squeezed her forehead as if working hard to catch up. "How did you? Why are you?"

"He's clear, Mags." Ryan walked up. "Grant is good to compete as your partner."

"I don't know." Maggie smashed her cowboy hat lower on her head.

The brim shadowed her face, blocking her gaze. Locking Grant out. But he wasn't there to find out if she'd slept as poorly as he had. Or if she'd replayed every bit of their conversation. Or if she still hurt like he did. He was there to compete. For her. Nothing else.

Grant's fingers tensed around the rope.

"Look, I spoke to Lewis Trumbly this morning. We ran into each other at the check-in at the arena. He's really looking forward to seeing you compete today."

"But the sponsorship was for Kelsey and me as a team." Maggie shifted and guided Lady Dasher closer.

"They sponsor individuals all the time, Mags," Ryan countered. "You have to ride and compete with Grant. Then talk to Lewis."

"What do you have to lose?" Grant pressed.

Maggie was silent. Then she exhaled a long breath. "You're right. A sponsorship was always the goal." She mounted Lady Dasher in one fluid motion, naturally and easily. She nodded at Grant, her chin firm. "Let's get warmed up."

Grant was as good as his word. He roped all four steers, not in the fastest time, but clean and quick enough to advance. Maggie was giving Grant tips for the second round when another roper Grant recognized from the first round approached. If he wasn't mistaken, the cowboy and his partner had clocked one of the fastest times.

Introductions complete, Maggie smiled at their competition. "You ready for the next round, Vince?"

Vince took off his cowboy hat and tapped it

against his leg. "That's why I'm here. I'm hoping you'd consider partnering for the final rounds."

Surprise crossed Maggie's face. "What happened to Ross?"

"Twisted his knee wrestling that steer earlier." Vince glanced at Grant. His cowboy hat stilled against his leg. Uncertainty filtered his words. "We were hoping Doc Sloan might have a minute to look at it. J.D. said you really helped him with his hip."

"I'm not here officially as medical personnel," Grant warned. "But I can give you my personal opinion."

"We'd sure appreciate it." Vince grinned and turned his attention back to Maggie. "About teaming up, Maggie. If you want to ride with Doc Sloan, I don't want to interfere."

"I'll make this simple." Grant stepped forward. "Maggie will ride with you. And I'll check on Ross and his knee if she's okay with that. That way we are all sticking to what we're good at."

Maggie nodded and shook Vince's hand. "Looks like I've lost my partner and gained a new one."

Vince thanked Grant, then settled his hat back on his head. "Well, Maggie, what do you say we go get ourselves a jackpot?"

Grant consulted with a handful more com-

petitors along with the medics on hand while
Maggie and Vince roped their way into the
finals. They secured a second-place finish
overall. Not the automatic bid Grant knew
Maggie had been hoping for. Yet, there was a
decent cash prize for second place. And Maggie seemed happy. She'd even given Grant a
quick, entirely too obligatory hug. Other than
that, she'd kept her distance from him the entire day. He should've been fine with that. This
was her community, not his. Now it was coming to a close and Grant was equal parts restless and frustrated, despite not having a right
to feel anything. He'd walked away last night.
Today was about Maggie.

They stood outside with Nolan and Kelsey
discussing where to go for dinner to celebrate.

"Nice riding with you today, Maggie." Vince
walked by and tipped his hat at Maggie. "My
cousin Shayna is looking for a new heeler. Her
partner is having a baby. Can I give her your
number?"

"Definitely." Maggie smiled. "And thanks
for giving me a chance today."

"Pleasure was all mine." Vince stopped beside her. "Are you heading to San Antonio for
the Rodeo Roundup? I could use a partner
there. Doc Sloan doesn't think Ross will be
back in the saddle that quick."

"I can make that work." Maggie avoided looking at Grant. "Text me the details."

"Check your phone." Vince laughed. "Already sent everything." With that he sauntered off to celebrate.

Maggie's name was called again. Grant turned to see Lewis Trumbly from Denim Country walking toward her. He wore a big smile and even bigger belt buckle. "Maggie, any chance you might be free for dinner? I'd like to discuss a potential business arrangement."

"Yes, she's free for dinner." That came from Kelsey. Maggie's sister gave Lewis Trumbly a gingerly hug before slipping her hand back into Nolan's.

Grant stepped back. Lewis kept the two sisters occupied with a quick rundown of the company's thoughts on sponsorship and expanded his dinner invitation to Kelsey and Nolan. The foursome turned and started walking toward the parking lot. Maggie never turned back. Never looked back.

That was because she had her goal in sight. And it had never been Grant. He should be satisfied. He'd played a small part in helping her that afternoon.

Grant spun around, headed for Ryan's camper, and told himself he would be happy soon.

CHAPTER TWENTY-SIX

KELSEY OPENED HER eyes to the smell of bacon sizzling and the feeling of pain throughout her body. An unexpected fall from a horse tended to leave bruises that didn't fade overnight. Still, she wasn't completely miserable. Maggie had secured sponsorship with Denim Country last night at dinner. And Kelsey couldn't have been more proud of her little sister.

Yet, the victory was slightly hollow. Kelsey wouldn't be joining her sister on her new journey. That left Kelsey adrift and, for the first time in years, without a purpose. Looking after her little sister had been Kelsey's purpose for so long now. Selfishly, she wanted Maggie to stick around, if only to give Kelsey a job to do. Who was Kelsey supposed to protect now? And what exactly was she supposed to do with her own life?

The bedroom door opened slowly. Nolan stepped through carrying a tray and wearing a less-than-confident smile. "I made breakfast.

But I wasn't sure if your stomach might be upset. Or even if you are a breakfast person."

She was quickly becoming a Nolan person. Kelsey scooted awkwardly into a sitting position. Nolan set the tray on the side table and was at her side in an instant, gathering pillows behind her and seeing to her comfort. Only Maggie had ever really taken care of Kelsey and that had only been when she'd let her little sister. Funny how she didn't mind Nolan looking after her all that much. Even more telling was that she looked forward to returning the favor someday. She was definitely Team Nolan, and they hadn't even gone on a first date.

Kelsey ordered her heart to stand down and stop rushing things. Then she glanced at the side table, rather than risk giving her thoughts away, and gaped. "Nolan, that's a mini-buffet."

"Like I said earlier, I didn't know what you preferred." Nolan shifted from side to side and presented each choice. "Butter toast is easy on an upset stomach. The scrambled egg toss is good protein. Fruit seems to be the go-to for lighter breakfast eaters. Fresh orange juice and crispy bacon for the traditionalist. A smoothie for the nutrition minded."

Kelsey snagged a piece of bacon and eyed him. "Careful, Chef. I could get used to this."

His smile grew. "I was sort of hoping you would."

Interesting. Her chef sounded like he might be Team Kelsey. She chewed on her bacon and tipped her head toward the empty side of the bed where Maggie had slept. "Why don't you put the tray between us, and then we can share?"

He picked up the tray. "I like how you think."

And she liked him. "But don't think I'm going to share that bacon."

"Have it all." Nolan settled on the bed, his movements gentle as if he was afraid of jostling her and causing her pain. "There's more in the kitchen. I wasn't sure if Maggie would want some when she gets back from tending to the horses."

Maggie had slipped out around dawn. Kelsey knew why. Her little sister did most of her thinking with the horses. And Kelsey suspected crying too. Maggie's pillow had been damp, when Kelsey touched it after her sister had left the bedroom. One more reason the victory of signing a national sponsor felt hollow. Her little sister's heart was broken. And no jackpot or sponsorship check would ever be large enough to mend that. Kelsey picked at the grapes. "Did you talk to Maggie this morning?"

Nolan shook his head. "I never heard her leave. She left a note stuck on the cabinet asking me to check on you."

Maggie trusted Nolan or she wouldn't have left. Would Maggie trust that Kelsey knew what was in her heart? Did Kelsey trust her own heart? Kelsey chewed on a grape, then said, "I need to talk to her about my surgery and what it all means."

"What does it mean?" Nolan offered Kelsey the orange juice. When she declined, he took a deep sip.

"It means my life is being turned upside down." Kelsey reached for the toast to calm her suddenly upset stomach. "I have no career. No prospects. Just a business idea, a whole bunch of rhinestones and a lot more hope."

"Sounds to me like you have a start then." Nolan took her hand in his and eyed her. His gaze warm and thoughtful. His words gentle and affectionate. "I want to be there with you while you figure everything out."

"Why?" Kelsey blurted.

He held her gaze. "Because I like you. A lot."

Kelsey curled her fingers around his. "Isn't it too soon? Too quick?"

"We can take things slow." Nolan squeezed her hand. "Maybe go on that first date finally."

"I'd like that." Kelsey smiled. "A lot."

"It's settled. I have a first date to plan." Nolan's thumb stroked across her palm.

A slow, steady caress that soothed and calmed her. That felt extraordinarily right.

"Now that we're dating," Nolan said. His half-grin lifted into his cheek. "We should discuss your living situation."

Kelsey blinked. Maggie would need the camper on the road. Kelsey needed a new career and a new place to live. But she'd only ever lived with Maggie. Never alone. Panic started to set in.

But Nolan blocked it as if he'd always been by her side. He said, "There's a vacant two-bedroom apartment behind the Owl. You could stay there after your surgery. You'd have a chef next door to cook every meal for you if you wanted. And Maggie would have a bedroom to stay in while she's in town."

Not so very alone after all. Kelsey opened her mouth.

Nolan stopped her and said, "Before you say no, I should tell you that Abby and Wes own the place. They're happy to let you and Maggie stay there."

"I don't know what to say." One minute she was adrift without direction. Now things were seemingly falling into place. With little assistance from her. Kelsey and Maggie always made their own way. On their own. But what if they didn't have to anymore?

"Just tell me that you'll think about it," Nolan said. "Run it by Maggie."

Kelsey nodded. Then, for the first time in too long, she listened to her heart and followed its lead. "Is it too fast if I ask you to kiss me before our first official date?"

Nolan grinned, brushed her hair from her cheeks and leaned forward. Their lips met. He kissed her as if he had all day to learn her secrets and nowhere else he'd rather be.

And right then, Kelsey knew exactly where she was meant to be.

CHAPTER TWENTY-SEVEN

IT WAS LUNCHTIME when Grant walked into the kitchen after helping Carter and Josh set a new copper still at the distillery. He wiped his boots on the mat and greeted his grandfather and uncle, telling them, "I called a family meeting. Everyone is on their way."

Sam's chin lowered to his chest and his wise gaze settled on Grant. "Looks like you'll have those loose ends tied up before you board your plane Tuesday night."

That was the intention. Grant had returned from Amarillo last night and found his grandfather sitting on the porch. He had bypassed the details of his fallout with Maggie, only relayed the relevant information about Kelsey's injury and Maggie's second-place finish. Then he got to the essential stuff like how he'd rescheduled dinner with his mother, having walked out on the first one, and planned to tell his brothers. Those were the loose ends. Things with Maggie were just at an end.

Ryan walked into the kitchen, washed his

hands, and glanced at Grant. "Want a sandwich? I'm making one."

Grant shook his head. "I'm good."

Ryan looked skeptical but kept his commentary to himself. Still, Grant saw the concern in his brother's gaze. And he appreciated it, although, it was hardly necessary. Grant was fine. Or he would be. In time. "Grandpa. Uncle. Now's the time to place your sandwich order."

"I'll take one of whatever anyone is making," Caleb called out from the laundry room.

Josh and Carter arrived soon after. Sandwiches assembled and everyone seated around the kitchen table, it was time to start the meeting. Grant glanced at Carter. "Where is Tess?"

"Out with Abby and Paige. They're getting ready for their girl's night at the Owl." Carter popped open a soda and took a sip. "They want Maggie to join them. And Kelsey too if she's feeling up to it. When will they be back?"

Grant shook his head.

"No, Maggie can't join them." Carter arched an eyebrow at Grant and frowned.

"Maggie isn't coming back." At least not to the farmhouse. And certainly not to Grant.

"Where is she?" Caleb dumped a pile of cheddar potato chips on his plate.

Grant flattened his palms on the placemat as if he needed to steady himself. "I don't know."

"Is that why we're here?" Josh reached over and grabbed the chip bag from his twin. "To find Maggie and bring her back home?"

"No." There was no finding Maggie. No bringing her back. No home without Maggie. Grant cleared that unsettling thought from his mind. This wasn't about Maggie.

His brothers all shifted to look at Ryan.

"Don't look at me." Ryan held up half of his sandwich and leaned back in his chair. "I have tried talking to Grant about Maggie. In Amarillo and again this morning. He's locked down tighter than Carter's single barrel bourbon whiskey."

"It's good to discuss and share these things with your family." Caleb considered Grant. He sounded very much like a school counselor speaking to an uncooperative elementary school kid.

Grant returned his younger brother's stare and remained silent.

"Carter and I were with you all morning, Grant. Why didn't you say anything?" Josh eyed Grant and scowled. "We're here to help, you know."

Not with Maggie. No one could help with Maggie. Grant tugged at his hair, then said, "This isn't to do with her. There's another family issue we need to talk about."

"More important to you than Maggie?" Ryan's eyebrows lifted. Disbelief cast a shadow across his face.

Grant was beginning to wonder if anything or anyone could be more important than Maggie. But that was for Grant to deal with. On his own terms. But still, there were things that he and his brothers needed to decide. "Mom is back."

"Back in New York?" Caleb crunched on a potato chip sounding completely unconcerned.

"Or is she back in the news again for creating an advanced artificial heart? The likes of which the world hasn't seen." Josh looked equally as unmoved as his twin.

Grant glanced at his grandfather and took a deep breath. "Our mother is back in Three Springs."

A stillness settled around the table. Constricting and uncomfortable.

Ryan was the first to recover. Though there was still shock on his face. "Who invited her here?"

"It's her hometown." Sam braced his elbows on the table. "Lilian doesn't require an invitation to return."

"The town is one thing." Ryan tapped his finger against the table. "But the farmhouse.

Here. That's another thing entirely. She absolutely requires an invite to come here."

Caleb crumpled a napkin in his hand and tossed it on the table. His natural good humor was gone. His shoulders were stiff. His face set. "What does she want?"

"What does it even matter?" Ryan crossed his arms over his chest and slipped into the same rigid pose as Caleb.

Grant wanted his mother's return not to matter. He wanted to ignore her and the past. But he didn't want to carry all that into his new life. Like he had told his grandfather last night on the porch, he wanted a fresh start on the West Coast. That meant wrapping up the unfinished things like long overdue conversations with his mother. Even if it might be difficult. He'd already walked away from Maggie. Nothing could be worse than that. He said, "She wants to talk."

"Have you seen her, Grant?" Carter's gaze was probing. His words solemn. "Have you talked to her in person?"

Grant nodded and met his older brother's stare. "I saw her last week. At the clinic, in exam room four, to be exact. She pretended to be a patient to see me."

Josh dropped his head in his hands. Caleb studied his plate as if searching for answers among the breadcrumbs. Carter opened and closed his mouth, then looked at Sam and Roy.

The older duo sat shoulder to shoulder. Each one had their hands folded together and resting on the placemat in front of them. If either one had an opinion, it wasn't being shared. As if they both understood the brothers had their own decisions to make. And those required time and deliberation, as much as each one needed.

"Why now?" Ryan tipped his chair back, braced his hands behind his head, and frowned at the ceiling. "Why is she here now?"

"I'm having dinner with her tonight," Grant stated.

Ryan's chair legs thudded against the floor and his wide, surprised gaze landed on Grant.

Grant added, "Hopefully, I'll find out exactly what she wants."

"Why are you even going to dinner?" Josh pushed away from the table, gathered several empty plates, and paced into the kitchen. Caleb was not far behind him.

"The truth is, I want closure." Grant looked around the table. "I want to close the past before I get on the plane for California on Tuesday."

The entire family frowned at the mention of California. Same as they'd been frowning since Friday morning at breakfast after Maggie and her sister had left for Amarillo. That was when Grant had told his family that his job at the West Coast clinic was official, and his flight was booked. Their upbeat congratulations had been forced. Their smiles more than a little strained. Even as they tried to be supportive of what Grant wanted.

Carter rubbed his chin and eyed Grant. "Do you want us to go with you to dinner?"

"I agreed to go. I never agreed for any of you to," Grant explained. "I'm only telling you so you can decide what you want to do. You can join me or not."

"Not joining you." Josh braced his arms behind him and leaned against the island. Caleb stood beside his twin, looking as if his mind was also set.

Carter said simply and firmly, "I want to talk to Tess first."

Grant envied his brother. He wanted to talk to Maggie too. Even more, he wanted Maggie to be with him when he went back to dinner with his mother. To hold her hand. To keep himself steady and anchored.

"If you want backup, just say the word." Carter's smile was there and gone. "You know I will be there for you."

"You are always there for us, Carter," Grant reassured his brother. . "I'll take this one."

"I'll drive you and wait in the parking lot, if you want." Ryan set his hand on Grant's shoulder. "But I won't promise anything about going inside."

"I got this." After all, Grant had to prove he was more than fine on his own. Just as he had been before he'd met Maggie. That, in fact, nothing had changed. And his life was as it should be.

At precisely six o'clock that evening, Grant walked into The Spiced Beehive Bistro in Belleridge. He greeted the hostess and saw his mother already seated at a private booth against the far wall. He headed to the booth and tucked his hands in his pockets, along with his apprehension. It was only one conversation. Not a commitment to be in each other's lives going forward. Unless he chose that.

"Grant. I'm surprised you called. And even more surprised you're here now." His mother motioned to the other side of the booth. "Please. Sit."

Gran slid into the booth. "I thought we should talk before I head to California."

"So, you're going then," his mother said. Surprise shifted swiftly through her gaze.

Grant nodded. "Is there a reason I shouldn't go?" Aside from Maggie. The woman he loved. Who'd left town too.

"I just assumed from talking to your grand-father the other night." Lilian picked up her wine glass and waved her other hand. "Never mind. You know what is right for you."

Grant ordered a Misty Grove straight bour-bon whiskey, one of his favorites from his brother's distillery, when the waitress arrived. Sipping the whiskey also gave him a sense that his family was with him. He glanced at his mother. "If you haven't tried Carter's whis-key, you should. It's award winning and some of the best out there."

"I have several bottles at home." Lilian watched him. "I keep up on the distillery and your brother's success. All of your successes."

But always from afar. Grant wasn't quite sure how he felt about that. Although he imagined he'd be following Maggie's success from the same kind of distance. But tonight was about finding answers. Getting closure. "Clearly, you've been content to keep tabs on us from the outside. Why are you here now?"

"I'm alone, Grant." His mother went straight to the heart of things too.

Grant appreciated that, despite being frus-trated by her revelation.

She added, "I find myself alone with the cold comfort of an illustrious career that is quickly coming to a close."

"You didn't have to be alone," he countered, unable to hide the decades' old anger and hurt. "You chose that path." Just as he was choosing his. He shifted in the booth, rolled his shoulders as if that truth no longer fit him quite so well.

"I came back, but you didn't know." Lilian sipped her wine, stared into the burgundy liquid, then looked at him. "You must have been around ten years old. I went to a baseball game. You and Ryan were on the same team. Carter was watching the twins. Your grandmother was selling snacks. Your grandfather was in the dugout with the rest of your team. No one noticed me up in the bleachers."

Grant searched his memory. Tried to place his mother in the metal bleachers and failed. Surely, he would've noticed her, if only for the simple fact that she would've stood out in her business suit and heels.

"My hair was longer back then, and at the time, I was a poor surgical resident." She gave him a tight-lipped smile as if she'd read his thoughts. "I wore scrubs a lot in those days and clothes I picked up at the thrift store."

"Why didn't you say anything?" he asked.

"Why sit on the bleachers and leave as if you'd never been there?"

"I didn't feel like I fit in. Everyone had a place. A role." She swirled the wine in her glass. "I figure you might know a little something about that."

Grant leaned back in the bench seat. "Why would I know about that?"

"We are doctors, not cowboys." She touched her pearl earring. "To truly fit in around here, you need to be a cowboy through and through."

Grant wasn't so sure. He hadn't felt out of place at the farmhouse. The clinic. Or with Maggie. He'd felt connected. Surely, he'd find those connections on the West Coast. Except his mother lived on the East Coast. Alone. And looking at her now, there was a fragile air of loneliness around her. Nothing obvious. There in the faint lines around her eyes. In her uncertain fidgeting as she checked her jewelry as if to make sure all was still as it should be. California seemed to be everything Grant ever wanted, but was it?

"When I came back, I saw how happy you and your brothers were. How genuinely alive my parents were with their grandsons. You'd all settled into this wonderful life without me." Lilian shrugged. "I didn't want to disrupt that."

"We had no choice. You didn't give us any

other," Grant argued. Same as he hadn't given Maggie a choice. Grant nudged that aside. "We would've made room for you. You were our mom."

"I couldn't see how at the time. How I could slot back into your lives without messing up everything you'd built together." She rotated a gold bracelet into place, then flicked her wrist. "Besides, your Gran Claire was always better at the mom thing than me."

Grant picked up his whiskey glass. "That's your excuse for not even trying to make it work? You weren't cut out to be a mother?"

"Those are the excuses I used to convince myself. To tell myself that I was making the right decision." Lilian toasted him with her wine glass. "The truth is something much simpler. Stubborn pride. I vowed never to return here. I told your grandparents I was always meant to be more than Three Springs. That my dreams were bigger than this place."

Grant had promised his Gran Claire he would pursue his best life, even if it meant leaving Three Springs. She'd never wanted him to feel tied down. He'd always wanted out. He'd left for college, more than ready to fly. Then medical school. Yet, when he'd returned this time, tied down wasn't how he'd felt.

"I kept my word and proved I was right."

There was no pride. No satisfaction in her words. Only disappointment. "Now I'm realizing Three Springs had much more to offer me. And I fear it's too late."

Grant took in the lost look shadowing his mother's face and the regret in her eyes. Grant hadn't been lost with Maggie. He'd been grounded and felt more like himself than he had in years. Would he look back at his life like his mother with more regret than gratification? "So, what are you saying? You wouldn't do it all over again. If you had a do-over, you'd give up all your achievements and success for a country life in Three Springs?"

"No." She tucked her hair behind her ear and shook her head. "I would still want my career. But I would do it all differently."

"How?" Grant leaned his elbows on the table.

"Easy." Her smile was genuine. Her gaze insightful. "I would've fought harder to have it all."

CHAPTER TWENTY-EIGHT

LATE MONDAY MORNING, Maggie sat on a metal bench outside Dr. Toro's SportsMed Clinic and waited for Kelsey to finish her pre-op blood-work. Sitting inside the clinic had been too distracting. She kept hoping Grant would appear every time an exam room door opened.

Ryan had pulled out of the parking lot fifteen minutes ago with the sisters' trailer, horses, and Nolan in the passenger seat. Nolan had convinced Maggie that the apartment behind the Feisty Owl was the most suitable place for Kelsey to recover after her surgery. Then Kelsey and Nolan had persuaded Maggie to let Ryan take the horses to the Sloan stables, where they would be safe and well cared for.

Maggie wanted to be in Ryan's truck, headed to the Sloan farmhouse too. She wasn't sure if Grant had already left for California, and she'd been afraid to ask Ryan. But showing up unannounced at the farmhouse would only remind Maggie how much she already missed Grant. And she certainly didn't need any more reminders. Her city doc who'd accused her of living other's dreams, who loved her but didn't want to be loved in return. Her city doc was infuriating. Then he'd stepped up and competed as her partner. To give her the opportunity to secure a sponsorship and reach her goal. He'd held his own in the competition. She'd been impressed. Grateful. Loved him even more. To top it off, the exasperating man up and left. Walked away. Again.

Maggie wanted to kick her doc. And kiss him. She stretched her legs out and stared at her new suede cowboy boots, courtesy of Denim Country. Grant loved her. She loved him. She should be dancing among the clouds in her sky-blue boots. Instead, she was parked on a bench. *Alone.*

Worse was what Maggie saw in her future. More time alone. But she'd gotten the national sponsorship. Reached their financial goal. Where was all the happy? Surely, she'd earned that.

Kelsey slid onto the bench, set her surgery information folder on her lap, and took Maggie's hand. "Ready or not, surgery in one week, Mags."

It was the first time the sisters had been truly alone since the accident. Maggie noted the relief she heard in Kelsey's words. That soothed her even as she stepped into another hard conversation. "There isn't going to be another roping competition for you, is there?"

"No." Kelsey tightened her grip on Maggie's hand and stared out over the parking lot. "Do you hate me?"

"Of course not." Maggie hated herself for letting it all get so far out of hand. Hated that they'd gotten to this place where her sister—her best friend—had to ask that. Maggie wrapped her arm around her sister's waist and set her head on Kelsey's good shoulder. "Oh, Kels, how did we get here?"

"Rodeo was a thing we could do with Dad. A way to spend time with him." Kelsey stretched her arm around Maggie's waist. "It just became our thing. You were hurting after your breakup, and I wanted you to have an adventure. Something to look forward to."

Maggie grinned. "We've certainly had an adventure."

"Yeah. We have." Kelsey released Maggie's hand and touched the bracelet wrapped around her wrist. "Now it feels like roping is the thing we do because no one ever told us it was okay to do other things."

"What does it look like from here on out, Kels?" Maggie straightened and shifted on the bench to face her sister. "Do those other things you want have to do with Nolan?"

"Yeah." Affection softened Kelsey's smile. "But it's not just about Nolan. I want to have a business with my clothing. A real one. And I want a kitchen window that overlooks a garden, not a highway or a barren campground. Silly, isn't it?"

"Not so very silly." Maggie folded her arms in her lap. She'd liked waking up at the Sloan farmhouse. Being a part of things there. Helping where she could. Cleaning the stables. Gardening with Tess. Joining a spontaneous card game after dinner. Even the midnight meet-ups. She hadn't known how much such simple things would fulfill her.

"I'm ready, Mags, to park and stay for a while." Kelsey leaned back and extended her legs as if practicing her new lifestyle. "I want to sit and watch the world go by. Not just spend every day getting by. I want to do all that in Three Springs."

"I'm really happy for you." Maggie squeezed her sister's arm. "You deserve to be happy. To have everything you want."

Kelsey covered Maggie's hand. "What about you, Mags? You deserve the same."

"The rodeo and I aren't done yet," Maggie confessed. "I'm going to partner with Vince Harrow and maybe even his cousin. But I really want to compete in breakaway."

"You never told me." Kelsey smiled.

"I didn't want you to think I was giving up on us," Maggie said. "On our team. I wanted you to know I was invested. That I believed in us."

"Oh, Mags, you kept me going," Kelsey said. "Through every injury. Every loss."

"I still need you, Kels," Maggie said. "Even if it's in the stands."

"I'll be there. You don't have to worry about that." Kelsey tipped her head and eyed Maggie. "There's someone else you need, Mags."

Maggie turned away from her sister. Frowned at the sky. "Don't say it, Kels."

"I sort of have to." Her sister's words were affection filled. "As your big sister, it's my duty to look after you and your heart."

"We aren't like Nolan and you." Maggie ran her hands over her faded jean shorts. She was denim and dust. Grant was dress slacks and silk. "We don't want the same things. In the same place. It wasn't ever going to work long-term. We both knew that." And if she'd hoped for a different outcome, she'd course corrected over the weekend.

"But you guys are good together," Kelsey argued. "Everyone could see it."

"Everyone but Grant," Maggie countered. "Besides, we both chose our careers over what we might have together." And one day Maggie would know that was a good choice. But that day wasn't today. Not when her heart was still bruised. And she wasn't feeling so good.

"It's what you do have together," Kelsey stressed. "There's no might about how you two feel for each other. Maybe it's time to let love back in, Mags."

Maggie kicked at a pebble on the sidewalk. "Grant wasn't interested in love."

"Did you tell him you love him?" Kelsey asked.

Maggie frowned and clenched her teeth together.

"Or, better yet, did you show him?" Kelsey rushed on. "Really show him what it means to be loved by you, Mags?"

"What are you saying, Kels?" Maggie asked.

"I'm saying if you love him, then show him that you really are better together. That being together is worth more than any career. Any belt buckle. Any medical award. Convince him that the love you share is worth fighting for."

Maggie eyed her sister. "How am I supposed to do that? He's in California."

"You pack your bags, little sister." Kelsey smiled at her. "And go get your doc."

CHAPTER TWENTY-NINE

IT WAS AFTER dinner when Grant dismounted from Moonshine and returned the gelding to the stables. He'd been restless after he'd returned from Dr. Toro's clinic where he'd spent the afternoon going over patient cases and notes with the rodeo doc. Then Ryan had arrived at the ranch with Maggie's horses and trailer and no Maggie.

Grant had unloaded Lady Dasher and taken the gelding to the pasture as if the horse would answer all Grant's questions about his cowgirl. Where was she? What was she doing? How was she? Ryan had trailed after Grant as if waiting for Grant to ask him about Maggie. Grant kept quiet. Hearing about Maggie would only make him want to see her. Be with her. So, Grant had saddled Moonshine hoping to exercise away his lingering fascination with his cowgirl.

Grant gave Moonshine an extra rub down and wondered if he'd ever stop thinking about Maggie.

His grandfather appeared outside Moonshine's stall and rested his arms on the stall gate. "Find what you were looking for?"

"No." Not even a glimpse of Maggie. Grant brushed the horse. "I was trying to gather my thoughts."

"Maybe you didn't ride far enough," Sam mused. "Your gran used to ride clear to the next county, trying to gather her thoughts."

Grant paused and looked at his grandfather.

"Sometimes your Gran Claire came back right as rain." Grandpa Sam touched the silver slide on his bolo tie. His expression thoughtful. "Other times she thundered in here like a storm."

Grant felt a bit like a storm tonight. Unsettled and unhappy without Maggie. Agitated and annoyed that his feelings seemed to be anything but fleeting. He asked, "What did you do when Gran Claire came in like a storm?"

His grandfather shrugged. "I let it pass, of course."

"So, this too shall pass." Grant nodded and continued brushing the horse. He just needed to wait it out. Have a little more patience with himself.

"I let your gran's sour mood pass," his grandfather corrected. His words were firm. "But not once did I ever leave your gran. There's a difference."

Grant had left Maggie twice now. His mood dipped past surly. It was the only choice. Except his mother's words at dinner came back to him. *I'd fight harder to have it all.* Grant hadn't fought at all. He glanced at his grandfather. "Gran Claire and you worked because you wanted the same things. Shared the same dream."

"We worked because we had the same values." Sam watched Grant, his gaze steady and shrewd. "We compromised. We tried to do what was best for us as a couple. But it took work to get to that mindset."

"But what if we're just too different," Grant said.

"Your Gran Claire wasn't a rancher or a farmer." His grandpa tossed that out like it was a well-known, unsurprising fact. "Your Gran Claire had dreams outside these county lines. Followed them, too, when we were just newly dating."

Grant finished brushing the horse, gave the gelding one last pat, and stepped from the stall. He dropped the brush in a bucket and faced his grandpa. "You're telling me that Gran Claire left Three Springs."

"She sure did." His grandpa chuckled and

smoothed his beard into place. "Packed up her car one night. Drove to my parents' place and told me she was heading to the city."

Grant had never heard this story. Not even a quick reference to it. "Why would she do that?" His gran Claire had only ever talked about her love for the pond. The farmhouse. His grandfather.

"Your gran claimed she had things to prove. Dreams to chase." One of his grandpa's white eyebrows arched. "Wings she claimed that needed to be spread beyond this small town."

Gran Claire had told Grant never to be afraid to spread his wings wide and go after his best life, even if it was outside his hometown. Now he learned she'd done the same. "How long was she gone?"

"A little over a year." His grandpa touched his watch as if he wanted to bring back that time.

Grant walked along beside his grandfather, trying to keep up. "Did you ever hear from her during that year?"

"Not a peep." Grandpa Sam stepped into the evening air and grinned at Grant. "Of course, we didn't have your fancy phones and all the gadgets to get in touch like you do now."

"But Gran Claire came back," Grant said.

"I got home one afternoon and found her sitting on the porch. Her suitcase sat beside the rocking chair," his grandpa explained. "Before I could greet her, she told me: Samuel Corbin Sloan I thought you'd like to know I'm done." His grandfather chuckled. "I looked at her and asked, 'Done with what, Claire?'" He smiled. "You know what she said?"

Grant shook his head.

"She looked me straight in the eye and told me she was done proving she could leave." His grandpa clapped his hands together and laughed. "Your Gran Claire sure had spirit. One of the things I loved about her."

Maggie had spirit. It was one of the many things Grant loved about his cowgirl.

"Well, I asked her what she intended to do then," his grandfather continued his story. "She stood up and said: 'Now, I'm going to prove I can stay.'" His grandpa's soft chuckle mixed with the evening breeze. "Can you believe that?"

Grant wanted to ask his grandmother why she'd left. But even more, he wanted to know how she knew it was time to come home.

"We were married six months later," his grandfather added. "That was a wonderful wedding day. But one of my favorite days was walking home and finding your Gran Claire on my porch like she hadn't left with her suit-case and my heart."

Grant knew a little something about losing his heart.

"Your Gran Claire stuck by me every day after that," his grandpa stated with pride and more than a touch of sweetness. "And I stuck by her. No matter what, we always knew we were in it together."

If you find a love that sticks when you're at your worst, Grant, you best pay attention. That's the important kind. More of Gran Claire's wisdom that today made even more sense. Grant finally understood. Understood the love he had with Maggie was the kind he needed to pay attention to. It was the kind that had brought his Gran Claire home. The same as it would him. Grant grinned. "Grandpa, I think I might have found what I was looking for after all."

"'Bout time if you ask me." His grandpa peered at him. "Now what do you intend to do about it?"

"Call a family meeting." Grant headed to-ward the farmhouse.

His grandfather kept pace beside him. "Your brothers already called one. That's why I came to the stables. To fetch you."

"What's it about?" Grant asked and crossed the porch.

"You'll have to ask them." His grandpa walked inside, went directly to the kitchen and announced, "Found him."

Grant barely stepped into the room when his brothers started in. All at once. About how they'd tried to be supportive, but it wasn't right. It was too far. He needed to stay. With them. They liked having him around again. Over and over they went for several minutes straight.

Eventually, they all quieted and Grant dropped into a chair at the table. He asked, "Are you guys about done?"

Carter rubbed his chin, eyed Grant, then asked, "What's there in California that isn't in Three Springs anyway?"

"Nothing." Grant paused and waited a beat. Then he smiled wide. "Which is why I've decided to stay. Here. In Three Springs."

All his brothers pulled back. Their grins were slow to arrive.

"You could've said something instead of letting us go on and on." Ryan punched Grant in the shoulder.

"It's nice to know how you all truly feel about me." Grant nudged his elbow in his big brother's ribs.

"Glad you know." Ryan squeezed Grant's

354 FALLING FOR THE COWBOY DOC

shoulder. Determination flashed through his gaze. Yet, there was a lightness in his words. "Don't think I'll be sharing my feelings with you ever again."

Grant chuckled, then sobered. "Speaking of feelings, there is someone I need to share mine with."

"Maggie." His grandpa clapped his hands together. Satisfaction was easy to see on his face. "Grant finally figured out what he needed to on his ride. That's the power of our place. It'll show you the way if you pay close enough attention."

Or rather their grandfather would if they only took the time to hear his message inside his stories. Grant rubbed his hand over his mouth and considered his family. "So, I've found what I'm looking for, but how do I get Maggie to hear me out."

"We got you covered on that one." Ryan lifted his eyebrows and glanced at Carter.

Carter set a small box on a placemat and slid it across the table toward Grant. Around the table, everyone grinned.

"What's that?" Grant eyed the box but didn't touch it. His heart pounded.

"That is how you show Maggie that you mean what you're saying." Delight was clear in his grandfather's smile and words.

"I was just going to tell her." Grant glanced at his brothers. No one seemed particularly inspired by his plan.

"Definitely not enough." Ryan wrinkled his nose.

Caleb and Josh nodded. Uncle Roy shook his head as if disappointed.

His grandpa motioned toward the box. "You have to think bigger than words."

Grant opened the box. Inside was a familiar ring with a round diamond in the center and small opals set into the rose gold band. "But this is Gran Claire's ring. Carter should have it. For Tess."

"I'm having something designed for Tess." Carter sat back and crossed his arms over his chest. "We discussed it earlier. Gran would want Maggie to have her ring."

Grant swallowed. Rings were for love that intended to stick. For the unwavering, unfaltering kind that Maggie had thought she had once. For the kind of love that Grant never thought he'd find.

His grandpa nodded. A sheen covered his gaze. "Can't think of anyone better than Maggie to wear it."

"Maggie loves horses. Same as Gran. She has Gran's spirit and passion and kindness."

Ryan ticked Maggie's attributes off on his fingers. "Maggie should definitely have her ring."

"What if she doesn't…" Grant started.

"Feel the same?" Ryan said. At Grant's small nod, his brother added, "She does."

"And if the ring isn't to her liking, you can have a different one designed for her." Carter smiled. "I happen to know a guy."

"It's the gesture you need to make, Grant," his grandpa urged.

It was the giving of his heart. Proving he was all in. Not just repeating some lines. But meaning everything Grant had told Maggie. Not only finally listening to his heart, but speaking from it too. Because Maggie deserved to be loved right. Grant slipped the ring from the box. Held it in his palm. It all felt right. Like it was meant to be. And that knowledge at long last settled him. No more running. No more leaving.

Grant nodded, knowing he was on the right track now. "Okay, if I'm getting on one knee, then it has to be perfect. The setting. The place. Every detail. I can't take any chances." Not with Maggie's heart.

"Where's her favorite place?" Josh took off his hat and chose a seat as if ready for a night of planning.

"The arena," Ryan joked.

"I suppose you could make the arena romantic somehow." His grandpa tapped his chin.

"It is Maggie's favorite place." Grant tucked the ring back in the box and closed it. He stuck the box in his pocket. "Ryan is right. It has to be at the arena. Now we need to turn it into something from out of her dreams."

"No problem." The sarcasm was thick in Caleb's words. His fingers drummed against the table.

But Grant's mind was already working out the details.

Ryan eyed him. His grin slowly appeared. "You already have something in mind, don't you, Grant?"

"I do." Grant smiled. "But I'm going to need help from all of you and then some to pull it off."

"Count us in," his grandfather said. "Whatever you need."

And that was just one of the many things California didn't have. But it was one of the most important: his family.

CHAPTER THIRTY

"MAGGIE," KELSEY SAID, walking out of the master bedroom at the Feisty Owl apartment on the night before her surgery, tucking her phone into her jeans pocket. "We need to go to the camper."

"Now?" Maggie looked up from her laptop. "Why?"

"I need my pink plaid pajamas for the hospital tomorrow." Kelsey fake-pouted, something which Maggie had never seen her sister do before. "I can't find them anywhere so they must be in the camper."

"You have other pajamas." Maggie waited for the airline webpage to load.

"Those are my lucky ones, Mags." Kelsey gripped the sofa, her words a plea. "I have to wear them at the hospital."

Her sister's surgery was the following afternoon. And Dr. Toro planned to keep Kelsey overnight in the hospital. "Okay. We'll go get them. Let me just book a flight first." Maggie tapped on her computer screen and scrolled through the flight options from Amarillo to California. "Do I fly into Los Angeles or Orange County?"

"I don't know." Kelsey picked up Maggie's purse and jingled the truck keys. "We can talk about it on the way."

"What if the flight prices change while we're gone," Maggie countered. What if she lost her nerve? "Just let me book a flight." Take the first step to winning back Grant.

"We won't be gone long." Kelsey opened the front door and motioned to Maggie. "I'll run in and out. It'll be super quick."

Maggie shut her laptop and hurried after her sister. The windows in the truck were rolled down, the summer night air swirled through the cab. Maggie's thoughts raced.

"What do I do when I get to California, Kels? Do I call Grant when I land? Or give him more warning? How does this work?" Maggie tapped a discordant beat with her fingers on the steering wheel. "Hey, Grant, surprise! I'm here in California. Oh, and I love you. Just wanted you to know."

Kelsey laughed.

"It's not funny." The warm breeze made Maggie restless, not relaxed. Her legs were sticking to the vinyl seats. She rolled up the windows and cranked up the air conditioning. "Grant could hang up. Or send me to voicemail. Then what do I do?" Maggie peeled her bare legs off the bench seat. "They make it look so easy in the movies. How do they do that?"

"It's going to work out." Kelsey's words were as smooth and calm as the night air.

"You don't know that." Maggie tossed her phone on Kelsey's lap. "Text Ryan for me. He'll know how to reach Grant."

Kelsey picked up Maggie's phone.

"Wait." Maggie chewed on her bottom lip. "Ryan hasn't answered my texts in the last day or so. He took Grant's side. As he should. I lost Grant and one of my closest friends too." Maggie frowned at her sister.

Kelsey's shoulder shook, but her laughter never filled the truck cab.

"Kelsey, stop laughing at me." Maggie tightened her grip on the steering wheel. "This is serious. We have to fix it."

"Sorry." Kelsey pulled herself together and straightened in the passenger seat. Her smile lingered. "I've just never seen you like this before."

"Like what?" Maggie shifted her focus back to the road.

Kelsey pointed back and forth, up and down at her. "This."

"I'm in love." And alone. And scared she'd waited too long. Scared she'd lost Grant for good. "This is what I look like in love. We can't all glow like you, Kels."

"You think I'm glowing?" Kelsey flipped the visor down and peered at her reflection in the mirror.

"Yes. You sparkle whenever someone so much as mentions Nolan's name." Maggie tucked her hair behind her ear. "When Nolan walks in the same room as you, then you literally light up."

"That's the sweetest compliment." Kelsey sighed happily. "I can't help it."

"Well, dial back the wattage on your sparkle meter and *help me*, please," Maggie said. She wanted to glow. Or sparkle. Heck, she wanted to feel like smiling again. That would be a good start. Grant had walked away with her joy and her heart. Maggie frowned and pulled into the Sloans' driveway.

"I'll be back in a flash." Kelsey reached over and touched Maggie's arm. "Then we'll put together a plan for you, okay?" Kelsey slipped out and headed toward the camper.

Maggie waited in the truck. The farmhouse was dark. Only a single light glowed in the kitchen window. Tess had mentioned her cousin, Abby, and Abby's husband, Wes, were hosting Sunday night dinner for the families at their house in town. She'd invited Maggie and

Kelsey. Thanks to Kelsey's limited diet before her surgery tomorrow and Maggie wanting to stay with her sister, Maggie had a ready and believable excuse.

If only that had been the only reason Maggie had declined. She knew she wasn't very good company lately. Broken hearts tended to ruin a pleasant mood. She also worried being around Grant's family would make her miss him more. As if that were possible.

Just sitting there staring at the farmhouse made her chest ache. She wanted that porch door to swing open. She wanted her city doc to walk out and climb into her truck. Give her one of his half-smiles. Take her hand. Take her anywhere as long as it was with him. The ache built. Maggie squeezed her eyes closed. No more tears. Surely, she'd cried herself dry the past week.

She wanted Grant back. And if the cowgirl had to move to the city to have him, then that was what she'd do. Maggie had to get back to the Owl apartment. She had flights to book. And a city doc to win.

She swiped at her damp cheeks, unbuckled her seatbelt, and hopped out of the truck. Where was her sister? It was one pair of pajamas. Maggie opened the door to the camper and called, "Kels? You need help finding those pajamas?"

Kelsey stood at the kitchen window. "Maggie, we should head over to the arena."

"Why?" Maggie climbed the stairs and stood by her sister. "What's wrong?"

"Probably nothing." Kelsey pointed out the window. "It just looks like there are lights on in the arena."

"Ryan probably left them on when he finished practicing. He was always leaving lights on in the farmhouse," Maggie reminded her. "Come on. Get your pajamas."

"I still think we should check it out." Kelsey bit her bottom lip. Worry shifted across her face. "Just in case. No one else is here."

"Fine." Maggie walked to the door. "But have your phone out and ready, okay? In case we need to call 9-1-1 or something."

Kelsey patted her back pocket of her jeans and grinned. "Got it right here."

Maggie picked up the flannel pajamas from the couch and tossed them over her shoulder. "Can't forget these."

"Right." Kelsey chuckled and followed Maggie outside.

The closer they got to the arena, the more Maggie's confusion grew. The lights weren't on inside the arena. She could see that much through the row of windows near the roofline. But there was definitely some sort of light coming from inside. There wasn't any smoke or the smell of a fire. Beside her, Kelsey kept wiping her hand over her mouth, then fiddling with her ponytail, and looking everywhere but in Maggie's direction.

Maggie gripped the door handle and glanced at her sister. "Kels, you okay?"

Her sister nodded.

Kelsey's face looked pinched, but Maggie blamed the nighttime shadows. She pulled the door open and gaped. The entire arena had been transformed into the lushest garden Maggie had ever seen. Pink roses. Deep purple lavender. Tall happy sunflowers. Cascading ivy wrapped around an arbor and so much more. The light Maggie had glimpsed came from hundreds of twinkling lights strung from the ceiling that gave a soft glow over the greenery.

Behind her, Kelsey tugged the pajamas off Maggie's shoulder and whispered, "This one is all for you, little sister." She nudged Maggie inside and shut the door firmly behind her.

A path led into the center of the garden and to the arbor. Maggie's boots crunched on the pebbles. She skimmed her fingers over the flowers and plants, stopping to inhale the sweet scent of the gardenias. The rich wisps of lilacs. And the velvety softness of petals from blooms she couldn't name.

The path ended at an intricate arbor, draped in white organza, stunning pink flowers, and thick vines. But it was the cowboy standing beneath the arch who stole her breath. The floral bouquet of scents was thicker than Maggie's voice. "Grant."

He walked toward her. His gaze took her in with one long, slow sweep. Head to boots and back. Maggie's gaze followed a similar route, as if she couldn't believe he was there, or that she was, either.

"Maggie." He stopped well out of reach. His grin barely creased his cheek. "I wasn't sure what a fairy garden looked like exactly. But I hope it's close to what you always imagined."

Fairy garden. Maggie's eyes widened and filled. She covered her gasp with her hands. He'd given Maggie her very own fairy garden. Her city doc, dressed like a cowboy and standing in a pretty garden he'd created. For her. Her voice was tear-soaked. "It's perfect." *You're perfect*.

"I was told that words weren't going to be enough." Grant stood tall, his expression hopeful. "But it needs to be said. I'm sorry, Maggie. I never should've walked away from you."

Maggie walked to him, paused outside of handholding distance. Because he was right. There were things that needed to be said. "I shouldn't have pushed you away. I should've fought. For you. For us."

"That's what I'm doing now. Fighting for us." He reached for her.

She met him, linked her hands in his. "I love you, Grant. I want to be wherever you are. If that is California, then I'll be there, as long as it's with you."

"It's not California. I'm choosing the woman I love instead." He cupped Maggie's face in his hands. "It's you, Maggie. I'm choosing you."

"But what about your career?" she asked.

"It's nothing if you're not with me," he said. "Wherever you are is where I want to be."

"What if I told you I want to be here?" Maggie smiled from within. Joy spiraled through her. "Right here in Three Springs. With you. With your family."

"I would thank you," Grant said. "Dr. Toro wants me to be a partner in his clinic and I wanted to tell him yes. But I needed to know first if you could call this home. Come back here between rodeos."

"I haven't been missing a place to call home. A place to come back to." Maggie framed his face in her hands. "I've been missing a person. You, Grant. You're my place. My home. The only one I ever want to come back to."

Grant gathered her in his arms, swept her off

her feet and kissed her. Her heart took flight. Love surrounded her. Filled her. He lowered her back to the ground, yet Maggie still felt as if she were floating. Soaring, really.

"There's more." Grant took her hands in his.

"I can't imagine what." She had everything. The man she loved and a fairy garden. Dreams did come true.

Grant lowered onto one knee.

Maggie gasped. She couldn't stop the tears splashing onto her cheeks or the sudden tremor in her knees.

"Maggie, I love you." Grant held onto her hands. His gaze never left hers. "It's that unwavering, unbreakable kind of love. I never thought..." His voice caught.

Maggie's tears fell faster. She'd never thought that, either. "That you could feel this much. Love this fully."

Grant nodded. There was a sheen in his own gaze. "Maggie, will you marry me? Will you let me show you every day that I'll fight for us—for you—for the rest of our lives?"

"Yes. I love you." Maggie threw herself into his arms. He caught her easily. Kissed her breathless. Under the arbor. In the garden of her dreams.

"There's one more thing." He kept one arm around her waist and smiled at her. Then reached into his pocket and pulled out a small box. "Sorry. I should've had this out earlier. I guess I should've practiced this whole proposal thing after all."

"It was exactly as it should've been." From the heart. She couldn't ask for more. Maggie opened the box and gasped at the beautiful rose gold ring inside.

"It was Gran Claire's engagement ring," Grant explained. "If you don't…"

Maggie shook her head, stopping him from going on. She carefully tried to touch the ring, but her fingers shook. "Can you put it on, please?"

Her ever-steady surgeon had the ring sliding onto her finger in a matter of seconds. He gazed at her hand in awe. "It's a perfect fit."

"Like us." Maggie curled her fingers around his. "What now?"

"We start building our life together." Grant held her close.

"I like the sound of that." She kissed him then. And knew, with the doctor of her dreams beside her, anything was possible.

EPILOGUE

ONE WEEK AFTER the proposal in Maggie's garden arena, she worked through her mental checklist for her first solo breakaway competition weekend. Lady Dasher and King were loaded in the trailer. The camper stocked and ready. Nothing to do now but get on the road. She stopped in the doorway of Carter's office. "I'm heading out."

"Tess and I will be watching this weekend down at the Owl, along with the rest of the town. We'll be cheering for you." Carter sat behind his desk and grinned at her. "Bring home a bigger buckle than Ryan, okay?"

"I'll see what I can do." Maggie laughed. She picked up her water bottle from the kitchen counter, walked outside, and paused on the porch. Most of the Sloan clan were gathered outside her camper. Assorted duffel bags and suitcases scattered near their boots. "What are you guys doing?"

Sam hooked his fingers around his bronze

belt buckle and beamed at her. "Going with you to San Antonio."

The twins grinned at her. Ryan lifted his eyebrows as if daring her to argue with his grandfather. Or try to stop them.

"With Kelsey still recovering from her surgery, we couldn't very well let you go alone." Uncle Roy picked up a small suitcase.

"But we couldn't decide who got to go with you." Sam spread his arms wide. "So, we decided to make it a family affair."

Family. This was what it felt like to be a part of a big family. To belong. It left her feeling so very grateful and somewhat speechless.

"Haven't been to San Antonio in a spell." Sam shrugged. His eyes gleamed. "Seemed like a good time for a bit of a road trip. Cheer on our favorite cowgirl and see the sites."

Roy scratched his chin and considered her. "You don't mind the company, do you, Maggie?"

"Not at all." If she couldn't be at the farmhouse with them, then the next best thing was to have her family on the road with her. She crossed the porch and joined them.

"Now, Roy and I have been discussing a few things." Sam brushed his hand toward his grandsons and smiled. His words sounding sly. "Seeing as my grandsons are coming along, we thought you could introduce them to some of your friends, Maggie."

"The single ones, preferably." Roy waggled his eyebrows.

"We were thinking the rodeo might be a good place to find them dates," Sam explained with excitement.

The three Sloan brothers frowned. Maggie worked to keep her laughter in check.

"We don't need dates, Grandpa." Josh set his arm around his grandfather's shoulders and steered him toward Ryan's truck. "But we do need to get on the road. We're stopping in Abilene along the way. I've got a lead on an Appaloosa gelding."

"Good horse for barrel racing." Roy nodded and eyed Josh. "Who did you say owns the ranch?"

"A lovely married couple, Uncle." Josh's words were dry and dull. "So, forget about any matchmaking opportunities."

"We still have the rodeo." Sam grinned. His eyebrows tilting up into this forehead.

"Josh is right. No dates. Besides, I'll be too busy working this weekend." Caleb tapped his fist against Ryan's shoulder. "Meet your new pick-up rider."

"You can't ever be too busy to meet your

perfect match," Sam argued and stared down his grandsons.

"Yes, we absolutely can be too busy." Ryan high-fived Josh. "Watch us this weekend. We're going to be really very busy."

"Well, all I'm saying is that you're gonna need dates for all the weddings coming up." Amusement curved around the warning in Sam's words.

Caleb wrinkled his nose. "Only Grant and Maggie are engaged. And they haven't even set a date yet."

"Kelsey and Nolan won't be far behind," Sam stated. There was a twinkle in Sam's gaze. "I can guarantee you that. That's a good match there."

Maggie hadn't seen her sister happier, even after her shoulder surgery earlier in the week. Kelsey had been smiling as soon as Nolan had greeted her in the recovery room. The doting chef hadn't left Kelsey's side much since then. And Maggie knew her sister didn't want it any other way.

"I suspect Carter will be asking for Tess's hand soon," Uncle Roy mused. "Though Carter has been mum on the details."

Maggie had asked Grant about Tess and Carter's possible engagement. She'd been worried Carter might've wanted Gran Claire's ring to give to Tess. Grant had kissed Maggie and told her they might've inspired his big brother to ask for Tess's hand, but Gran Claire's ring was meant for her. Maggie touched the rose gold diamond ring on her finger. Her heart swelled with a love she hadn't known she'd been missing, but very much needed.

Caleb and Josh looked slightly ill at ease. Caleb spoke up first. "That's like an entire wedding season right there. I don't usually attend one wedding a year."

Uncle Roy slapped Josh on the shoulder with one hand and Caleb with his other. "That's why you two need to find yourselves dates."

"Grandpa. Uncle Roy. You sure you guys don't want to stay home this weekend?" Josh rubbed his forehead. "I think the rodeo is supposed to be televised. Carter mentioned watching it at the Owl."

"What's the fun in that?" Sam opened the door of Ryan's truck. "Come on, let's get in and get comfortable. We need to talk about what you're looking for in a perfect partner. Roy and I need to know so we can be on the lookout."

Maggie burst out laughing at the brothers' collective reactions as if they'd all suddenly gotten carsick.

"Maggie." Tess hurried across the porch, carrying two coolers. "This one is lunch. This one is snacks. But put them in your truck; otherwise, they'll be gone before you get there."

Maggie found herself once again touched by the support. "I cannot believe you put all that together. When did you do that? I could've helped."

"It was nothing. Now, Paige wanted me to remind you that it's girls only next weekend." Tess put the coolers on the floor behind the passenger seat. "Riley already has her bags packed. But I think I might be more excited than her. I've never been to a women's-only rodeo."

And Maggie never had so many people looking out for her. Or so many friends. Maggie smiled. "I'm looking forward to it too."

"Have fun. Ride hard. Win." Tess hugged Maggie. "And don't worry about Kelsey. Nolan and I will take good care of her." Tess released her. "I'm going to make sure everyone is good in Ryan's truck."

Maggie didn't doubt Tess for a second. Her sister had two of the very best taking care of her. And Maggie was beginning to understand how many people cared for her too. And the feeling was mutual.

"I guess I don't need to call shotgun." Grant walked across the porch, a duffel bag on his shoulder and a half-grin on his lips.

Maggie took in his cowboy boots, jeans, and

plaid shirt. "Dr. Sloan. You're not dressed for the clinic. Where are you going?"

"I'm dressed for a rodeo." He kissed her cheek. "You didn't think you'd be going to your first breakaway competition alone, did you?"

Maggie's heart was full. She didn't know it could get any fuller. But her doctor found a way. Every day.

"I'll also be acting as on-site medical support." He set his bag down and reached for her. "Will that be a problem?"

"Nope." Maggie threw her arms around him. She set her head on his shoulder and watched the others decide who was riding with who. "But if everyone decides to keep joining us, we might need to invest in a bigger camper."

"Not if we make them stay in Ryan's camper instead." Grant hugged her and chuckled.

Maggie lifted her head and eyed Grant. "Ryan told me he prefers to stay alone."

"Not anymore, I hope." Grant's laughter erupted.

"Should we help him?" Maggie asked.

"He'll figure it out." Grant's gaze settled now on Maggie. Her heart soared. . She never knew she could love so deeply. Or so much. "Well, Dr. Sloan. I have something to tell you."

He gave her that half-smile again. The private one, meant only for her. He asked, "What's that?"

"True story." Maggie watched his eyes light and his smile stretch. Oh, she had his full attention. And he had hers. There was nowhere else she wanted to be but right there in his arms. "I came to town and met a handsome city doc."

His arms curved tighter around her waist. His voice was low and tender. "Is that right?"

"Turns out he's also a cowboy." Maggie put her arms around him, closing the space between them.

He gathered her even closer. "Then what happened?"

"I fell in love with that cowboy doc and decided to stick around." Maggie leaned in.

He met her for a kiss that wrapped two hearts together as one.

They continued that way for a long moment, until he ended the kiss and tipped his head back to look at her. The affection in his gaze was something she'd never forget.

"True story," he said. "This cowboy doc opened his heart, lost it to a cowgirl and ended up finding his home."

* * * * *

*Don't miss the next installment of
the Three Springs, Texas miniseries,
coming from Cari Lynn Webb and
Harlequin Heartwarming in
fall 2023!*

Get 3 FREE REWARDS!

We'll send you 2 FREE Books <u>plus</u> a FREE Mystery Gift.

FREE Value Over **$20**

Both the **Love Inspired®** and **Love Inspired® Suspense** series feature compelling novels filled with inspirational romance, faith, forgiveness and hope.

YES! Please send me 2 FREE novels from the Love Inspired or Love Inspired Suspense series and my FREE gift (gift is worth about $10 retail). After receiving them, if I don't wish to receive any more books, I can return the shipping statement marked "cancel." If I don't cancel, I will receive 6 brand-new Love Inspired Larger-Print books or Love Inspired Suspense Larger-Print books every month and be billed just $6.49 each in the U.S. or $6.74 each in Canada. That is a savings of at least 16% off the cover price. It's quite a bargain! Shipping and handling is just 50¢ per book in the U.S. and $1.25 per book in Canada.* I understand that accepting the 2 free books and gift places me under no obligation to buy anything. I can always return a shipment and cancel at any time by calling the number below. The free books and gift are mine to keep no matter what I decide.

Choose one:
- ☐ **Love Inspired Larger-Print** (122/322 BPA GRPA)
- ☐ **Love Inspired Suspense Larger-Print** (107/307 BPA GRPA)
- ☐ **Or Try Both!** (122/322 & 107/307 BPA GRRP)

Name (please print)

Address   Apt. #

City   State/Province   Zip/Postal Code

Email: Please check this box ☐ if you would like to receive newsletters and promotional emails from Harlequin Enterprises ULC and its affiliates. You can unsubscribe anytime.

Mail to the **Harlequin Reader Service:**
IN U.S.A.: P.O. Box 1341, Buffalo, NY 14240-8531
IN CANADA: P.O. Box 603, Fort Erie, Ontario L2A 5X3

Want to try 2 free books from another series? Call 1-800-873-8635 or visit www.ReaderService.com.

*Terms and prices subject to change without notice. Prices do not include sales taxes, which will be charged (if applicable) based on your state or country of residence. Canadian residents will be charged applicable taxes. Offer not valid in Quebec. This offer is limited to one order per household. Books received may not be as shown. Not valid for current subscribers to the Love Inspired or Love Inspired Suspense series. All orders subject to approval. Credit or debit balances in a customer's account(s) may be offset by any other outstanding balance owed by or to the customer. Please allow 4 to 6 weeks for delivery. Offer available while quantities last.

Your Privacy—Your information is being collected by Harlequin Enterprises ULC, operating as Harlequin Reader Service. For a complete summary of the information we collect, how we use this information and to whom it is disclosed, please visit our privacy notice located at corporate.harlequin.com/privacy-notice. From time to time we may also exchange your personal information with reputable third parties. If you wish to opt out of this sharing of your personal information, please visit readerservice.com/consumerschoice or call 1-800-873-8635. **Notice to California Residents**—Under California law, you have specific rights to control and access your data. For more information on these rights and how to exercise them, visit corporate.harlequin.com/california-privacy.

LIRLIS23

THE NORA ROBERTS COLLECTION

40% OFF!

Get to the heart of happily-ever-after in these Nora Roberts classics! Immerse yourself in the beauty of love by picking up this incredible collection written by, legendary author, Nora Roberts!

HARLEQUIN
PLUS

Try the best multimedia
subscription service for romance
readers like you!

Read, Watch and Play.

Experience the easiest way to get
the romance content you crave.

Start your **FREE TRIAL** at
<u>www.harlequinplus.com/freetrial</u>.